Marin waited until Adam was out of earshot

This situation was unacceptable. There was no way she would spend her days—days she needed to figure out what she would do now that her life had imploded—with *children*.

She spun around to confront her parent who had put her in this predicament. "Are you out of your mind, Mother?"

"No." Angelica grinned. "What I am is damned happy to have purpose to my days. It's not the editor job, but it's something to keep me busy while we're here, and those children need someone. So does their father. The kids, I can help with. The man?" She stared at Marin. "I'll bet he'd take your mind off Colin."

"He has kids, Mother."

"No one said you had to marry him, Marin."

Dear Reader,

It seems like yesterday that Mirabelle Island started taking shape in my mind. A glimpse of a storefront here, a horse-drawn carriage there. A stately Victorian or lonesome lighthouse. A colorful marina or rocky beach on the shores of Lake Superior. There were times I had to remind myself that Mirabelle wasn't real.

Unfortunately, every miniseries must come to an end. And so, it is with this seventh An Island to Remember book I say goodbye to the place and the people that have filled my thoughts and dreams for almost four years. Mirabelle and its islanders will always be in my heart, and who knows? Another story or two might pop up down the road.

For now, though, it's onward and upward as a new town and new characters fill my thoughts. Right now I'm thinking about three brothers, their best friend and the town they call home. After all, romance is always about the heroes for me! Stay tuned for more details.

I love hearing from readers, and you can contact me at helenbrenna@comcast.net.

My best,

Helen Brenna

Redemption at Mirabelle

Helen Brenna

TORONTO NEW YORK LONDON
AMSTERDAM PARIS SYDNEY HAMBURG
STOCKHOLM ATHENS TOKYO MILAN MADRID
PRAGUE WARSAW BUDAPEST AUCKLAND

Recycling programs
for this product may
not exist in your area.

ISBN-13: 978-0-373-78476-9

REDEMPTION AT MIRABELLE

ABOUT THE AUTHOR

Helen Brenna grew up in central Minnesota, the seventh of eight children. Although she never dreamed of writing books, she's always been a voracious reader. So after taking a break from her accounting career to be an at-home mom, she tried her hand at writing the romances she loves to read. Since she was first published in 2007, her books have won many awards, including a Romance Writer's of America's prestigious RITA® Award, an *RT Book Reviews* Reviewer's Choice, a HOLT Medallion, a Book Buyers Best and a National Readers' Choice Award.

Helen lives happily ever after with her family in Minnesota. She'd love hearing from you. Email her at helenbrenna@comcast.net, visit her website at www.helenbrenna.com or chat with Helen and other authors at Riding With The Top Down.

Books by Helen Brenna

For Paul Twomey
Thanks, little bro, for walking in the rain!

Acknowledgments:

Thanks to fellow writer and editor, Sarah Tieck,
for her friendship, always supportive critique
advice, and insight into the children's book
publishing business. You make every day brighter!

And thanks to my editor, Johanna Raisanen,
for her editorial insight with all my books
and this story in particular.
You help me make every book better!

You guys are the best,
Helen

CHAPTER ONE

THE ONLY DIFFERENCE BETWEEN Mirabelle and Adam Harding's life was that this island would be good as gold by Christmas. Maybe that's why there was nothing he liked better than a good, old-fashioned natural disaster—tornadoes, floods, hurricanes. As long as no lives had been lost in the happening.

He could fix roofs and replace windows, repair roads and replant trees, putting everything right again. It's what he did best. He fixed things. That's why the folks here on Mirabelle had hired him, to get their town, their businesses and their lives back on track.

As a gentle, late summer breeze laden with dust blew from the interior of the island out toward Lake Superior, Adam glanced up and down Main Street, taking note of his team's progress in cleaning up after the tornado that had ripped across this island. When he'd first arrived, shattered glass, crumbling bricks, torn shingles, shredded awnings and twisted lampposts, as well as the remnants of uprooted trees and broken branches, had been scattered this way and that across town. Unfortunately, there was still much to be done before any rebuilding could start.

"This cleanup isn't happening fast enough," Adam said, addressing his crew. He could mollycoddle with the best of them, but every once in a while a man needed a swift kick in the rear to make something happen. "Initial supplies are getting dropped off in the a.m. That means no one leaves tonight until this place is ready for the shipment. Understand?"

"It would've been a hell of a lot easier getting rid of all this debris if we'd brought a couple of our semiloaders over on a barge, and drove them right up that pier and onto the island," said Ray Worley, one of several operations foremen. "We'd have had this whole place cleaned up in a couple days."

"And in the process we'd have destroyed all of Mirabelle's cobblestone," Adam said, staring pointedly at his foreman as he referred to the street below his feet. He made eye contact with as many of his crew as he could. "Every job we've ever done has had its own special problems and opportunities," he said softly. "One of the objectives on this island is to do no more damage while we're here. Tread lightly. Be respectful of Mirabelle's history. Understand?"

The men nodded, most of them having been with him for years. They understood he took pride in making good on his promises, and that's why his company had one of the finest reputations in the country for restoring towns devastated by natural disasters.

"I've promised these people that we'll have their island up and running before Christmas, and they've put their lives in our hands. Let's get this done."

His cleanup crew dispersed, a small team, relatively speaking. In a couple days, the real work would start and his main construction crew would be crawling in full force all over this island.

"Ray," Adam called.

"Yeah."

"In the past, you've disagreed on occasion with my messages to the men, and I've asked you to voice your objections in private," Adam said quietly. He didn't get angry, and he never raised his voice. He simply stated his expectations, and if those expectations weren't met then there would be consequences. "Contradict what I say one more time in front of anyone, and you're fired."

"Yes, sir."

Adam turned away, felt the heat of the man's irate stare on his back and impassively headed to his trailer set up on the street bordering the city park. He'd positioned his mobile office in about as centrally located a position as he could get while still being able to survey most of main street Mirabelle on which he and his crew would be focusing their efforts. There'd been some minor damage out at the Rock Pointe Lodge resort, up on the golf course and at Mirabelle Stable and Livery, but the rest of the mayhem wrought by the tornado had been concentrated in the village center.

As he crossed the street, his personal assistant, Phyllis Pennick, came out of the trailer holding a stack of messages. Phyllis was in her mid-fifties and of medium height with short, salt-and-pepper hair. She was rail thin, no doubt from smoking—outside, he'd always insisted—a pack of cigarettes a day. Some managers might begrudge the time she took away from her desk to appease her habit, but as far as Adam was concerned she more than made up for that one flaw with her organizational skills. Her husband had died almost a decade ago, so she had no problems traveling on the job, and, as with most good executive assistants, he didn't know what he'd do without her.

"Darwin called," she said. "His bus broke down somewhere in Iowa last night and they're waiting for a part. He figures they're going to be at least a day late."

That meant the initial supplies would be here tomorrow, but a big part of his crew wouldn't. It wasn't the first—and it certainly wouldn't be the last—time that's ever happened. Although he tried to hire as much local labor as possible, knowing an area devastated by a tornado could usually use the inflow of employment dollars, he brought the majority of his construction workers, including several foremen and supervisors, along with him to every job.

"I'm going to get myself a sandwich while I can," she said. "You want one?"

"Sure." He reached the steps to his trailer office and noticed his kids' nanny, along with his daughter and son, coming down the hill from the house he was renting up in the residential section of the island. Carla had standing, strict orders to not bring Julia and Wyatt anywhere near his construction sites and had never once violated the rule in the three years she'd been working for him. This had to be something big.

As they neared Adam, Wyatt caught sight of him. "Daddy!" he called.

Adam waved. Carla quickly bent down to Wyatt's level and pointed at the play equipment. Then she let go of the four-year-old's hand, and he ran over to the play equipment without a second glance toward Adam. His seven-year-old daughter, Julia, on the other hand, never took her eyes off Adam's face.

"Hi, Daddy," Julia said, looking more than a little worried as she and her nanny approached him. "I know we're not supposed to come down to your work, but Carla said it was important."

"It's all right. I'm sure Carla had a good reason." The nanny's eyes were red and puffy as if she'd been crying. "Julia," he said. "Go play with your brother for a few minutes while I talk with Carla."

"But, Daddy—"

"Julia," he said calmly. His soft-spoken strategies

in dealing with his employees worked just as well with his kids. "What did I ask you to do?"

Crossing her spindly little arms, she frowned at him, but then headed over to Wyatt.

As soon as his daughter was out of earshot, he turned to Carla. "What's going on?"

"It's my mother," she said, her voice breaking. "I don't know if you remember, but she's been sick."

He remembered.

"They found lung cancer."

"I'm sorry."

She closed her eyes for a moment, gathering herself.

"Do you know what you want to do yet?" he asked softly, bracing for the worst. The only thing he'd ever been able to count on in the construction business is that he couldn't count on anything. He'd deal with this problem the way he dealt with everything else.

"I have to go home to take care of her."

"How long will you be gone?"

"Could be two months. Could be a year. I don't know. I'll be staying as long as she needs me. I think it's best for the children if you find another nanny."

Something bad happened without fail on every single one of his jobs. This was the construction business, and what he did, moving from town to town, rebuilding after disasters, had more than its fair share of plans going awry. Last time they'd been to Arkansas, his roofing crew had been late by more than a week. In east Texas, one of his foremen, a good friend of Ray Worley's, had shown up on the job site in the morning still drunk from the previous night of partying and Adam had had to fire him. In Oklahoma, they'd had another tornado come through not a month into the job, forcing them to start almost from scratch. He'd gotten used to problems, had accepted them as par for the course. But this? This was different. This impacted his kids.

Carla had been his children's nanny ever since Beth—ever since his wife had died three years ago. Carla had been the only constant in their ever-changing landscape. Wyatt, too young to understand much of anything, went about playing on the park equipment as if nothing was amiss. But Julia? She was watching him. Always, she watched him. No child should have to grow up so fast.

"The children." Tears streamed down Carla's face. "I'm so sorry, Mr. Harding."

"It's all right, Carla. We'll survive."

One way or another, they always did, but he was getting a very bad feeling about this Mirabelle project.

"MEN." MARIN CAMDEN GLANCED at the group of construction workers eyeing—no, more like ogling—her as she and her mother took a ferry across the choppy surface of Lake Superior to Mirabelle Island. "They're all pigs."

"I imagine Artie and Max might just take issue with that very generalized opinion." Marin's mother,

Angelica Camden, chuckled softly. "Your brothers—
my sons, mind you—are definitely not cut from the
same cloth as those crude strangers. Or, for that
matter, Colin."

At the mention of her ex-fiancé, Marin turned
around and gripped the ferry's railing. "That's what
you want to *think*, but how do you really *know*? Men
hide their affairs very well these days, and Artie and
Max would hardly spill to either one of us."

"Well, I know this isn't what you want to hear,
but affairs are just one of the many ways men break
their vows," Marin's mother said, frowning as she
adjusted her dark sunglasses. "Sometimes the most
subtle infractions can be the most painful."

There was a great deal of truth to that statement.
Discovering Colin had been screwing around behind
Marin's back almost since the day they'd started
dating more than six years ago hadn't been quite as
shocking or cutting as discovering the identity of his
lover when she'd returned home early from a work
conference and found them in bed together. This, on
the same day she'd discovered the top management
at the Wall Street firm she worked for were under
investigation for ethics violations and had decided
to quit her job.

She still wasn't entirely sure what to think. Was
Colin's betrayal her fault? Had she been just too assertive and demanding? Not sexy or sensual enough?

"Still," Angelica continued, "I refuse to believe

that there are no men worthy of love and commitment."

Marin shot a glance in her mother's direction. She'd known her mother and father had been having a few spats of late, but when her mom had asked if she could tag along in Marin's escape from the media frenzy surrounding her breakup with Colin, she'd assumed it had been nothing out of the ordinary. Now she wasn't so sure.

"Forget about me and Colin," Marin said. "What's going on with you and Dad? Did he do something? Something serious or subtle?"

Her mother looked away. "I'm sorry, Marin. He's your father. I don't want to say anything that might color your opinion of him."

"Oh, come on." Marin shook her head. "How many times have I told you to divorce the arrogant, self-absorbed asshole? Have you finally decided to do it this time?"

Only silence from her mother.

"Mom?" Marin felt her eyes widen. "Did you actually file for a divorce?"

"I saw an attorney last week."

Holy hell. This from her patient, calm, always loving and forgiving mother. What had happened to the sermon about how a person doesn't throw away thirty-five years of marriage on a whim? Anyone can get a divorce. Making a marriage work? That's the hard part.

"Well, this probably doesn't help much." Marin

wrapped her arm around her mother. "But I would've left him decades ago." Of course, Marin never would've married the opinionated, sexist, controlling United States senator in the first place. She loved Arthur Camden as a father, but she'd never liked him as a man. "Do you want to talk about it?"

"Not just now," Angelica said, smiling slightly. "Suffice it to say, I needed a little time away. Thanks for letting me tag along with you."

But then the quaint and quiet Mirabelle Island with its Victorian bed-and-breakfasts, cobblestone streets and horse-drawn carriages wouldn't have been Marin's first destination pick. She would've much preferred a month at an adults-only resort on St. Barts in the Caribbean. Sand, surf and ice-cold drinks—Sex on the Beach—would've done wonders for her frame of mind.

Then again, hanging with her sister, Melissa, after she'd estranged herself from the family all these years held a certain appeal. It'd be nice getting to know her again and her new world. Although Marin would venture to guess that her husband, Jonas, was as much an ass as the rest of his sex.

"You know I've never been off on my own like this away from your father," her mother whispered. "For more than a weekend here or there."

"Then you were long past due."

"A month on Mirabelle. What in the world are we going to do all day long?"

"Unwind and relax."

Easier said than done. Marin might have a multi-million dollar trust fund inherited from her famous Camden grandfather sitting at a bank, making quitting her job financially feasible, but she'd also inherited her grandfather's work ethic. Other than to pay Harvard tuition and buy her Manhattan apartment, she'd never relied on that trust money for support. Until now. It didn't sit particularly well, but Marin was going to attempt to give lazy a good go for the first time in her life.

A brisk but warm wind hit the ferry as it crossed Lake Superior, and Marin secured her baseball cap lower over her brow. It was late August, near the end of Mirabelle's typical tourist season and while the ferry wasn't crowded, the last thing she and her mother needed right now was to be recognized.

Then again, Melissa had promised they wouldn't have to worry about crowds or the media on her little island. The tornado that had passed through Mirabelle only a short time ago had put an abrupt end to tourist season. From what Melissa had said, the island had emptied like water spiraling down a drain. They'd have plenty of peace and quiet.

The ferry docked at the pier. Marin grabbed both their bags and stepped off the ferry, following her mother. The large group of construction workers had exited ahead of them.

"Melissa said she would meet us," her mother murmured. "Do you see her?"

"Not yet, but I'm sure she'll be here."

"Marin! Mom!"

Marin spotted her sister waving near the edge of the pier. "Melissa!"

After a round of hugs, Melissa smiled. Marin wasn't sure she'd ever seen a woman look quite so happy. "Call me Missy, okay? If you keep calling me Melissa, no one here on the island will have a clue who you're talking to, including me."

In trying to slough off the expectations—and more—of the Camden name, Melissa had divested herself of most things Camden, including her name, years ago. "Missy Charms." Marin shook her head. "Where in the world did you come up with that name, anyway?"

"It's Missy Charms Abel now." She shrugged. "And Jonas called me Missy from the beginning. It just seemed to fit."

As did motherhood, or so her sister claimed. Missy and Jonas had no sooner agreed to adopt than found out they were pregnant. How any woman could be so happy with two children under the age of two was anyone's guess.

Marin had accepted the inevitability of someday getting married, but children were out of the question. All she'd had to do was look at her mother's life—or lack thereof—to firm up that decision. Angelica Camden had given up a promising editorial career at a large New York publishing house to stay home and raise a family, and look at her now. In

her late fifties, soon to be divorced and no life of
her own.

Marin was far too absorbed in her career and enjoyed her single life far too much to ever get tied
down by a child. Besides, she despised sticky fingers, chicken nuggets and cartoons, not to mention
she had absolutely no patience. She was a bit too
much like her father in that regard.

Missy grabbed their mother's suitcase, tossed it in
the rear of a golf cart and hopped behind the wheel.

Marin raised her eyebrows. "I take it there are no
cars on Mirabelle?"

"Nope. Only horse drawn carriages and golf carts.
Although with all the construction that's going on
with the rebuilding, there's bound to be some construction equipment here and there."

With the big water behind them, the marina still
dotted with several shapes and sizes of boat, quaint
gingerbread houses sprinkling the hillside, and
a majestic lighthouse visible down the shoreline,
Mirabelle reminded Marin of a smaller and slightly
less sophisticated Nantucket. But as Missy drove the
golf cart away from the ferry pier, the reality of the
devastation caused by the tornado put the island in
an entirely different light.

The roof on what appeared to have been a restaurant nearest the pier was partially destroyed, its
blue shutters hung limply as if they might fall to
the ground at any moment, and its windows were
smashed in and had been boarded up with plywood.

Several windows of the little white church on the hillside were boarded up as well, the stained glass having been broken and blown who knows where. In the other directions, historic brick buildings lay in various stages of destruction. The lucky buildings were only missing roofs. The unlucky ones were missing entire exterior walls. The most amazing thing was that no one had been killed.

"Stop," Marin said.

"Main Street," Missy whispered, tears gathering in her eyes. "What's left of it, anyway."

The town looked like Marin felt. As sure as she was standing here a tornado had ripped through her life. Her fiancé was a lying cheat, her parents were getting a divorce, and she'd lost faith in the people for whom she'd been working for the past eight years. The foundations on which she'd based her entire life had been ripped out from under her and she didn't know where to stand, let alone how to walk.

"Missy?" Marin asked. "Your gift shop?"

"Whimsy fared better than some shops, not as well as others," Missy said, taking a deep breath. "We had some roof damage and lost all our windows, so most of my inventory was ruined. But the restaurant of one of my best friends, Duffy's Pub, was hit the hardest. They don't even know if the structure is sound enough to rebuild or if they'll have to bulldoze everything over and start from scratch."

"There must be some way we can help them," their mother murmured.

For as long as Marin could remember her father had drummed into her head that philanthropy was an integral part of the responsibility of being a Camden. Although she disagreed with his delivery, she couldn't argue his logic. As a result, a large percentage of her trust fund dollars every year went toward charitable projects.

Marin rested her hand on her mother's arm. "We'll find a way to help, Mom."

"Let's go," Missy finally said. "I can only look at it for so long." She drove the golf cart up a hill and into a residential area that didn't seem at all impacted by the storm.

"The tornado didn't come through here?"

"No. It came through the golf course and slipped down into town over by the central park, missing most residential sections."

"Thank God for small favors," their mother mused.

Missy pulled the golf cart in front of a neatly kept yellow-and-white Cape Cod. "This is where you guys will be staying. The couple who'd been renting this place had just moved here last year to start up a new restaurant. But the storm destroyed their building, so they've decided to start over in Door County."

"Where's your house?"

"Right next door." Missy pointed. "How's that for convenient?"

As if on cue, Missy's husband, Jonas, came out the front door of their house, a much larger Cape Cod, carrying two small boys. "Hello, ladies," he called. "Welcome to Mirabelle." The moment he cleared the steps, he set the toddlers down in the grass and they ran somewhat clumsily toward Missy.

"Look at you two go," Missy said, smiling.

Angelica Camden had come to Mirabelle no less than three times to visit Missy these past couple of years, so the boys likely remembered her. Marin, on the other hand, had never met either one of the kids. "Who's who?" she asked.

"Nate is the towheaded one," Angelica said. "And Michael has dark hair."

She bent down and held out her arms. "Come say hello to Grandma!" The boys ran toward her and she hugged them both at the same time. "Thank God one of my kids finally gave me grandchildren."

"Well, don't count on me ever adding to the lineup."

"Never say never," Angelica murmured. "Now go give your auntie Marin a big sloppy kiss."

They both turned to Marin with their big, round eyes and messy mouths.

"No, that's okay." She smiled and waved. "Hi, boys."

Jonas laughed and grabbed the suitcases from Marin. They followed him up the sidewalk, the boys holding Grandma's hands. Everyone piled inside the house Marin and her mother would be renting for the duration. Immediately, the boys went racing from room to room and Marin flashed on what the next several weeks could look like if she didn't set some ground rules with her mother right off the bat. The boys screamed and raced by Marin. The vision wasn't pretty.

"If Grandma wants to see her grandbabies," Marin suggested, "I think she'll be going over to Missy's house from now on."

"I don't think you'll need to worry about your peace and quiet, Marin," Missy said, smiling. "The boys have a pretty good sense of self-preservation."

"I'm going outside with my grandsons," their mother called from the kitchen a moment before the back door opened.

"I'll keep an eye on them." Jonas headed outside.

"Hey," Marin whispered, pulling Missy aside. "Heads-up. Mom just saw a divorce attorney last week. That's why she came along."

"If I say it's about time will you be mad at me?"

"No." Marin sighed. "But I have this feeling she and I are both a bit raw."

"I'd say I'm sorry about what happened with Colin, Marin," Missy said. "But the truth is you dodged a bullet."

"I know. It's still hard to switch gears. I thought I'd be spending the rest of my life with him."

"Well then, you came to the right place. This

island has a reputation for creating matches made in heaven." Missy winked at Marin. "Who knows? Maybe you and Mom will both get lucky."

"Oh, no." Marin smiled grimly. "I need another man like I need a hole in the head."

CHAPTER TWO

"No!" WYATT STOMPED HIS FEET. "Carla can't go!"

"She has to, Wyatt," Adam said calmly. "Her mother is sick and needs her."

"But we need her, too, Daddy," Julia said. "What are we going to do without her?"

"I've already made some calls to people who help match nannies with families." Adam pulled lunch meat, cheese and a couple apples out of the refrigerator. It'd be cold sandwiches and fruit tonight. With Carla leaving, he wasn't losing only his nanny, he was also losing cook and housekeeper. "We'll find someone new. Someone you'll like just as much as Carla. In the meantime, Phyllis will take care of you."

They both groaned.

"She's boring," Wyatt said.

"She never plays with us," Julia complained.

"Why can't you take care of us?"

"I have to work, Wyatt. You know that." Adam slapped together some sandwiches. "I've made a commitment to this community to help its residents get their businesses up and running before Christmas. I can't let them down."

Pulling her suitcases, Carla came out of her rooms, mother-in-law quarters located in an addition built just off the kitchen. This rental house had been the perfect setup for a live-in nanny. So much for that.

Wyatt cried. Julia's lower lip trembled.

"Oh, *niños.*" Her eyes were even redder and puffier than earlier in the day. Carla got down on her knees. The kids flew into her open arms the way Julia used to jump off the end of the dock at his parents' house on Lake St. Louis. "I will never forget you."

Foregoing dinner preparations for the moment, Adam looked away.

"Both of you...be good for your father. He's a very busy man with important work to do."

Sniffles and sobs and sucked in breaths. If he had to listen to another minute of it, he just might... No. Adam refused to let this get to him. This situation was no one's fault. It was entirely uncontrollable. What point would there be in getting angry, anyway? That emotion was particularly unproductive. Not to mention distracting and draining.

"I called Arlo for a carriage to take you down to the ferry," he said gently. "Looks like Austin is waiting for you on the porch to take your luggage."

Carla stood, sucked in a big breath and, trying for stoic and dismally failing, headed toward the front door. "Thank you, Mr. Harding." She shook his hand.

"Thank you, Carla. Take care of your mother."

"Find someone good," she whispered as she slipped out the door.

The kids watched her through the front picture window. They both stayed there long after she'd disappeared. Adam had no more a clue what to say now than when he'd had to find the words to tell them their mother was gone. Forever.

"Come on, kids, let's get something to eat."

They slowly followed him into the kitchen.

"I miss Mommy," Julia whispered.

"Me, too," Wyatt agreed.

Redirect them. That's all he could think to do. He cut an apple in quarters and cored a section. "How 'bout we take our sandwiches out into the backyard for a picnic?"

"No!" Julia yelled. "I don't want to go outside! I don't want to play! And I don't want to be a good girl!" She glared at him. "This is all your fault. You did something to make Carla go away just like you did something to make Mommy go away. I hate you." She pounded up the steps, went into her bedroom and slammed the door.

Sobbing, Wyatt followed her up the stairs, slamming himself in his own room.

Feeling a little as if his heart had been ripped from his chest and thrown in a blender, Adam finished coring the apple. The sharp knife slipped, grazing his thumb. He stared at the blood pouring from the small cut and immediately memories flashed through his mind. *Don't go there. Don't.* Nothing good could possibly come from remembering.

He slapped a Band-Aid over his cut, threw the lunch meat and cheese into the fridge, tossed away the apple and then slowly made his way toward the patio doors at the back of the house. *Stay calm. It'll be all right. Everything will be all right.* He slid open the door and stepped outside into the warm early evening air.

"Adam!"

His stomach flipped. The last thing he needed at the moment was a visit from his sugary sweet, always jovial neighbor Missy Abel from two doors down. As he took a deep breath, turned and saw three women coming toward him, one trailing several feet behind the other two, it was clear that was exactly what he was going to get. Client, he reminded himself.

"I want you to meet my mother and sister," Missy said. "They'll be renting the house next to yours."

Great. Two more chipper females like Missy living next door. Could this night get any better?

"Mom, this is Adam Harding. Mirabelle's savior."

"Oh, no," Adam insisted, shaking his head. Since he'd arrived on Mirabelle, every resident had either rolled out the welcome mat for him in a big way or treated him with kid gloves, sometimes both. "Savior I am not, but it's a pleasure meeting you."

"Angelica Camden," the older woman said, smiling as she extended her hand.

"This is my sister, Marin."

The sister looked about as happy to be meeting him as he was to be having this conversation. "Never met a savior before," she muttered, shaking his hand. Although both sisters were attractive little things, Marin's demeanor was as assessing as Missy's was inviting.

"They say there's a first time for everything." Clearly, all the charm in the family had gone to Missy and her mother.

Normally, he wouldn't have paid the slightest bit of attention to what a woman was wearing, but the sisters not only acted like polar opposites, they looked it, too, making a comparison of the two unavoidable. Missy had curly sandy-blond hair, Bohemian in style, and wore a tie-dyed skirt and loose-fitting blouse. A hippie. Marin's brunette hair was stick-straight and all business, cut shoulder-length with stylishly long bangs swooping down over her forehead. She wore a pair of pencil-thin pants and a pale blue silky-looking T-shirt topped by a casual black blazer. Strangely enough, their mother appeared to be a clear-cut mix of the two.

"Adam owns the construction company that will be putting Mirabelle back to rights," Missy explained.

"That sounds like a big job," Angelica said.

"It gets a little easier with every town."

"He's not giving himself enough credit," Missy said. "His is the most highly recommended company in the country for this type of work."

Not really feeling like carrying on this conversation, he glanced away, trying to think of a way of extricating himself.

"Is everything all right?" Missy asked. "You seem troubled."

It was possible she might know of someone who might be able to help on a temporary basis. "The kids' nanny just quit today." He explained the situation with Carla's mother.

"Oh, that's terrible."

"Do you know anyone on the island who might be willing to babysit until I can find another nanny?"

"I'll ask around, but it's not likely." Missy cringed. "After the tornado hit most of the teenagers looked to the mainland for jobs. I'm having trouble finding babysitters myself."

"Let me know if you have any luck."

"Will do." Missy turned to her mother and sister and explained, "Adam's a widower."

He hated being described that way. People generally had two reasons for the clarification. Either they wanted to set him up with some eligible female—which, based on a quick glance at Marin's left hand, she was—or they pitied him and wanted everyone else to pity him, as well. Normally, he could decipher right off the bat a person's motivations. Missy, though, was hard to read.

"I hope your nanny leaving won't negatively impact your work here on Mirabelle," Marin said.

"Marin!" Her mother admonished, raising her eyebrows.

Surreptitiously, he studied Missy's sister. She had to be either a lawyer or an accountant, possibly both, and he guessed she came by her analytical attitude naturally. He prided himself on straightforward business dealings and respected the same from others. So why, all of a sudden, should the comment of a virtual stranger strike a chord?

"What? It's just a question." Marin shrugged. "There seem to be a lot of people depending on him here. They deserve to know if he'll be delayed."

"That's no excuse for being rude," her mother said.

Adam almost smiled. "Actually, she's right, Mrs. Camden. I'm sure that will be the first thought that crosses many minds here on Mirabelle." He'd worked hard over the years to not let anything influence his work. Nearly having to declare bankruptcy after Beth's death had taught him the hard way that emotions had no place in business. He turned to Marin. "And to answer your question," he said. "No. No one needs to worry about this impacting this project. I always honor my commitments."

BY THE TIME MARIN AND HER mother had gotten settled in their rental, it'd been dinnertime. They'd immediately headed to Missy's for a special welcome meal and were now visiting in the spacious family room off the kitchen. Trucks, cars and toy airplanes were strewn on the floor, along with books, wooden blocks and sippy cups.

Close to reaching her child tolerance level for the day, Marin sat on the couch with Missy's short-haired black cat, Slim, on her lap. She scratched the cat's muscular neck, and while he appeared to appreciate the attention, he never took his eyes off the two toddlers playing on the floor. Who could blame him? The two little monsters had more than likely grabbed, kicked or fallen on the poor cat more than once.

Monsters. That's what they were all right. Missy had bought at least two of every toy, but the boys still managed to find something to fight over.

Nate suddenly picked up a block and hit Michael with it. "No hitting, Nate," Missy said to her little blond. "Just because you're mad doesn't make it okay to hit."

"Yeah, right," Jonas muttered under his breath to Marin. "Two boys only a couple months apart? We'll be lucky if they don't kill each other by kindergarten."

"I know you're mad because Michael took that toy away," Missy went on. "But use your words. Tell him he has to share."

Marin was fascinated watching her sister interact with her kids. Her sister was gentle, loving and patient. Compared to her, Marin felt like an old spinster hag. The mother gene had obviously been either buried so deeply under the thick skin Marin had developed after years on Wall Street or she'd been missing it entirely in the first place.

When the boys started in on the tug-of-war over the toy, Angelica tapped Missy on the shoulder and snuck down the hall.

"Oh, oh!" Missy said, feigning surprise. "Where did Grandma go?"

"I don't see her," Jonas added.

Wide-eyed and innocent, the two boys forgot all about fighting over the toy as they glanced around the large, open family room. Just then, Angelica jumped out from her hiding place in the hallway and announced, "Boo!"

The boys screamed and ran toward their dad, scrambling into his lap. "I don't know," he said, teasing them. "She looks pretty mean."

Oh, puhleese. Marin rolled her eyes. Missy was letting the boys stay up late tonight, as it was their first night on the island, and Marin felt obligated to hang with the family. In truth, though, she'd had all the Kodak moments she could take for one day.

"I'm going to call it a night," she said during a break in playtime. "See everyone in the morning."

After a round of pleasantries, she went out Missy's rear patio door, letting Slim out with her, and walked through the backyard toward her house. Slim took off toward the front yard, but the moment Marin exited the periphery of glowing lights from Missy and Jonas's house, she stopped.

The glow of stars in the dark sky was magnificent, a spectacle that was almost too vibrant to be real. Missy's backyard was at the top of the hill overlooking Mirabelle's village center. The view of Lake Superior, black as ink this time of night, was amazing. It was a warm, balmy evening and in no real hurry to go to bed, she moved even farther away from the lights and let go a long sigh as the sky turned even more brilliant.

"Beautiful, isn't it?"

She spun and found their neighbor Adam sitting behind her and leaning up against the trunk of a large oak tree. Apparently, she'd wandered closer to his yard than she'd realized. "It's gorgeous," she said. "Never see anything like it living in Manhattan, that's for sure."

It wasn't apparent now, given that he was sitting, but he was a tall man, over six feet. It was one of the first things she'd noticed when they'd met earlier that day. That and his disheveled hair. Even now, he looked as though he'd just dragged his fingers straight over the top of his head.

Was his hair always a mess? Probably. It was a bit too long, for one thing, as if he were a few weeks late making an appointment with his barber. The slight wave in texture was more than likely the cause of his bangs hanging down over his forehead and the rest of his hair appearing tousled. Add a five o'clock shadow to the picture and he should've come across as rumpled. Except that even after what had likely been a long and drawn-out day for him, his shirt was still crisp, his khakis creased. What he looked was tired.

That's when she noticed his fingers curled around a bottle of beer, and the six-pack, one bottle already empty, sitting in the grass next to him. He still wore a wedding ring, and she couldn't help but wonder how long ago his wife had died.

"Would you like a beer?" he asked with a touch of a Southern accent.

"Sounds good." She was on vacation, right? She could talk, just talk, to a guy. It wasn't as if anything was going to happen between them. Cross-legged, she sat in the grass next to him, cracked open a bottle and took a long swig. "That hits the spot."

"That's what I thought."

He had the most amazing lower lip, full and almost too lush for a man. The most striking thing about their neighbor, though, was his eyes. Dark brown and soulful, slanting downward ever-so-slightly, they could only be described as puppy-dog eyes. Eyes that very likely made women incapable of deciding when looking at him if they should sigh, "Oh, poor baby," or "Oh, baby, *baby*." Marin sure couldn't make up her mind.

I honor my commitments.

Adam's comment when she'd cornered him about the impact his nanny leaving would have on his job came back to her as if he were whispering in her ear. She had no doubt he believed what he was saying, but after the stunt Colin had pulled Marin was going to have to see that kind of follow-through to believe it from any man.

"Your kids asleep?" she asked.

"Finally. They're having a hard time without Carla."

"How long do you think it'll take to find a replacement?"

"A couple weeks, at least. The agency sent me the first round of prospects today. Only five of them. It's difficult finding a person on a long-term basis who's willing to travel the way we do from town to town."

"How long was Carla with you?"

"Three years."

Probably since his wife had died. That was a long time to still be wearing a ring. "And you traveled that entire time?"

He nodded. "We go to where the jobs are. Tornado Alley, for the most part. Oklahoma, Arkansas, Kansas, Nebraska, Tennessee."

"You're a bit too far north, aren't you?"

"They made me an offer I couldn't refuse. Besides, most of the work will be done before Christmas. We'll be gone before the worst of the weather hits, and then a small crew will return in the spring to wrap up any loose ends."

"Ever work on areas hit by hurricanes?"

"Once or twice. It depends. Dealing with water damage from hurricanes and floods is different. Tornadoes are my specialty."

"How did you get into this line of business, anyway? It seems like a strange specialty."

"I suppose it does." He studied her. "I guess I fell into doing this so naturally, I never thought of my business as unusual. One day I was a successful commercial contractor and the next day I couldn't win a bid to save my soul. A small town near my home where a friend of mine was mayor was hit by a tornado. He asked me to fix them up. To treat the entire town as one client to generate overall cost savings and that was that. One thing there's never a shortage of is tragedy."

"So where are you from originally?" Someplace a little south of here, she'd wager, based on his accent.

"Missouri," he said, sounding sad. "Outside of St. Louis."

"You still have family there?"

He nodded. "We see everyone a couple times a year. Between jobs. And I take several weeks off over the holidays and head home." Then, as if the turn in conversation toward family had made him uncomfortable, he asked, "So what do you do in Manhattan?"

"I work…used to work…for a Wall Street investment firm."

"Used to?"

"I quit. Last week."

"Sounds like a spur-of-the-moment decision."

"You got that right." She took a swig of beer.

"So now what?"

"Your guess is as good as mine."

"What brings you to Mirabelle?"

"Needed some time away. A lot of time away."

"Hmm." He considered her. "Something else happen?"

"I suppose you could say that. Nothing short of my world collapsing around me." She took another drink of beer. "The firm I work for had been cheating customers without my knowledge. My parents are getting a divorce. And the last straw was finding out my fiancé of the last four years has been cheating on me almost since day one."

"Huh. That all?"

The words themselves could have been taken in a compassionate context, but the tone of his voice sounded rather unsympathetic. She studied his face, trying to discern exactly what he'd meant by those two words. "Excuse me?"

"I thought something really bad had happened."

"I tell you my life is falling apart and that's what you come up with?" She shook her head. "Wow."

"So you found out there are unethical people in this world and some of them work at your firm. Your mom and dad made some mistakes in their lives, but they're no different than, what, fifty percent of this country? And you found out in the nick of time that your guy is a lying, stinking excuse for a man. But is your world collapsing around you? I don't think so." He cracked another beer. "Now if you couldn't make your mortgage payment, then I'd agree you had a slight problem."

It didn't happen very often—no, make that it never happened—but Marin found herself completely speechless. She wanted to be angry with him, but couldn't seem to drum up the slightest bit of censure, given there wasn't an ounce of sarcasm or bitterness in his tone. He was merely stating the cold, hard truth.

"Sorry." He looked down at his beer. "Working around disasters for a living, I guess I have a tendency to minimize things."

"That's putting it mildly."

"Think about it for a minute. The world is full of people with stories a lot more heart wrenching than yours. Save your self-pity for those times in life that are truly deserving of the indulgence."

That comment stung. "Times that you're such an expert at, obviously."

"My story's bad, yeah, but it's not as bad as some of the folks living right here on Mirabelle. Look at what the tornado did to their town, their businesses. And if that's not bad enough, take the guy who lives on the other end of the island in the summer. His first wife and kids were killed in a car accident. He was driving. Then there's one of Missy's best friends who adopted her nephew because her sister, the boy's mom, was murdered by an abusive husband. The son of the island's retired chief of police, a game warden, was shot and killed by poachers." He took a swig from his beer. "Those are tragedies. The things that have happened to you sound a bit like stumbling blocks."

What the hell could she say to that without sounding bitter and petty? Maybe her problems were nothing in the grand scheme of things. His problems, on the other hand, involved the lives of children and the death of their mother, his wife, and he seemed to take it all in stride.

Or did he?

"Maybe you're right," she said. "But it's one thing to put life with all its ups and downs in perspective. It's quite another to deny that bad things even happened in the first place. Which one have you done with your life, Adam?"

Silently, he held her gaze.

She stood and headed for her house. "Thanks for the beer."

[faded text from previous page showing through]

CHAPTER THREE

MARIN WOKE AT THE CRACK of dawn her first morning on Mirabelle and glanced at the clock. By this time back in Manhattan she'd have already read the *Wall Street Journal* while working out on her elliptical, showered and dressed, eaten breakfast, had three cups of coffee and caught up on email, phone messages and the up-to-the-minute financial news on CNBC.

How many times over the years had she intently watched those news reports waiting for changes in the Federal Reserve's monetary policy? Then there were statistics on new home sales and jobless claims, along with the CPI, PPI and GDP. Any minute now the unemployment figures from last month were due to be released and every person on Wall Street was anticipating their next move in the financial markets.

Not your concern any longer, Mar.

She snuggled under the covers, closed her eyes and tried to go back to sleep. Instantly, the memory of how Adam Harding had looked in the moonlight last night flashed through her mind and her body came fully awake. Had she really been so frank with him as to suggest he was in denial? Yes, but then hadn't he suggested she was nothing more than a drama queen? The man had balls, she'd give him that. After shifting from one side to the other, flopping onto her back and then onto her stomach, she realized more sleep was simply not on her horizon.

She hopped out of bed and grabbed her cell phone to find Colin had already called twice this morning. *Too bad.* After shutting off her phone, she went downstairs to find her mother already up and sipping a cup of coffee in the kitchen, the patio door open to the sounds of chirping birds. "Morning, Mom."

"Good morning." She glanced at Marin. "Sleep well?"

"Actually, very." Marin poured herself a cup of coffee and noticed the sun rising over Lake Superior. A thin strip of hazy clouds obstructed an otherwise clear sky and in the distance she could just make out the shape of some kind of huge cargo ship heading, no doubt, to the port of Duluth.

"Isn't the view stunning?" her mother murmured.

"Yeah." Marin took a sip of coffee. Curious about those unemployment figures, she reached to turn on the small TV on the kitchen counter.

"Don't you dare turn that on."

"Why not?"

"The last thing I want to hear over the sweet chirping of chickadees and cardinals is the drone of CNBC."

Marin laughed.

"Sit down and relax."

"You're kidding, right?"

"Marin—"

"I'm going to work out." Figuring there wasn't a gym on Mirabelle, she put on her running gear. A glass of water and a yogurt later and she was outside stretching in preparation for a run. It was a gorgeous morning. Crisp, cool and she simply could not get over how clean the air smelled. She was bent down touching the sidewalk with her fingertips when the front door of the Harding house opened and Adam came outside.

Dressed in khakis and striped polo shirt, he looked cool and composed. Except for the fact that his still damp hair hung haphazardly over his forehead. "Morning," he said, a travel mug in one hand and a roll of what looked like some kind of building designs under his arm.

"Hi."

"You run every day?"

"No, I have an elliptical at home and a gym membership. Running's my stopgap."

He smiled and headed toward the street. "Do a few sit-ups for me, okay?"

From what she could tell, the man got enough of a workout on the job. Sit-ups didn't appear to be the least bit necessary. "Will do," she said, in any case, as she headed toward the street. "Who's taking care of your kids?"

"My assistant, Phyllis. For now, anyway." He hit the boardwalk at about the same time as did she. "Hey, and about last night," he said. "Sorry about what I said. I had no right to make light of what you're going through."

"No worries. Besides, I'm the one who should apologize. I was pretty blunt back at you."

"You live your life. I'll live mine." His cell phone rang. "I have to answer this. Have a good run." Without taking his eyes off her, he answered the call.

As she took off down the canopied residential street, a breeze came toward her bringing along with it the scent of a man's spicy aftershave. Damn, but that man smelled good. Was it wrong for her to want to turn around and bury her face in his neck? She almost stopped and turned, but she couldn't shake the feeling that he just might still be watching her.

"WHY HAVEN'T YOU STARTED *doing* anything yet?"

"Where are all these crews you promised us?"

"Start construction already, would ya?"

Adam sat at a table at the front of a large room in the community center, letting the islanders spill their guts for several long and drawn-out minutes. Several members of Mirabelle's city council were sitting alongside him, trying to keep the audience calm. On Adam's right were Carl Andersen, mayor and owner of the Rock Pointe Lodge, the largest resort on the island, and Garrett Taylor, the island police chief. Sarah Taylor, Garrett's sister-in-law and island wedding planner, and Marty Rousseau, manager of the Mirabelle Island Inn, were off to the left.

Carl, Marty and, to a lesser degree, Sarah, had been on board with Adam and his company from the initial phone call Carl had put in to Adam's company asking for a bid. Garrett, on the other hand, was still skeptical about working with one general contractor.

While Adam would've preferred not holding these meetings at all, he'd learned the hard way over the years that he could either face everyone at once at a time of his own choosing, or he could deal with them one at a time over the phone. Day in and day out.

Questions came at Adam like rifle fire, but he was used to this kind of reaction, at least initially. It had been the same in each and every community he'd rebuilt, especially at the beginning of every job. Everyone in this filled-to-capacity room was worried. Everyone was impatient. Everyone wanted his or her house repaired, street fixed or business up and running first. They wanted their lives back as quickly as possible and it was hard to fault any of them for being human.

"All right. All right." Adam finally stood and held up both hands. He connected eye-to-eye with as many individuals in the room as possible. His gaze caught with Missy Abel's and he found himself unaccountably searching for her sister, Marin. As he recalled her fresh, energetic appearance in running gear at the start of this very long and drawn out day, he forgot what he'd been saying, and everyone in the room stared at him expectantly.

Oh, right. Questions.

"One person at a time, so I can hear you," he continued. "I will answer questions until every person in this room is completely satisfied. I promise."

Hands flew into the air.

Adam made it a point to memorize as many names as he could prior to starting every job. If there was one thing that helped people in these situations feel better, it was being treated like a person as opposed to a number. He pointed first at an older man in the front row who owned buildings on Main Street that had gotten hit head-on in the storm. "Ron Setterberg, correct?"

The man nodded. "How long before you'll know if my buildings are structurally sound?"

Adam felt Garrett glance sideways at him. The worse the structural damage, the longer repairs would take, and Ron's buildings had suffered some of the heaviest damage from the storm. Garrett's wife, Erica, owned Duffy's Pub, the most popular bar and restaurant on the island which also happened to have been located in the hardest hit of Ron's buildings.

"I have a crew of experts making assessments as we speak," Adam said. "They have assured me they will have their findings on every single building impacted by the tornado ready for me by the end of the week—"

"But what's your gut feel?" Garrett blurted out.

Adam turned to the man sitting next to him. "I'm sorry, Chief Taylor, but I don't guess when it comes to ensuring people's safety. I deal strictly with facts. By the time we're finished here, I will personally guarantee you that every building will be one hundred percent safe to be open for business."

Adam held Garrett's gaze. He'd never been stared down by a police chief, and Garrett Taylor was one intimidating man.

"How will you communicate these findings?" Ron asked.

He caught Missy's gaze again. Marin apparently wasn't here. He took a deep breath and continued. "My admin team has already set up a Mirabelle website which is noted in the pamphlet of information you were given when you walked into the room. This site will be updated at the end of every day with any notices or changes in project status. The experts' findings will be posted on this website as soon as we have them."

He'd learned the hard way on his first job that a website was the only way to minimize the chances of getting woken up at ungodly hours with anxious phone calls. So he'd hired a communications specialist to update the website and field calls who was based at the home office outside of St. Louis, along with his accounting staff.

"You can call me directly, if you prefer," Adam went on. "But you'll likely get my voice mail given the amount of time I spend on the jobsite. I do return every single call, but it might take a few days. You're more likely to get the information you need in the timeliest manner from the website. The website knows what I know."

Ron nodded, as did several others in the audience.

Adam pointed to a middle-aged woman in the third row looking as if she was going to bite his head off. Another thing he'd learned? It didn't do any good to try and stall the disgruntled. "Delores, you have a question?"

"I own the—"

"Bayside Café with the reputation for the best cheeseburgers in Wisconsin," he said giving her a slight smile. "Yes, Mrs. Kowalski, I know."

With that acknowledgment, a little of the heat had gone out of her gaze. "Well, I'm losing more than just tourist business right now. I'm missing local business and I could be servicing your construction crews, as well. Why can't the Bayside get repaired right away? We didn't have that much damage."

"That's a good point. Your café is scheduled to be one of the first businesses completely up and running. I guarantee that." But it still wouldn't happen fast enough for her. Nothing ever happened fast enough for people whose livelihood had been destroyed. "The priorities as stated in our bid will be… first businesses crucial to the day to day lives of the island residents. The businesses that are geared toward tourism will be lower priorities given this is the off-season—"

"But what about our fall Apple Festival?" someone called out from the audience. "That's a big weekend."

"And the snowmobilers?"

"Not to mention the skiers and snowshoers?"

Heads bobbed up and down in agreement, and Adam could've sworn he heard Garrett growl beside him.

"I understand everyone's concerns." He looked around the room. "Believe it or not, I've studied your hotel occupancy reports. I know which weekends are the busiest. My crews and I will do our best to have as many businesses up and running by the Apple Festival, but our agreement for full functionality was Christmas."

That met with murmurs of disgruntled acceptance.

"Remember, folks, our biggest enemy in this process is going to be the weather," he said, glancing out over the entire group. "Our goal is to repair all exterior structural damage, such as roofs, windows and doors, and outside walls well before the first snowfall. Then we can concentrate on interior repair."

He pointed to an older woman in the front row. Mrs. Miller. Before she opened her mouth, based on her pursed lips and superior air, he would've put money on her being a bad apple in the group.

"You've been here more than a week, and it looks to me as though nothing is getting done. I could probably fix my ice cream shop faster myself."

He was tempted to tell her to go ahead and try and he'd have one less thing to worry about, but that wouldn't solve anything. "Well, Mrs. Miller, it looks as though things are moving slowly because, quite frankly, they are. For now. We're still organizing things, making assessments, and getting supplies ordered and delivered. When my core construction workers are operating at full steam, things will come together pretty fast. If you still have a complaint two to three weeks from now, you let me know."

And she would. He had no doubt about that.

He answered dozens of questions before the group seemed to start running out of steam. Several people had already left or were standing up to leave.

"One more thing," said Missy Abel. "What can we do to help?"

Adam smiled at Marin's sister. Already, he liked some of these islanders much more than others, but unfortunately, Missy's store, Whimsy, wasn't going to be one of the first businesses back up and running. "The most important thing you can all do is to be patient. The less time I have to spend making you all happy, the more time I have for making your community whole again. If you happen to have construction experience, that's a different story.

"I'll hire anyone who knows what he's doing. Understand that you will be working for me. Taking orders from my foremen. If you can work toward a common goal rather than setting your own agenda please see me after this meeting."

More people left. "I want you all to know that I will have Mirabelle one hundred percent open for business by Christmas. We'll have to put a few finishing touches on in the spring, but she'll be better than ever by Memorial Day and the start of your tourist season. Thanks for coming."

"That went pretty good," Carl said.

"Yeah, not bad." Adam gathered up his files.

"If there's anything at all you need…"

"I'll call."

Carl nodded and headed toward the door while Sarah and Garrett hung back. "You got a second?" Garrett asked.

"Sure." Adam turned and reminded himself that the intimidation radiating off this man was all because he cared deeply about this island and its residents. "What can I do for you two?"

"My brother, Jesse, is the best carpenter on the island," Garrett said.

"Jesse's my husband," Sarah added. "He couldn't be here tonight, but I know he'd want to work for you."

"Tell him to stop by my trailer as soon as he can and we'll figure out what crew to put him on."

"No references, or resume?" Sarah asked.

"Nope. I don't say this about everyone I meet, but your word's good enough for me." He paused and turned to Garrett. "By the way, Duffy's was in a pretty old building. The layout of the place was a bit antiquated by today's standards. It wouldn't cost any more for you and Erica to sit down with an architect and tweak the designs a bit. It might even save some money."

Garrett nodded. "That's a damned good idea. I never did like the fact that I couldn't see the lake from the bar."

"There's your silver lining." Adam patted him on the back. With the way this project was going, he had a feeling he was going to need every friend he could get.

CHAPTER FOUR

"FREE TRADE GOODS. MADE BY women in the U.S.A."
Marin analyzed the Whimsy business files on
Missy's home computer. "I hate to tell you this, sis,
but you're spending way too much for the inventory
at your gift shop."

"And I hate to tell you this," Missy said as she
continued folding laundry at her kitchen table. "But
that's exactly the point."

Frustrated, Marin flipped through month after
month of profit and loss statements. Some months,
her sister was barely making any money and others
she was losing her shirt. "Who does your accounting?"

"I do my monthly stuff and an accountant in Ashland does my taxes. A payroll company pays Gaia
and any other summer help I need."

"Speaking of which, you're paying your employees too much."

"College is expensive these days. I'm doing what
I can to help my staff."

Marin pulled up several more files on Missy's
computer and continued poring through one spread-

sheet after another. Her sister was the worst businesswoman Marin had ever run across. "Your profit margins suck. In some cases, you're actually losing money on the stuff you sell."

Missy smiled. "I know."

"You need to raise your prices and start buying cheaper goods from China."

"Next thing I'll be outsourcing everything." Her sister laughed. "Marin, my gift shop isn't about making money. I'm lucky enough to have a balance in my trust fund that lets me do whatever I want. And part of what I want is to give back. My gift shop helps me do that by buying goods from people all over the world who are struggling so that they can put food in their mouths. And help to support single, working moms here in the U.S. so they can feel good about getting a fresh start."

Marin sighed. "Okay, I get it."

"Do you?"

"Kind of." Marin shrugged. "But I guess it's hard to slough off the whole bottom line thing."

"Tell me something," Missy said, snapping out a T-shirt. "Do you really like all that business stuff? I mean really, really love it."

"Well, I—"

"Just think about it for a minute."

"There are parts of it I enjoy. Like the fact that it feels vital and in the moment. But I have to admit that there are days I'm not crazy about what I'm doing."

"So do something else."

"Like what?"

"I don't know. Why don't you take this time on Mirabelle to get all that finance mumbo jumbo out of your head so you can recharge. Get some perspective on life."

"And how do I manage that?"

"I don't know. Paint your nails. Daydream. Read a book."

Snorting, Marin returned to analyzing the spreadsheets.

Missy stalked over to her then and flipped a switch on the computer, shutting it down.

"What did you do that for?"

"When's the last time you read something other than the *Wall Street Journal*? Something purely for entertainment?"

"High school."

"Then you're long past due." She grabbed a book down from the stack on her desk hutch and held it out toward Marin. "Here."

The book cover depicted a bare-chested man and a woman in a flowing gown in what looked like a desperate embrace. Marin laughed out loud. "A romance? Seriously?"

"Try it. You might like it."

"HIGHER, GAMMA!"

"Higher!"

"Okay, here we go!" Angelica announced as she

pushed the two boys in their swings, one part of an elaborate backyard play system that Jonas had built.

A picture-perfect late summer day, like all the others had been since they'd arrived on Mirabelle, the sun was shining, a light breeze was blowing and the scent of petunias was in the air. Marin was bent over weeding Missy's vegetable garden when Missy came outside with a pitcher of iced tea and several glasses. "Time for a break, Marin."

Marin slipped off the gardening gloves she'd borrowed from Missy, sat beside her on the patio and took a long drink of cold sweet tea.

Missy sat on one of the other chairs and watched their mother with her two boys. "What do you suppose is the crux of the issue between her and Dad?"

"He's a self-absorbed ass and she's fed up."

"It's never that simple." Missy sighed. "She's such a good grandma."

"Not surprising, considering how devoted she's always been as a mother."

Suddenly, Michael started fussing for no apparent reason. A moment later, Nate followed suit.

"Time to go read, boys." Missy stood. "Aka, naptime," she whispered to Marin.

Their mother lifted the boys out of their swings and walked them across the yard. "I'll see you boys later."

"Bye, Gamma," they both called together. "Bye, Mairn."

"It's so cute the way they say your name."

"Yeah. Cute."

The minute the door closed, Angelica sat in the chair next to Marin and sipped her iced tea. "I love the city," she said. "But I might be able to get used to this."

"We've only been here a few days," Marin said. "Wait a few weeks. I have a feeling you'll be bored out of your mind."

"Oh, I'm already a bit bored, but I'm sure I could find plenty to do here."

"Do you mean you're thinking of, like, living here?" Marin asked, astounded. For as long as she could remember, her parents had split their time between D.C. and Manhattan. The Camden idea of wilderness had been Cape Cod.

"Goodness, no." Angelica shook her head. "I love being here and getting to be grandma, but I'd miss the hustle and bustle of the city too much. Some extended time over the summer, though, would be nice."

Angelica glanced out across the yard and seemed to focus on something in the distance. "We need to meet those children," she murmured almost to herself.

Marin followed her mother's gaze to find Adam's kids taking turns going down the rickety slide of a rusty old swing set while his assistant, a tall, thin woman with short salt-and-pepper hair who appeared to be in her late fifties, stood nearby talking on a cell phone. The picture had been some variation of the same theme for each of the past several days. The children entertained themselves while the woman talked on the phone or worked on her laptop.

Just then the woman started pacing. A moment later, she stopped at the picnic table where her laptop was running and lit a cigarette.

"I wonder how their mother died," Marin's mom said as she set down her tea.

"I should've asked Adam."

Her mother raised her eyebrows. "When did you talk with him?"

"The other night when I went home early. He was sitting outside having a beer."

"And you joined him. Hmm. He's a handsome man."

"Don't even think about it, Mom. Me getting involved with any man right now is entirely out of the question. And a man with children? Never, ever gonna happen."

The kids, bored with the slide, wandered over to a large, but sickly looking pine tree. The girl boosted her brother up to the lowest branch and slowly but surely they both climbed up the tree. *Get off the phone, lady, and take care of those kids.* Hell, even Marin, as inexperienced as she was around children, could tell that was an accident waiting to happen.

"Good Lord," her mother murmured. "If they're not careful, they're going to break their little necks."

They climbed higher and higher.

"That's it," her mother said, pushing off from her chair. "I can't stand it."

Oh, oh. Knowing exactly where this was going to lead, Marin followed her mother across the lawn. Angelica Camden was the sweetest person in the world until she was crossed or found a cause to support, and then the barracuda in her came out with a vengeance.

"Hello, I'm Angelica Camden," Marin's mother said as she approached the other woman.

Clearly surprised, the woman spun around. "I'll have to call you right back." She flipped her phone closed and set her cigarette in an ashtray on the picnic table. "Phyllis Pennick. Adam Harding's personal assistant."

"Did Mr. Harding ask you to watch his children?"

"Yes." She didn't look happy to be caring for two youngsters, but was entirely resigned to her fate. "Just until he can find a replacement nanny."

"Well, in that case, I suggest you pay more attention to your charges, or there won't be a need for a new nanny." Angelica stalked over to the tree. "Children, why don't you come down? You can play in the playhouse in my daughter's yard."

"We can?" the little girl said, her big brown eyes widening with excitement.

"Absolutely."

"Awesome!"

"Only for a little while," the assistant added.

The two kids scrambled down the tree, ran to

Missy's backyard, and immediately climbed the ladder into the tree house. The assistant, on the other hand, stayed in Adam's yard, but now kept vigilant eyes on the children.

The little girl poked her head out from the window. "This is high," she said, smiling at Marin and exposing permanent teeth that looked too big for her little face. For a kid, Marin had to admit, she was adorable. With brown hair, cut in a long bob, much like Marin's, and brown eyes, she looked like her father.

"What's your name?" she found herself asking.

"Julia."

"And your brother's name?"

"Wyatt." He poked his head out from one of the other windows and smiled. His brown hair was cut very short, showing off cute little ears that bent a bit outward at the top like an elf. "And I like this."

"Well, you both can come over here anytime you want," Angelica said to them. "As long as it's all right with your dad."

Soon they were alternating between the slide, the fireman's pole and the monkey bars, and Angelica was having the time of her life. "How old are you, Julia?"

"Seven and a half. I'll be in second grade this year. But I don't know anyone in my class."

"Well, there must be other kids your age on the island."

"Hello, there." A man's voice sounded behind them.

Marin turned. Adam. His gaze caught with Marin's first and she couldn't for the life of her stop the little flutter in her stomach at the sight of him. "Hi," she barely managed to get the word out of her mouth. Dressed in jeans and a black polo shirt, he was the best thing Marin had seen all day.

He glanced from her to her mother. "Mrs. Camden."

"Please call me Angelica."

"I thought I'd stop up here and give Phyllis a break." He glanced at his assistant. "You ready for some lunch?"

She nodded vigorously. "And I have several urgent emails that need to be addressed."

"Go ahead. I got my kids."

The woman nabbed her laptop and disappeared into Adam's house.

Adam waved to his kids and turned back to Marin and Angelica. "So how are things going?"

Angelica raised her eyebrows. "Other than your assistant being too busy talking on the phone to pay proper attention to your children?"

Oh, God. Marin rolled her eyes.

Adam's expression was completely unreadable. He could have been upset with his assistant, worried about his kids, wishing Angelica Camden would butt out of everyone else's business, or any combination of the three. Then again, it was possible he found the entire episode entertaining. Marin had no clue.

"They were just climbing the tree, Mom," she said, interrupting. "They were fine."

"That's what everyone says until a neck gets broken."

"Mother—"

"How long until you find a replacement nanny?"

At that, he displayed his first show of emotion. Clearly, more than anything, he was worried for his children. "The agency said to expect it to take at least a month. I don't want to rush things and get just anyone in here because I'd like to make sure whoever I hire is in for the long haul." He paused. "Once school starts, things will be a lot easier."

"Will they both be in school full-time?" Angelica asked.

"Yes, ma'am. Both of them." Adam nodded. "The school on the island offers a full-day kindergarten option, so even Wyatt will be gone all day."

"In that case," Angelica said, "I can take care of your children, Adam, until you find a new nanny."

What? Marin swung her head so quickly toward her mother she wouldn't have been surprised had she snapped a vertebra in the process.

Adam smiled indulgently. "No offense, Mrs. Camden, but—"

"Oh, I suppose I'm not as limber as most nannies and I don't have an education degree, but I do love children," Angelica said. "Raised four of them virtually on my own. U.S. senators, you know, don't have much time for parenting. And you won't find me talking on a cell phone while they're in my charge."

"I didn't mean to suggest you weren't qualified," Adam said. "Only that I need someone until I can find a permanent nanny."

"Well, I'm here for at least a month with nothing much to do other than play with my grandsons. And they have a mother to take care of them. I don't want to put you on the spot, though, so you think about it and let me know what you decide."

For a long moment, he studied Marin's mother. Then he shook his head. "I don't have to think about it. If Missy's disposition is any indication of your child-rearing abilities, then I have nothing to worry about."

Marin felt her mouth gape at his implication that her disposition, as opposed to her sister's, was less than ideal. But that was beside the point. She still couldn't believe her mother was serious about babysitting these kids. "Mother, are you sure—"

"When do you need me to start?" Angelica asked. "Monday morning at eight?"

"Perfect." Angelica smiled. "And don't you even think about paying me. I do not want your money."

"You're sure about that?"

"I'm the wife of Arthur Camden, Mr. Harding. I would prefer that you send any money you'd be paying me along to Carla. Under the circumstances, her family will likely need it."

"In that case, I'll add the funds to the severance I

was already going to give her." He nodded. "Would you like to work the details out now?"

"You're still busy with work." She smiled. "Monday morning is fine."

"Okay, then." He turned to walk away, but then stopped and turned. "You're sure about this?"

"Positive. It'll be my pleasure. One more thing, though?"

He held her gaze.

"If I were in the construction business, I'd be ashamed of that swing set in my backyard."

Adam glanced at the old metal set and chuckled. "Point taken." Then he turned and walked on.

Marin waited until he was out of earshot before spinning around. "Are you out of your mind, Mother?"

"No." She grinned. "What I am is damned happy to have a purpose to my days and those children need someone. So does their father. The kids, I can help with. The man?" She chuckled. "I'll bet he'd take your mind off Colin Everett Masterson III."

"He has kids, Mom."

"No one said you had to marry him, Marin."

CHAPTER FIVE

THE CAPE COD MARIN AND HER mother had rented had only two bedrooms, and Marin's mother had chosen the one on the first floor, leaving the entire upstairs, basically, a remodeled attic, to Marin. Pale moonlight streaming through her bedroom window, Marin flicked through her cell phone messages as she walked into the bathroom getting ready for bed.

Her father had called Marin at least four times since she and her mother had arrived at Mirabelle and had left two voice mails. As she brushed her teeth, she quickly texted to let him know they were fine. What else was she supposed to do?

Colin, on the other hand, had left no fewer than twenty messages, text and voice mail combined. They ranged from soulful apologies to frantic appeals to angry outbursts, and she'd deleted every single one of them.

How could he have done this to her? She rinsed out her mouth and washed her face, scrubbing roughly. They'd been as good as soul mates practically since the day they'd met in grad school. They'd been cut from the same cloth, both of their families coming from old, East Coast money. They liked the same books, movies, TV shows, food, colors, decor and even hand soap. They'd fit together, their lifestyles, their dreams and aspirations. And he'd been entirely content with her decision to not have children.

All in all, they'd wanted the same things in life. Or so she'd thought. Shutting off the water, she dried her face. Then he'd broken her heart. She slathered on a moisturizer.

Or had he?

Shouldn't she be more inconsolable if her heart truly had been broken? Shouldn't she want to throw her phone across the room, smashing it into a thousand pieces? Shouldn't she be unable to sleep or eat? Shouldn't she have cried at least once?

Instead, it was almost as if she'd expected this outcome to their relationship. Maybe that's why she'd kept delaying the wedding date, almost as if her subconscious had known that when she'd come home early from that conference that she was going to find Colin in bed with someone. What she hadn't expected was for that someone to be Colin's best friend. Marcus.

It explained so much. She padded to her bedroom. It probably even explained why she'd found herself so undeniably attracted to their neighbor Adam, a man as virile and down-to-earth as Colin was cerebral and refined. And gay.

Pretty simple, really. Available woman in need

of an available, attractive—very clearly heterosexual—man. No reason not to act on it, right? Except that she wasn't entirely sure Adam was attracted to her. Maybe there was something wrong with her. Maybe she just wasn't feminine enough to attract a masculine man.

With a heavy sigh, she climbed onto her bed and dialed Colin's number. He picked up on the first ring. "Marin, thank God, you called. Where are you? Your doorman said you'd left the city."

"I'm on Mirabelle," she said quietly, not wanting to wake her mother who'd gone to bed almost an hour ago.

"You went to Melissa's? Why?"

"You expected me to stay in Manhattan? With everything that's going on?"

"The paparazzi have been hounding me to death."

"Better you than me. This is, after all, your doing."

"I didn't mean it like that." He sighed. "Oh, Mar, I'm so damned sorry. I don't know what else to say."

What else could he say? She knew his family well. His father and mother wouldn't just be surprised. They'd likely disown him if they found out. Colin wasn't a bad man. In fact, he'd been her friend before they'd gotten engaged. He was still her friend.

"I have to know," she said. "Did I do something? Not do something to…cause this?"

"Oh, Marin, how can you say that? Think that. It's not you. It's me."

"How long have you known?" she asked, trying to understand.

"Do we have to go there?"

"I do. Did you know before we started dating?"

He was silent for a moment. "Yes."

"You son of a bitch." The words came out of her mouth without heat. As much as she tried, she couldn't seem to summon an appropriate amount of anger, let alone indignation.

"I guess I thought you knew," he said. "Inside. I mean, come on, Mar. We weren't exactly a match made in heaven, but I assumed it was a match that suited you. Your needs. The way the facade of our engagement suited mine."

"I was convenient, is that it?"

"No. You were…content with…mediocrity."

That made her angry. "Content with—I thought I loved you! I thought you loved me. I thought we were good together! I thought—"

"Marin, you've worked ten- to twelve-hour days from the day I first met you. Between your career, your volunteer gigs and your workouts we barely saw each other. Maybe, if we were lucky, we ran into each other in bed in the middle of the night once a week and made love. The truth is that I spent more time with Marcus than I did with you. And you can almost include the time we spent sleeping together in that equation. Can you honestly tell me that's a vibrant, healthy relationship?"

He was right. She swallowed. But he was wrong,

too. Maybe she'd worked so many hours and kept so busy because she'd been, underneath it all, so dissatisfied in her relationship with Colin. She remembered the nights he'd turned her down when she'd wanted to be intimate. When she'd wanted more from him. She hadn't understood her own frustration. Now, she wondered.

"I think there was a part of me that felt like…like there was something wrong with me, Colin. Sexually. For wanting more. For not turning you on."

"I'm sorry," he said. "That's my fault entirely."

"Does anyone in your family know? Your sisters? Your brother?"

"Good God, no! And I'd very much like to keep it that way."

"You should tell them."

"Can't we just let this…die? I'll do whatever you want. Tell everyone I was cheating. With a woman, please. Tell them I beat you. That I have gambling debts. However you want to handle the breakup, I'll go along. Just don't tell my family. The press. My coworkers. Please, Marin."

"Tell me this. Would you have gone through with the wedding?"

A long pause followed, and then he admitted, "Probably."

"Wow." She shook her head. "Fine. Tell everyone you had an affair with some woman, if that makes it better for you. I really don't care anymore."

Marin hung up the phone, flicked off her light and

stared outside. A full moon shone down on the trees, casting creepy shadows on the grass. She cracked open the window, letting the still-warm late summer breeze flow through the room. It was quiet here, so quiet she could hear the wind rustling the leaves of the towering old maple just outside her window. Maybe Saint Barts wouldn't have been a good idea. She needed this time away more than she'd realized.

All her life, she'd swallowed hook, line and sinker her father's rhetoric about how Camdens being Camdens needed to lead by example. She'd meticulously dotted her *i*'s and crossed her *t*'s. She'd been a high achiever, some said overachiever, in both academics and athletics throughout her childhood. She'd graduated summa cum laude from Harvard. She donated heavily from her trust fund to worthy causes. She spent every Wednesday night at the women's shelter, every Sunday at the food bank. Worst of all, through it all, she'd even imagined herself happy and in love. It had all been a lie.

Well, now she had to find out what she wanted from life.

Her gaze was suddenly, inexplicably drawn to Adam Harding's backyard. Would she find him, once again, leaning against his tree? But no. He was inside, his house completely dark but for one dim light at the first floor. Pale sheers fluttered with the breeze blowing through his open window. His bedroom? Probably not. The bright glow of a computer screen indicated it was likely an office. He was working late.

She would've sworn she could hear him talking, possibly on the phone. Holding her breath, she strained to listen. Whether real or imagined, there was no doubt he had a nice voice, deep and calming. And that faint touch of a Southern accent? *Mmm.* What would it feel like to kiss that lush lower lip? To nip at him softly? To feel that big, warm body around her, over her?

Oh, hell.

Needing a distraction, she picked up the romance Missy had given her the other day. If nothing else, it would put her to sleep. By page ten she realized her mistake. She was going to be up for a long, long while.

"WE'RE LATE," MARIN WHISPERED as she followed Missy into the large room at the community center amidst an uproarious discussion.

The town meeting, apparently one of many that would be had over the coming months to discuss the progress on Mirabelle's rebuilding, had started several minutes earlier. As quietly as possible, she slid after Missy into the first available seats in the last row.

"Didn't you just recently have one of these meetings?"

Missy nodded. "The engineers finished with

their building assessments and Adam wanted to go through the results in person."

"So what was the point in dragging me here?"

Missy grinned. "Because I want you to come to the yoga class I'm teaching right after this."

"Yoga?" Marin rolled her eyes. She should've guessed something was up when her sister had also suggested Marin wear something loose fitting and comfortable. Why did it not surprise her that her vegetarian, tree-hugging little sis was also a yogi?

"And I wanted to introduce you to some of my friends." Missy pointed toward the front of the room. "Sarah is one of the council members. She's sitting up at the table next to Garrett."

An old woman in front of them shifted and glared pointedly at Marin. "Shh!"

After the hag turned back around, Missy grinned and whispered in Marin's ear. "Mrs. Gilbert. Runs a mean bed-and-breakfast inn."

Marin snapped her mouth closed and looked toward the front. Several townspeople were sitting behind a long table, but it was Adam who captured and held her interest. For close to an hour, she listened to him field one question after another in a detached and unemotional, but somehow compassionate, mode.

People were angry and frustrated. There were any number of times islanders said things clearly inflammatory in nature and Adam not only didn't react, he also managed to defuse every one of those situations, turning them to his advantage. You couldn't teach a man that kind of control over his emotions.

What would it feel like to snap his concentration? To release his power, his energy behind closed doors, to feel his passion running wild? Nothing like Colin's lukewarm attention, that's for sure. She'd always dated professional, white-collar men. Intellectuals. Thinkers, not doers, but Adam seemed to bridge that gap. Maybe her mother—her own mother—had been right. Maybe what Marin needed right now more than anything was no-strings-attached sex. Hot, passionate, burn the bedsheets sex. Maybe Adam Harding *was* man enough to wipe away every bad memory of Colin. But was Marin woman enough?

The thought had barely entered her mind when the town meeting abruptly wrapped up. Suddenly, Missy was introducing Marin to several people. Then she asked, "Coming to my yoga class?"

Marin shrugged. "No offense, but I'm not really into yoga."

"You should try it," Sarah said. "Missy's a very good teacher."

"I'm sure she is." Marin chuckled. "But I'm more of a…kickboxing kind of woman. I think I'll just go home."

Missy looked disappointed, but she'd live.

Marin turned to head for the exit and almost ran into Adam's back. She put her hands out to steady herself. "Sorry. Wasn't watching where I was going."

He turned. "Hey, there. I'm surprised to see you here. Find it interesting? Or entertaining?"

"I thought you were nothing short of amazing," she said honestly.

"I'm not too sure about that." He laughed, although he looked tired and wrung out, and who could blame him after the way the locals had raked him over the coals.

"How do you do what you do?"

"What do you mean?" he said as they pushed through the exit doors and stepped out into the cool evening air.

"There was so much emotion in that room. At one point, it was so tense you would've needed a stainless steel blade to cut the air."

"I guess I've gotten used to it."

By unspoken agreement they both turned in the direction of their tree-canopied street. "I don't think so," she said, shaking her head. "Either you have an incredible gift, or you have ice running through your veins. Which is it?"

"Those are the only two options?" He grinned. "Then I'll go with ice."

No way.

"I've been in the construction business a very long time," he explained. "Something always manages to go wrong, no matter how well you plan. There are just too many variables out of a contractor's control. You either learn how to deal, or you get ulcers. Maybe I like spicy food too much." He stuffed his hands into his pockets. "What about you? Wall Street can't be a cakewalk."

"It's a bit on the intense side, yes."

"Coming to Mirabelle must be like going from sixty to zero in the blink of an eye. You missing it yet?"

"The first couple of days were tough, but now?" She thought for a moment. "I don't miss it much. Surprisingly."

"What about your fiancé. Missing him?"

"There's another surprise. No." She laughed. "Finding the man you're about to marry in bed with his best friend has a way of altering things…in the blink of an eye."

"His best friend?" He narrowed his eyes at her.

"You know, I don't really want to talk about him." She managed a smile. "There was a lot of truth to what you said that first night. I dodged a bullet."

He frowned, clearly still disconcerted about making light of her situation. By this time they'd reached their houses. Rather than head up his sidewalk, he stopped and held her gaze. "He lied to you. That's not your fault."

"No, but it doesn't stop me from wondering if I'd somehow caused it." If maybe it was her fault that she didn't turn him on. Maybe she wasn't feminine enough. Not sexy enough. There was one way to find out. "So I was thinking…maybe we could…I don't know. Go out to dinner some night."

"Dinner?" His entire body went still. "You mean just the two of us? That's not a good idea."

The intensity of his eyes belied his words. "I'm not talking about anything serious, Adam. Just dinner." Dessert, hopefully, would come later.

"Sorry. Widower, remember? The kids. The way I move around." He shook his head. "I don't date."

"So that's it?"

His gaze traveled all over her face and settled on her lips. His eyes darkened, almost as if he might reconsider. Then he turned and started up the walk. "That's it."

Apparently, she wasn't woman enough for Adam Harding, either. That is, if she bought his excuse lock, stock and barrel. Which she didn't. Colin and his betrayal might've thrown Marin for a loop, but she was pretty sure Adam was attracted to her and fighting it.

This wasn't over. Not yet, anyway.

A DATE. ADAM HADN'T BEEN on a real date since high school, since Beth. Even if he could fathom returning to that scene, he wouldn't have had a clue what to do, how to act, what was appropriate. Not that Marin hadn't tempted him with her offer.

As he opened the front door to his house and stepped inside, he glanced back at Marin. Head down and lost in thought, she was stalking back to her house like a woman on a mission. Very likely, she wasn't used to taking no for an answer. Cool, calm and all-business women had never really been his type, but she sure filled out running gear nicely.

Not gonna happen. Not now. Not ever.

On a sigh, he walked into the house and Phyllis, looking stressed out, met him at the door.

"It's about time." She handed him a stack of phone messages. "These are critical. The rest I've left for tomorrow."

"Thank you, Phyllis." He glanced through the calls he'd missed. "How did it go with the kids?"

"Fine. They're playing outside." She grabbed her laptop and several files. "I'm out of here, thank God. I can get back to my real job on Monday morning, right?"

"Yep. Angelica's set to go."

"Great." She was already halfway out the door. "See you Monday."

Adam set his own laptop and messages on his home office desk and then walked toward the rear of the house.

Julia spotted him in an instant and came running inside. "Hi, Daddy!"

"Hey, sweetie." His gaze caught a basket full of clean clothes that still needed to be folded and another load lying on the floor still needing to be washed.

Wyatt ran at him from outside and hugged his leg. "Daddy! I'm hungry."

"Me, too!" Julia said, bouncing up and down. "Can we go out to dinner tonight and go shopping?"

"Shopping? For what?"

"School starts soon. We need to get stuff."

He stopped and closed his eyes. He'd all but forgotten about school starting, and it'd take a trip to Ashland to get what they needed. All the work he had to do between now and then piled up like a checklist inside his mind. "Honey, Mirabelle doesn't have the kind of stores we need, and I'm not sure—"

"Daddy, it's a...ritual. Everybody goes school shopping."

"I want a backpack," Wyatt added. "I need one, right, Julia?"

"You need supplies, too," Julia said, nodding. "And a jacket. And some new jeans."

She was right. The island was going to start getting chilly and most of Julia and Wyatt's clothes were suited to warmer climates. Still, he couldn't afford a day away from the construction site.

"I can't manage the time away right now," he said. "I'm sorry. We'll get on the computer together tonight and order online what you need for the first couple weeks of school. I'll make sure it's shipped here on time. That's going to have to do."

"Okay," Julia said, sounding miserable. "Will you take us another time?"

"Sure."

"Promise?"

He wasn't going to promise. He'd done that and hadn't followed through too many times. "I'll do my best. Now let's go figure out what we're having for dinner." He was going to have to make time to go grocery shopping this weekend, too.

A date. As if Adam had the time.

CHAPTER SIX

"YOUR HOUSE LOOKS JUST like ours." The young girl's voice came from the kitchen along with the sounds of the patio door sliding open and an umbrella being shaken out.

What were they doing here? Marin frowned. Her mother had promised she'd babysit the Harding kids where they belonged. At the Harding house.

From Marin's position, stretched out on the couch in the living room reading—*devouring*, might be a better word—another one of Missy's romance novels, she couldn't see the three, but she could hear them. All morning, as a warm, late summer rain had been drizzling down, she hadn't moved off the couch except to eat, drink and use the bathroom. Now, she wondered if she shouldn't head upstairs in an effort to maintain this uncharacteristic sense of tranquility.

"I hadn't noticed until now, but our house does look a little like yours, doesn't it?" Angelica said. "Except you have a fireplace."

"That rain makes me thirsty," Wyatt said.

At that, Marin smiled. Rain always made her thirsty, too.

Marin's mother and Missy both appeared in the entryway to the living room. Missy was holding a clear plastic storage box filled with what looked like art supplies.

"I thought we agreed you'd be watching those kids at their house," Marin whispered.

"We did, and I will," her mother replied. "Most of the time. But I wanted to do a messy project with them."

"So you'd rather destroy our kitchen," Marin said. "Why don't you go over to Missy's?"

"Jonas is getting the boys down for a nap and we didn't want to keep them awake," Missy explained. "What have you been doing all day? I thought you might stop by to visit."

"Reading."

"All day? You? Lying on the couch?"

"Miracles do happen." CNBC was surprisingly quickly losing its draw on her.

"Well, just keep reading," her mother said. "We won't disturb you. I promise."

Famous last words. Marin returned to her book. Within seconds, she felt eyes on her. Both Julia and Wyatt stood in the archway to the kitchen watching her.

"Are you reading?" Julia asked.

Desperately trying to get back to it. "Yes."

"My mommy liked to read, too."

Oh, God. "Did she read to you?"

"Every night." Julia frowned. "My daddy doesn't like to read, though."

"Nope." Wyatt shook his head.

Marin didn't want to care about the problems these kids were going through, but as if a weight was pressing down on her chest, her heart ached all the same. She refocused on her book, hoping they'd take the hint.

"We're going to make something for Carla," Julia said.

"So she won't forget us," Wyatt added.

"Okay, we're ready," her mother called from the kitchen. "Come to the table, kids."

For the next half hour, Marin lay there, half reading, half listening to what was happening in the kitchen. A large part of her wished they'd leave, a small part of her somehow enjoyed the commotion, and, surprisingly, there was even a tiny part of her that wanted to join them.

Eventually, that tiny part won out. Closing her book, she went into the kitchen. "Oh, my God," she murmured, her eyes widening in horror. Colored rice, feathers and all different shapes and sizes of pasta noodles had spilled onto the floor. Paint and glue had dribbled onto the table. And glitter was stuck to everything, everywhere. "Look at the mess you're all making."

"I know." Missy grinned. "Isn't it great?"

"No, it's actually not." Marin picked up a colored pom-pom that she'd almost stepped on. "It's a mess."

Julia held up a frame made from wooden Popsicle sticks. Loose ribbons and glitter fell to the floor. "I'm going to put a picture of me in here and mail it to Carla."

"Me, too!" Wyatt's eyes sparkled as he held up his frame.

She had to admit it was a thoughtful thing to do for both the kids and Carla. "Who's going to clean this mess up?"

"I think you should," her mother said, chuckling.

Marin raised an eyebrow at her mother.

"You know what your biggest problem is, Marin?" Missy cocked her head. "You've never been a kid yourself."

"Well, that's not entirely true." Their mother looked from Missy to Marin. "You had quite a whimsical nature when you were very young. Do you remember the plays you two used to put on for me?"

"What I remember is Marin always getting the good parts," Missy said. "She was the fireman while I had to be the damsel in distress. She got to be the princess and made me, not a horse mind you, but a donkey."

Marin laughed. "But you were so good at braying, Mel."

Missy glared good-naturedly at Marin.

"I loved listening to you both write the lines and

make the sets. You were quite artistic, too, Marin. Do you remember those watercolors you used to do?"

"I remember," Marin murmured. She'd absolutely adored painting, and yet she hadn't picked up a brush in years. "Why? Why did I change?"

"I have no clue," Missy said. "But you turned sixteen and turned into a by-the-numbers stick-in-the-mud."

"Oh, it didn't really happen overnight," her mother said. "You started working for your father here and there. Slowly, but surely, as you matured, I guess your priorities changed."

That made sense. She'd enrolled in an after-school painting program in junior high and taken several art classes in high school. Once she'd gotten into college, though, it seemed she never had time for those liberal arts classes.

As if she was curiously listening to their conversation, Julia quietly set aside her finished frame, went to the rain-spattered patio door and looked outside. The next thing Marin knew, the young girl had opened the door and was putting her arm outside. She grinned as raindrops accumulated on her skin.

"All I remember is when you babysat on Friday nights," Missy went on. "You wouldn't let me sneak in any TV shows or movies Dad had on his taboo list, you made me and Max go to bed exactly at our bedtime, you wouldn't let me have a candy bar if I didn't finish all my supper, and you stood next to me in the bathroom with a timer set for five minutes when I brushed my teeth."

"I did do all that, didn't I?"

"You were more strict than Dad."

"I'm sorry."

"I don't want you to be sorry, Marin." Missy wrapped her arm around Marin's shoulder. "I want you to get in touch with that long-lost inner child."

"Sorry to disappoint." Marin chuckled. "But Wall Street has a way of smothering inner children."

"So revive her," her mother said softly. "Take your father's tapes out of your head and listen to your own."

Suddenly, Julia turned toward Angelica. "Can I go outside?"

"Oh, good heavens, it's raining."

"So." Julia shrugged. "It's warm rain."

Her sister thought Marin was a stick-in-the-mud and her own mother thought Marin had lost her priorities. Maybe they were both right.

"I want to go outside," Julia said.

"Is there lightning?" her mother asked.

Marin went to the patio door and looked up into the sky. "No. No lightning." She'd always wondered what it would feel like to walk in the rain. *I do remember how to have fun. I can let go.* Without giving it a second thought, she walked outside.

"Marin, you're going to get soaked," Missy said, laughing.

"Isn't that the point?" Marin put out her hands and spun around as the fat, wet drops hit her head, arms and shoulders, drenching her in minutes.

"Can I go, too?" Julia asked.

Wyatt came to stand beside Julia. "Me, too?"

"Marin, are you sure there isn't any lightning?" Angelica called.

"No. Just rain." Marin opened her mouth and put her face up to the sky. "Warm, wet rain."

"Okay," Angelica said, smiling. "Go for it!"

A moment later, both Julia and Wyatt squealed with delight as they stepped outside. Laughing, Wyatt grabbed her leg and wiped his face on her jeans. Julia took Wyatt's hand and pulled him out into the yard. Before she knew it, Marin was running through the grass and jumping in every puddle she could find. She was wet, a little bit chilly, and she couldn't remember having felt this alive for a long, long time.

"THE BAYSIDE CAFÉ IS completely finished?" Adam asked one of his foremen over his cell phone as he walked home in the rain.

"Yes, sir, and Newman's will be finished in the a.m."

"I'll do my walk-throughs after lunch tomorrow." He already knew they were still behind on the library and Duffy's, so there was no point in beating that dead horse. "Have a good night," he said, wrapping up the call as he headed up the sidewalk to his house.

Adam shook out his raincoat, hung it out on the porch and walked through the front door. There were no lights on inside the house and all was silent. For a moment, he was more than a bit concerned, but then he remembered the Camdens were a well-known family. Angelica wasn't about to run off with his kids. "Hello?" he called out. "Anyone home?"

When no one answered, he walked into the kitchen and found a note on the table. Angelica and the kids were over at her house working on an art project. He was thankful for the opportunity to let his head clear. It'd been a long day.

He walked over to the kitchen window and saw the lights on in the Camdens' kitchen window. Angelica and Missy were standing at the patio door laughing. But what—

He followed the direction of their gazes and found his kids skipping through a small river running through the far side of the backyard. His first instinct was to call them inside and give Angelica Camden a piece of his mind. They were going to catch a cold. What a mess, cleaning up those wet clothes. Was it lightning out?

Then the sheer joy on their faces registered, and he couldn't help but smile. It wasn't often he saw his normally reserved children let loose like this. It was good to see them laughing, to see them blissfully happy for a change. Then he noticed Marin out in the rain. For a moment, he watched the three of them interact. Although Julia seemed to keep her distance, strangely enough, Wyatt seemed to really like Marin.

And no wonder. Marin, for her part, looked as though she was having as much fun as they were. Kicking the water with her bare feet and splashing him. Chasing him around the yard. Her hair was plastered to her head, but her face, wet and glowing with life was the prettiest thing he'd seen in many, many years. She turned her face to the stormy sky and spun around like a child.

Suddenly, he couldn't take his eyes off her. Her clothing, a white V-neck T-shirt and faded low-slung jeans, clung to her like a second skin, and it was clear that sweet creature splashing in the rain was no child. She was a voluptuous and curvy...woman.

His smile slowly disappeared as a jolt of awareness spread through his body like a shot of an old single malt whiskey, warm, strong, heady. He wanted to feel those curves. That skin. Those wet lips. He wanted to hold a woman in his arms again, but not just any woman. He wanted this one. He wanted—

I want.

The realization that his body was firing to life again after all these years stunned him motionless. He'd completely forgotten what it had felt like to be a man, to feel raw desire course through his veins. He was alive. He was still alive.

Marin caught him watching her through the

patio door, and the look on her face said she understood exactly what was on his mind. Even more astounding, though, was her reaction to him. Instead of being embarrassed or indignant, she was right there with him every step of the way. Instantaneously aware of him, wanting back. She licked her wet lips, and her mouth went slack. Her gaze homed in on him, his face, his body. Then, as if snapping out of it, she steadied herself by reaching for the trunk of the nearest tree.

No. He couldn't do this. He had no right to feel this way. Mentally shaking himself, he grabbed several clean towels from the bathroom and opened the patio door. "Julia! Wyatt!"

"Daddy!" Julia stopped and waved to him. "Come out. It's fun."

"Daddy, Daddy!" Wyatt yelled. "Get wet with us."

"Oh, no. You two had better come inside now before you catch cold."

"Ahh," they both groaned.

"Come on, guys." Marin came to the door, but the kids kept playing in the rain. "I'm sorry," she said, slightly out of breath as she ran a hand through her wet hair. "The rain is warm, but I hope you don't mind the kids getting wet. They were over at our house doing a craft project with my mom and we... It was just kind of spur-of-the-moment."

"No apologies necessary. I'm glad they had a good day with your mom. And you."

Water dripped off her nose and eyelashes, and his

gaze was drawn to the rivulets of rain trailing down her cleavage and the lacy outline of her bra under the wet, translucent cotton. He wanted nothing more in that moment than to strip those wet clothes right off her.

They stood there for a moment, neither saying anything, only the soft sound of her breathing filling the silence. Suddenly, he wanted so badly to kiss her, to feel her, to hold her. As if she could read his mind, she let go a low sigh and moved toward him, her mouth slightly parted.

"Marin, don't," he said. "You don't know—"

"Shh." She spread her hands on his chest, suffusing his core with warmth. Then she moved slowly toward him and kissed him. Softly. Her touch so light, so sweet.

It was at once both the strangest and the most wonderful feeling to have her warm, wet lips touch his. So different from Beth. Her taste. Her smell. The feel of her. He closed his eyes and drank in the sensations. "I've never kissed any woman other than Beth," he whispered against her mouth. "In my entire life."

"Never?" She drew away slightly. "But that—"

"Shh," he whispered, kissing her again. "I like it." The wetness of her shirt under his hands registered, and he realized he'd gripped her shoulders and pulled her tight against him. She wasn't nearly close enough for what he wanted—

"Daddy, that was so fun!"

Adam jolted away from Marin only a second before the kids came running inside.

"You should've come out with us!"

"We got so wet!"

Confused, he glanced at Marin. She looked as dazed as he felt. "Here." He handed her a towel. Then he turned away and focused on the kids. On and on, they chatted and animatedly described the rain, their day, and all the while Adam barely heard a word they said.

All he could think about was Marin still standing too close beside him. That the front of his shirt felt wet where her breasts had pressed against his chest. Of the drop of rainwater falling from the end of a strand of her bangs and landing on her cheek. Her skin was so clear, so soft-looking, it was all he could do not to use the water droplet as an excuse to reach up and touch her again.

The kids wound down and dried themselves off and an awkward silence filled the kitchen. "By the way, Marin." He cleared his throat. "Could you tell your mom that I'm interviewing nannies? Should have someone here in three to four weeks."

"Sure," she said, backing away. "Well, I should go."

Yes, she should leave. Now as a matter of fact.

"Thanks for the towel." She handed it back to him.

"Bye, Marin," both kids called.

Adam couldn't seem to find his voice and she ran out into the rain. All these years, he'd been able to go about his business, day in and day out, not thinking about sex. He'd fooled himself into believing desire was all a matter of control and that he was a disciplined man. Now he realized his mistake. All these years, he simply hadn't been tested. No amount of control was going to keep him from wanting Marin.

Well, he might not be able to stop himself from wanting her, but he could—he would—stop himself from doing anything about it. After all, it was his fault—*his* fault—Beth had died. He should've taken better care of his wife. He should've done... something, anything to save her. But he didn't. He'd failed.

So go ahead. Want away, you fool. Torture yourself to death if it makes you happy. That's not going to change anything. You still can never let yourself have her. Never.

CHAPTER SEVEN

IT WAS HERE. THE FIRST DAY of school.

"Come on, Wyatt, finish your cereal," Adam said. "We have to leave in a few minutes, and I want you to brush your teeth."

"I don't feel so good," Wyatt said, looking into the bowl.

Adam's cell phone rang and his laptop dinged with incoming mail, but he ignored the intrusion and knelt down in front of Wyatt. "Are you sick?" he asked Wyatt. "Or are you just nervous?"

"I don't know."

Adam felt Wyatt's forehead. No fever. "Well, don't worry about finishing." He took what little remained of the bowl of cereal and dumped it down the garbage disposal. "Go on up and brush."

As Wyatt raced up the stairs, Julia came into the kitchen. She unzipped her backpack and looked through everything for the millionth time. "Are you sure you got everything, Daddy?"

"Positive, but let's check one more time." He didn't blame her for a minute. There had been too many times in the course of the past several years that she'd been the only one in class unprepared for this, that or the other thing simply because he'd forgotten or didn't know about something happening at school.

He produced the supply list. "I'll read everything off and you can check your backpack." A few minutes later, every item was accounted for, and Adam smiled at his daughter. "Satisfied?"

"I guess."

"You sure look nice."

A few of the things Julia had ordered online had been delivered, so she'd laid out what she was going to wear the night before, a lime-green knit skirt with a matching hooded sweatshirt. Wyatt on the other hand, in a pair of new sweats and a long-sleeved rugby shirt, had chosen comfort as opposed to style.

"Daddy, are you going to walk us to school?" Julia asked.

"Of course. Haven't I always taken you on the first day?"

Holding one child's hand in each of his big mitts, they took off outside. As they passed Marin and Angelica's house, he glanced up. It'd been several days since that kiss in his kitchen, and while he'd seen plenty of Angelica in the interim, he'd seen neither hide nor hair of Marin.

More than once he'd wondered if he hadn't just imagined what had happened between them. Three years was a long time for a man to go without touching a woman, but then the very real feel of her warm, wet lips and the scent of rain on her skin came back to him, reminding him that moment they'd shared had been all too real.

You've got more important things to worry about this morning.

Putting aside the unsettling thoughts, he refocused on his kids and they walked the several blocks down to the small elementary school. No school buses on Mirabelle. Everyone walked or rode bikes.

As they approached the building, it became apparent that he was, as usual, the only father amidst a sea of mothers. The women were lining kids up outside and taking pictures. Adam had forgotten a camera again, but he had his phone. "Do you kids want pictures?"

"Naw," Wyatt said.

"I do." Julia grinned. "Come on, Wyatt."

"Yeah, Wyatt," he said. "It's your first day of kindergarten."

Julia bent down slightly, put her arm around Wyatt, and Adam snapped off a couple pictures. "There. You two look good." He turned his phone around and showed them the shots he'd taken. The school bell rang and Adam realized that they were the only ones still outside.

"Daddy, we have to go!" Julia grabbed his hand and tugged.

Adam reached for Wyatt and they walked down the main hall to the classrooms. They dropped Julia off first. She was a bit hesitant, but she went into the room without incident. "Bye, Daddy. See you later, Wyatt."

Adam and Wyatt turned toward the kindergarten room.

Suddenly, Wyatt looked up at Adam. "I don't feel good." His face was as white as a sheet and his eyes seemed unfocused. He looked as though he was going to—

Oh, no.

Wyatt bent over and threw up all over the hallway outside of his classroom. The moment Wyatt straightened and realized that the kids in the surrounding area had either stopped and stared or screamed and ran away, tears pooled in his eyes. Then he turned toward Adam and buried his face in Adam's gut.

Wyatt's teacher came out of her classroom. "No worries. Maintenance will be here in a jiff. Are we sick or nervous?"

"Nervous, I think," Adam said softly.

The janitor came to clean the area.

"Why don't you head to the nurse's office and let her decide, okay?" the teacher said.

As Wyatt turned down the hall, Adam said to the maintenance man, "Sorry about that."

The guy smiled. "Happens every year on the first day. Usually more than once."

Adam took Wyatt into the nurse's office, saw the worry had returned to his son's face and bent to talk to him. "You okay?"

"Daddy?" Wyatt looked up at Adam, worry creasing his little brow. "What if my teacher's mean?"

Adam swallowed. Maybe he should hire a nanny who was capable of homeschooling and call it a day. Although that was a good thought, it was too late for this school year.

"You know, son, I just don't think that could happen in a place as nice as Mirabelle. Everyone knows everyone else, and all I've heard are good things about the teachers. Remember, you're going to be in the same classroom as Julia at least part of the day. You'll be all right."

Trooper that he was, Wyatt nodded, turned and went into the nurse's office. Now it was Adam's turn to feel as if he might throw up.

THE FIRST DAY OF SCHOOL.

Marin had to admit that, despite her every effort to the contrary, she'd thought of Julia and Wyatt—not to mention Adam—several times that morning. To keep herself occupied, she'd gone to Missy's first thing after breakfast to help wash windows. The construction down on Main tended to kick up a lot of dust that, of course, ended up on every glass surface.

"Mom said she's staying on Mirabelle for at least another month," Missy said, spraying down the window in the family room.

"Yeah, I know."

"What about you? You going to hang around a little while longer?"

Marin had been debating that for the past few days. There was nothing holding her to Manhattan other than her apartment and a few close friends. She paid her bills online, and the company that managed her apartment building was handling her mail for a small fee. She had no plans, no pets, no job.

"I don't have anything to go home for, yet," Marin said on a sigh. "I might as well stay."

"Good." Missy smiled. "It gives us more time together."

It also gave Marin more time to sort out what was happening between her and Adam. A kiss didn't have to mean anything, but, oh, what a kiss it had been. She touched her lips, remembering. *That* was the way a kiss between a man and woman was supposed to feel. Colin had been so right. She had been settling for mediocrity all these years.

If that was how Adam kissed, what would sex with him be like? Her knees almost weakened at the thought. Just sex. That's exactly what she needed. Especially with a man who came with a complicated package including kids.

The thought of Julia and Wyatt had her glancing at the clock for the third time in the past half hour. It was only a little past noon.

"You keep looking at the clock," Missy said. "Marin, if you have something else to do, you should go. I'll manage."

Might as well fess up. "It's the first day of school." Marin wiped down the front storm door. "And I'm wondering how Julia and Wyatt are doing."

"Well, that explains it. You always hated the first day of school."

"Actually, I hated every Monday."

"I remember. Sunday nights were the worst." Missy paused. "I have something that might take your mind off things." Grinning, she raced into the kitchen and returned with a package. "I ordered a few things for you and they were delivered yesterday."

"What is it?"

"Open and see."

Marin slit the tape and opened the package flaps. Inside the box were tubes of watercolor paints, several pads of paper in varying weights, colors and textures, a variety of sable brushes and natural sponges, a couple of palettes, and a variety of mediums to be added to the paints to create differing washes, textures and transparency.

"You did your research," she whispered, more than a little impressed with her sister's thoughtfulness.

"I found supply lists on the internet. Along with several courses you can take through reputable colleges online."

"Online, huh?"

Missy nodded. "And now that you've decided to stay on the island a little while longer. Here." She tossed a notebook down. "Illustrate those for me. Children's books I've written."

"You've written children's books?"

"I wanted something different to read to the boys and decided to teach them a little about Lake Superior. One thing led to another, and I ended up with a separate book about each of the Great Lakes. I've tried drawing pictures, but all my attempts look silly and amateurish."

"You think mine would look any different?" Marin laughed. "The only formal training I've ever had was in high school."

"I remember your paintings were beautiful, and I was so jealous that I had no talent."

That was nice she remembered. "But I haven't painted in years."

"I'll bet it's like riding a bike."

"I'll bet it's not. Besides, I've heard children's publishers like to match the artist with the book. So why bother?"

Missy smiled. "I think the better question to ask is why not?"

MISSY'S WINDOWS NOW SPARKLING, Marin, Angelica and Missy sat at Missy's kitchen table for an afternoon snack with the boys. While the boys were quietly occupied eating chunks of cheesy crackers and drinking fruit juice, Marin glanced at Angelica. "You ready to tell us what's going on between you and Dad?"

Missy raised her eyebrows. "Believe it or not, I was about to ask the same thing."

Her mother looked up from her cup of hot tea. "I think you hit the nail on the proverbial head. This situation is between your father and me. It wouldn't be right to lean on either of you."

"That's bullshit," Marin said. "I'm fully aware of Dad's failings as a man. But he's my dad, and I love him. I don't think there's anything you can say that will change that."

"Divorce him and just be done with it," Missy said, putting a few more crackers on each boy's tray. "No one would blame you."

"You should know by now, Missy, that it takes two to make a marriage and two to break it up."

"You're right." Missy sighed.

"Still," Marin said. "It never hurts to talk things through."

"It seems so silly, really."

"Spill it, Mom."

Her mother stirred her tea. "In a nutshell…I've been thinking for years that I'd like to go back to work, and I finally got up enough courage to put out some feelers with friends. The week before I came to Mirabelle, I was offered a job as a children's book editor at a major New York publishing house to start in the new year."

"That's wonderful, Mom!"

"Well, your dad doesn't think it's so great because I'd have to spend a lot of time in Manhattan. He said his senate career isn't just his. It's ours. I've been on board with him all these years and he still needs me."

"Well, that's awfully selfish."

"Actually, he made several good points."

"Such as?"

"Married couples shouldn't make unilateral decisions in situations where that decision might impact the other person. So I shouldn't have been out looking for a job without discussing it with him first."

"But he would've just shot you down."

"Exactly." She munched on a couple of the boys' crackers. "I've always felt uncomfortable with being a senator's wife. The entertaining. The constant limelight. Life in the public eye."

Her mother had never talked about this before, but given she was relatively quiet and introverted it made perfect sense to Marin.

"This has been creeping up on me for years," Angelica continued. "And it comes down to this—I can't be who he needs me to be any longer. The life of a senator's wife is killing me."

"Oh, Mom." Marin reached out and put her hand on her mother's arm. "I didn't know you felt that way."

"I've gotten to where I need something of my own," she said. "Something interesting and challenging that I can jump into with both feet. And if Arthur won't jump with me, I don't see any alternative but divorce."

"Do you want a divorce?" Missy asked.

"That's the crazy part of all of this. I don't. I know you've had your issues with your father, and rightly so. He can be demanding and unforgiving, but he has many admirable qualities."

"Such as?" Missy asked, clearly unconvinced.

"He's passionate and dedicated. He's generous, not just with money, but with his time and ideas. He's a good man. And I know you won't believe this, but he can be so thoughtful and romantic."

"Our father?"

"Yes, your father."

They all chuckled, but then Angelica's eyes misted. "I'm so glad the three of us are here together."

"Me, too." Missy leaned over and kissed their mother's cheek. "And I want you to know that whatever you decide about Dad, I'm here for you."

"Me, too," Marin added.

The boy's started fussing to get out of their high chairs and quiet time was over. Angelica glanced at the clock. "Well, girls, I have to run. School's just about over, and I need to meet Julia and Wyatt and walk them home."

"And I'm going to get the boys down for a short nap," Missy said.

"All right, I'm out of here." Marin picked up the box of painting supplies Missy had given her and walked to her house, all the while thinking about her mother's issues with her father. Her parents could actually get divorced. The thought was surprisingly unsettling.

With a heavy sigh, she set the box on the kitchen table and glanced down at all that nice, blank paper and those plump tubes of brilliant colors. She had no intention of illustrating Missy's children's books. To begin with, it'd been so many years since she'd painted anything, including the walls in her Manhattan apartment, she'd be starting from scratch. She had the time, no doubt, but not the inclination.

She smoothed her thumb over the fine sable brushes, delighting in the needle-sharp point of the liners, the fullness of the rounds, and finally, the thick softness of the flat brushes used to wash both water and color onto the paper.

Then again, where was the harm in just fooling around? Watercolors had been fun, and nothing said she had to paint Missy's books. For that matter, she didn't have to paint anything in particular.

She grabbed a big sheet of textured paper, a cup of water and, dipping a wash brush into the cup, dampened a small section on the paper. Now what?

Blue. Easy. Once upon a time, she'd quickly mastered the sky and the look of water. She squeezed out a small smudge of color and gave it a shot. After several attempts, she was frustrated. First the color was too dark, then her paper had dried out, and then she had too much water. Crumpling up the paper, she tossed it in the trash and started over. After several more attempts, she'd finally managed a halfway decent sky. Painting water, she remembered, had been more difficult, but this time she painted quickly before her paper could dry. The results were less perfect, but more interesting.

Time to play. She toyed with the blurred image of a boat and the detailed lines of a bare tree. Flowers, faces, buildings. She outlined, highlighted and washed. She used every single brush and played with mixing colors. By the time she was finished, she'd filled up several pages of paper with sophomoric, uninspired creations. Clearly, any talent she may have had when she was younger had dried up like the watery paints drying on the paper in front of her.

That was that. She set Missy's notebook of children's stories on the counter with the intention of returning it to her sister. Then she washed out the brushes, stacked everything back into the box Missy had given her and carried the box upstairs, kicking the whole kit and caboodle under her bed. Out of sight. Out of mind. Just like Julia, Wyatt and Adam Harding.

CHAPTER EIGHT

"Put on a sweatshirt because you're coming with me." Missy charged into the rental house, snapped the book out of Marin's hands and plopped it down on the coffee table. "When I suggested you pick up reading for enjoyment again I wasn't talking 24/7. Today's the start of Mirabelle's Apple Festival, and we're going to pick some apples, clamber around the pumpkin patch and go on a hayride."

Over my dead body. Not only did none of that small town festival crap sound even remotely interesting, the last thing Marin wanted to do was take a chance on having to face Adam after that kiss. Two weeks. Two blissfully uneventful weeks since the rain kissing incident. "Go without me, Mel. I'm quite content right where I am."

"Come on, Marin, it's gorgeous out. A perfect day to get out and enjoy autumn."

The trees in the backyard had somehow turned the richest shades of red, gold and yellow almost overnight, it seemed, indicating the days were getting shorter and colder. Today there wasn't a cloud in the sky and it was warm enough outside that Marin had cracked a nearby window for a whiff of fresh fall air.

"What are you hiding from, Marin?"

"Nothing."

"In case you haven't figured it out by now, us Camden women have an uncanny ability to read other people. Which means I know you're lying. Something happened. I want to know what it is."

In high school, Marin and Missy had shared almost everything with each other. Then they'd become adults and went their separate ways, only Marin had never been as close to a girlfriend as she'd been with Mel. "I kissed Adam Harding," she said, blurting it out like a schoolgirl.

"Seriously?" Missy's mouth gaped. "When?"

"Remember that day you and Mom were at our house doing an art project with Julia and Wyatt and I went outside in the rain? When Adam got home and I went into their house, it just kind of happened."

"Who kissed whom?"

"Oh, there's no doubt I kissed him." She chuckled as her forwardness in his kitchen came back to her, and then sobered as she remembered his intense reaction, the way it felt to have his arms around her. "But then we…he kissed me back."

Missy chuckled. "Okay. So when this kiss happened, the feeling, the moment, was mutual, right?"

"Oh, yeah." Very mutual.

"Then why is there a problem?"

"A problem?" She hopped up and went to the window. "Trust me. There's more than one."

Missy sat on the edge of the coffee table. "Like…"

"I'm rebounding from Colin." That was a stretch, but she was still in no position to get this serious this quickly. "Adam has children. I don't want children." She paced. "And to top it all off, he is far from over the death of his wife. Can you believe that kiss we shared was the first time he's ever kissed a woman other than his wife?"

"Ever?"

"Ever."

"Whoa."

"See what I mean?" She plopped down on the sofa.

"Was it just a kiss?"

Just a kiss. That was like saying just a tornado. Or just a hurricane. "Yeah. Just a kiss."

"How was it?"

Marin's body flushed with heat at the memory of Adam's mouth, his tongue, his hands on her. "Let's just say I didn't know what I'd been missing."

"So that explains why you've been hiding in here."

Marin held Missy's gaze. This time with Missy had brought back memories of the two of them talking until all hours of the night. Laughing, crying, teasing one another. Because of their family situation, the wealth they'd grown up around and their father being a senator, there were times when all

Marin had was Missy and their two brothers. It felt good to have Missy back.

"You know when you first disappeared," Marin whispered. "After what happened with Jonas all those years ago. I was really angry at you."

"I know that now," Missy said. "Back then, though, I wasn't thinking about you. I'm sorry."

"Don't be. You were hurting. I just wish I'd had the chance to be there for you."

"You're here now." Missy smiled. "Come to the Apple Festival with us."

"Is he going to be there?"

"Probably. It's Sunday. He and his construction crews will have the day off. There'll be a lot of people there, though, so you should be able to avoid him."

Famous last words.

"And I've invited John Andersen to join us." She grinned. "One of the island's most eligible bachelors."

Marin rolled her eyes. "Missy, please don't go trying to set me up."

Her sister laughed out loud. "Well, unless your tastes run along the lines of men old enough to be your father, I don't think you have anything to worry about."

"Good." She breathed a sigh of relief until the implication hit her. "Mom? You're trying to set up Mom?"

"I just want her to know there are other fish in

the sea. He's our island's retired pastor and his wife died last winter."

"But she hasn't even decided yet if she's going to file for a divorce."

"Well, maybe this will help to resolve things. And Doc Welinski will be there, too. He's put together a band that covers old classic rock."

"This I gotta see. All right. Let's go to this Apple Festival."

"DADDY, COME ON!" JULIA grabbed his hand and pulled him along. "I want to climb the haystack, too!"

Wyatt had shot toward the mountain of hay the minute he'd seen it and was already halfway to the top.

"I'm coming." Adam let himself get pulled along.

The minute her tennis shoes touched the hay, Julia dropped his hand like a hot potato and raced up the slippery hill.

"I'm gonna get there first," Wyatt called, laughing.

"No fair!" Julia yelled. "You got a head start."

While the kids played in the hay, Adam found himself perusing the crowd, but he wasn't just killing time. He was looking for Marin and there was nothing unconscious about it. He'd barely been able to stop thinking about her since kissing her that day she'd come in from the rain. She had to come today.

Everyone on Mirabelle was going to be here, that is if they hadn't already arrived.

The place was crawling with people and activity. Doc Welinski led a band of retirees who played classic light rock. Mrs. Miller had set up an apple doughnut stand that was selling the fresh pastries covered in cinnamon sugar as fast as her crew could make them. There was apple cider, popcorn and, of course, bratwurst. Kids were climbing a mountain made of hay, and families were traipsing through the orchard picking apples.

Just as Julia came rolling down the hill of hay, Adam caught sight of Jonas coming toward the haystack, his head sticking up a bit from the rest of the crowd. He was lugging the two boys around in his arms. Only a few feet behind him were Missy, Angelica, John Andersen and Marin.

One look at Marin's face and he could tell she didn't want to be here. She'd been avoiding him, and he didn't blame her for one minute. What woman in her right mind would want to get involved with him?

"There's Angelica!" Julia exclaimed.

"I see that."

"I'm going to say hi." She ran toward them and stopped in front of their group. "Hi!"

Angelica's face lit up. "Well, hello there, Julia."

Marin immediately glanced up, clearly looking for him. The moment her eyes caught his, she looked away. He'd been right. She had been doing her best to steer clear of him. He reached the group and greeted everyone.

"Where's Wyatt?" Angelica asked.

He pointed at the haystack. "King of the hill by now, no doubt."

Missy's boys immediately wriggled down from Jonas's arms and beelined it to the mound of hay.

"No fear," Missy said, shaking her head. "Those two."

Adam went to Angelica's side. "I keep forgetting to update you on the nanny search."

"Ah, don't worry," she said, dismissing him. "I love watching your kids, and it gives me something to do while I'm hiding out here on Mirabelle."

"Well, I'm interviewing a couple of candidates, so I should know something soon."

"When you find one, you find one."

What had Adam done to deserve her? "Anyone up for some caramel apple slices?"

When several in the group nodded, he asked Marin, "Will you watch Wyatt and Julia?"

"Sure," she said, her gaze intense.

He returned several minutes later with a couple baskets of apple slices and cups of gooey caramel to share. As they stood munching on apples and watching the kids play, several people stopped and shook his hand. Most of them he knew, but several he wasn't able to immediately place.

"We sure appreciate everything you're doing for our island."

"Looks like things are moving along pretty good these days."

"Don't know what we'd do without you and your men, Adam."

"Sure glad the Bayside's open."

"Good, hardworking crews."

He was surprised to hear almost exclusively positive comments from the islanders. Normally, he had as many people dissatisfied as satisfied, that is, until all was said and done. Then everyone was happy. By the time the last person left, he and Marin were standing side by side, alone. The others had moved closer to the hay. Angelica and John were nearby listening to Doc Welinski's band.

"My, aren't you the man of the evening," Marin said with a smile.

"For now. Next week, everyone just might hate me."

"I doubt it. From what I hear, the first couple of weeks were tough. People didn't see any progress, but things are coming along now."

"Slowly, but surely, everyone's opening for business. Unfortunately, the block hit the worst, Duffy's Pub, Whimsy and Sarah's flower shop, will be some of the last to be open."

"You can only do what you can do." She scooped some caramel with her last bit of apple and popped the treat into her mouth.

A dab of caramel stuck to her lower lip. He'd enjoyed the fresh taste of rain on her mouth. How sweet would caramel and apples taste on her? For a long, quiet moment, they said nothing, but as her gaze darted from his hair to his mouth, it was clear she, too, was thinking of that kiss.

"Listen, Marin—"

"Daddy, Daddy!" Julia raced toward him. "We have to hurry if we want to catch the hayride."

A trailer stacked with bales of hay, loaded down with people, and being pulled by two big draft horses came rolling down the road. In seconds, the haystack was all but forgotten as the kids raced to get in line for a hayride.

"Marin?" her mother called. "Go on the hayride and pick us out a couple of pumpkins."

Marin narrowed her eyes at her mother.

"Go quick! Before they leave!"

"Fine."

Adam helped Marin up onto the bales of hay and found the only place left to sit was next to her, but with his kids on board, he couldn't very well wait for the next ride. He had to squeeze in close to make room for another family, and to steady himself, he put his arm behind her and ended up brushing against the edge of her breast. She stiffened.

The hayride started, rumbling slowly down the road. He leaned toward her. "Marin, we need to talk about the other day," he said quietly. "When you came out of the rain. I—"

"Don't worry about it." She smiled. "It just happened. Doesn't need to mean anything."

"Well, it doesn't just happen to me. Beth and I were childhood sweethearts. Got married right out of high school. She's the only woman I ever dated."

"No wonder you turned me down for dinner." She shook her head. "Obviously, that kiss shouldn't have happened."

No. Mostly because he was beginning to wonder if anything except the both of them naked and sweaty and twisted up under a set of sheets would ever be enough. For either of them.

"You're not ready," she continued. "I'm not ready. I asked you out on a date to, basically, take my mind off Colin, my ex-fiancé." She paused. "You're not really what I want."

Ouch. He wasn't easily riled, but her comment struck a chord. "And what is it, exactly, that you want?"

"A man who neither has kids nor wants them is at the top of the list. You have two. They're nice, sweet kids. I just don't plan on ever being a mom."

"Well, that settles it then, doesn't it?"

"Yep."

"Not that it makes any difference, but I'm curious. Why?"

"I've always been focused on my career. I travel a lot for work. I haven't even bitten the bullet and gotten a cat. How could I raise children?"

"That was then, this is now. You quit your Wall Street job and aren't going back."

"Let me get this straight." She turned to face him

head-on. "Are you saying that you want a relationship with me?"

"Just playing the devil's advocate."

"Oh, really?" She studied him. "All right. Here's the bottom line. I'm too selfish, and I know it. I've known since I was a little girl that I would never have kids."

"That's pretty young to be making such a big life decision."

"I used to watch my mom and dad, living their lives, and I never wanted to be my mom."

"Your mom is a wonderful person."

"I know that. She's my mom. I love her. But for years on end, I watched my dad go off doing exciting things, making things happen while my mom stayed home with us kids. I couldn't help but think that there was more to life."

The horses stopped at the edge of the pumpkin patch and everyone jumped down to run into the field, except for Marin. "Come on, Marin," he said, throwing a note of challenge into his voice. "Don't you want to find the perfect pumpkin for your mom?"

"Is there such a thing?"

"Of course." He held out his hand. "I promise I won't bite."

She laughed, grabbed his hand and jumped down.

"Look at this monster!" Wyatt suddenly exclaimed from the edge of the field. Julia was already well into the pumpkin patch.

"Oh, my!" Marin laughed. "That just might be the biggest pumpkin in this entire field, Wyatt."

He grinned up at her. "You think?"

"Could be. We'll have your dad guard this one while we go look."

Wyatt looked up at his dad.

"Go," he said. "I'll watch it for you."

Wyatt ran off.

"And you said you don't like kids," he whispered to Marin.

"I don't."

Adam smiled as he watched her take off with Wyatt. He had a feeling that whether she liked kids or not, she'd probably make a good—no, a great—mom. His smiled waned. Someday she was probably going to make some lucky man an even better wife.

"THEY'RE VERY GOOD," Angelica said as she and John stood listening to the band of retired gentlemen covering old rock songs.

John nodded. "Willard put the band together over the past year."

"Which one is he?"

"The lead singer and guitarist."

As they snacked on apple slices and caramel, they chatted for a while about how Angelica's visit was going and how the tornado had impacted the lives of his two grown children, Carl and Grace, who lived on Mirabelle.

It was a beautiful afternoon and she was happy to be outside around all this life, but it was a bit disconcerting to have found out Missy had invited a single man just a few years older than her. She might be a bit out of touch, but she wasn't stupid. Then again, maybe it was best to get some more information before she jumped to conclusions.

"Are you fairly close to Missy?" she asked.

"Not particularly." He took another apple slice. "I mean…Mirabelle's a small place. Anytime there's a gathering of locals, we tend to see each other, but she's never before specifically invited me to something."

In that case… "This is a little awkward for me," she said. "I'm not entirely sure what Missy told you when she called, but—"

"It's all right, Angelica, no worries. I know you're married, going through a tough time right now, but you don't need to worry about me muddying the waters for you. My wife just died last January and I'm nowhere near ready to date."

That was a relief.

"But if I was," he said, smiling, "you'd be the first one I'd ask."

"I'm sorry about your wife."

"Thank you." He glanced up at the band and grinned. "Now, Willard, on the other hand. You're going to have to watch out for that man."

He'd no sooner made the comment, than the band announced a break and Willard joined them. He reached out for her hand. "You must be Angelica, Missy's mother."

"I am."

"Nice meeting you. Enjoying the music?"

"Very much, thank you."

"I've only got a few minutes here for a break." He held her gaze. "We're scheduled to play until seven tonight, but how would you like to shoot a round of golf with me sometime in the next week?"

She'd have been lying to say she wasn't appreciative of the attention, but she was still married. "Oh, I don't know—"

"How 'bout we make that a threesome?" John said with a smile.

"How 'bout we don't." Willard frowned at him.

Angelica laughed. "A threesome sounds wonderful."

"All right, then."

As Willard rejoined his band, Angelica noticed Marin traipsing through the pumpkin patch with Adam. The way they looked at each other and talked, if that wasn't attraction sizzling between those two, she wasn't a grandmother.

More than likely this wasn't serious for Marin. She was probably taking her mother's advice, and looking beyond Adam's two kids for something, or someone, to take her mind off Colin. What little Angelica knew of Julia and Wyatt's father, though, indicated he might have a tough time acting on his draw toward Marin. At least not without a little push.

And that is where Angelica came in.

"Would you like some hot cider?" John asked, pulling her out of her musings.

Angelica smiled as a plan formed in her mind. "Apple cider sounds absolutely wonderful."

CHAPTER NINE

"SLOPPY FACES AND MESSY diapers," Marin's mother said. "Or straightforward, clean school-age activities. Take your pick."

Marin paused in the task of washing her breakfast dishes at the kitchen sink to stare at her mother. "But it's Monday. Why aren't the kids in school?"

"They have the day off for some reason."

"This is not what I signed up for when you talked me into coming to Mirabelle."

"So go to Saint Barts next month. Today, I need your help."

Her mother had been watching the Harding kids after school for the past couple of weeks without mishap. Until today. Apparently, Missy had a doctor's appointment scheduled on the mainland. She'd been planning on doing some shopping at the same time and was expecting Jonas to watch the boys while she was away for most of the day. Jonas, as her mother had explained, had just gotten word that he had to fly out immediately to Washington, D.C., and they needed someone to babysit Nate and Michael.

Marin did not want to be having this conversation. "You should know Dad left a couple of messages on my cell phone."

Her mother was silent for a moment. "Did you call him back?"

"Yeah. I left him a message to let him know everything is fine."

"That's it."

"That's it. You want to talk about Dad some more?"

"No. And I know why you're changing the subject. That's enough stalling, Marin. Your nephews or the Harding kids?"

"Doesn't Mirabelle have a doctor?" Marin muttered.

"Yes. Sean Griffin. But he's Missy's close friend and she feels a little strange going to him for, you know, women's issues."

"Is Missy all right?"

"She's fine. It's her annual physical."

"Then it's not a big deal. She can reschedule."

"Well...that won't work."

"Why not?"

"She—she's already rescheduled twice before because she had no babysitter for the boys." Her mother put her hands on her hips. "Marin, come on. You were raised to step up to the plate when asked. I'm asking. You can take care of either Missy's two boys or Julia and Wyatt. Take your pick."

"The Harding kids." Somehow taking care of

two-year-olds, nephews or not, held worse than no appeal.

"Thank you. I'll head over to Missy's. You're on with Julia and Wyatt. I already told Adam you'd be taking care of his kids today."

"Oh, you did, did you?"

"The little darlings are waiting for you." Her mother chuckled wickedly as she headed outside and across the yard to Missy's house.

Feeling as if she'd just been played, Marin finished the dishes, grabbed the book she'd been reading and went to the front door of the Harding house. She knocked and waited.

A moment later, Adam, holding a cell phone, opened the door and waved her inside. "No, you can't do that, Ray," he said, his voice calm. "We already talked about this. The roof on all the building needs to get finished before your men start the interiors." He paused. "No." He paused again. "Ray, you're not listening to me. Do this my way, or find another job." He clicked off his phone.

"That sounded serious," she said.

Dressed in a pale blue dress shirt and crisply pressed khaki pants, his face cleanly shaven, he looked and sounded entirely prepared for the day. He smelled good again, too, thanks to his aftershave. She found herself having to stifle the urge to take another whiff of him.

"Serious seems to be par for the Mirabelle

course." He sounded awfully calm for a man with all hell apparently breaking loose around him.

"Are you sure this is okay?" he asked, holding her gaze.

It was babysitting, not rocket science. "Positive."

"I appreciate it. I really need Phyllis today and, honestly, the kids don't like her all that much."

"Well, I'm not sure they'll be all that excited to have me, either."

"Before I forget, a crew will be coming by today to put up some play equipment in the backyard."

She rolled her eyes. "I still can't believe my mother said that to you."

"I'm glad she did." He smiled. "She was right, and I might not have thought about it until it was too late for the kids to enjoy it."

They walked into the family room and found Julia and Wyatt, still in their pajamas and looking a little sleepy, snuggled on opposite ends of the couch watching cartoons.

"Hey, kids," Adam said. "Marin's here."

They both looked up.

"Are you taking care of us today?" Wyatt asked.

"Yep. Is that okay?"

Julia nodded, apparently uncaring.

Wyatt's eyes grew wide and he grinned. "Is it going to rain again?"

Marin laughed. "Sorry, I don't think so."

Adam was checking messages on his phone. "I have to go." He kissed the tops of his children's heads. "Be good for Marin, and I'll see you for supper."

"Bye, Daddy," Julia said, her eyes following him as he headed toward the front door.

"Bye," Wyatt said absently, his attention returning to the TV.

Marin walked with Adam to the door.

"My contact numbers are on the refrigerator. If all else fails, you know where to find me." He glanced again toward his kids. "Marin, I—"

"Go." She smiled as reassuringly as possible. "They'll be fine."

He turned and walked across the porch. The second his feet hit the sidewalk he was back on his phone. She remembered well those stressful days at her old job. Checking messages almost from the moment her alarm clock went off in the morning. Returning calls the whole way into the office. Eating lunch and sometimes dinner at her desk. Going home in the dark.

Suddenly, she realized, she didn't miss a single thing about her old job. Not the stress. Not the people. Not the hustle and bustle of the city. It should've been a weight lifted off her shoulders. Instead, she was left with a sense of uncertainty with regard to her future. What the hell was she going to do? She couldn't hide out here on Mirabelle forever.

When no answer miraculously came to her, she tore her gaze away from Adam, sat in the family room and grabbed her book. The kids ignored her and she ignored them. Perfect.

She picked up reading where she'd left off the previous night. What seemed a short while later, she'd just turned to a new chapter when a voice interrupted her story. The little boy was standing in front of her chair. "Did you say something?"

"I'm hungry."

She glanced at the clock and realized she'd already been here more than an hour. "You haven't had breakfast yet?"

"No. We woke up just before Daddy left."

"We can get it ourselves." The girl jumped up from the couch. "Come on, Wyatt." She pushed a kitchen chair over to one of the cabinets, climbed onto it and grabbed two bowls from the cupboard. "Get the milk, Wyatt."

Marin watched them, wondering all the while if she should be doing something, but they seemed fairly self-sufficient. While the boy took a carton of milk from the refrigerator, the girl set two boxes of cereal on the table next to the bowls and spoons. Julia managed pouring the cereal just fine, but Wyatt dumped out far too much.

Marin snapped her book closed. "Do you need some help over there?"

"No," Julia said, glaring at her. "We can take care of ourselves."

My, aren't we snippy?

"I need help," Wyatt said.

"I'll do it." Julia scooped up a handful of the cereal Wyatt had spilled and dumped it back into the box. Then she poured milk into Wyatt's bowl.

As they ate, Marin returned to reading her book. She wondered if she should have an ear toward what these kids were doing, but soon she was lost in her story. Sometime later, her foot having fallen asleep, she shifted and became aware of an all-too-quiet house. The milk, bowls and open boxes of cereal were still on the kitchen table, but the kids were nowhere to be seen.

"Julia! Wyatt!" she called, jumping up from her chair.

No answer.

Oh, hell.

They weren't in the kitchen, and they weren't upstairs. She poked her head out the back door and saw them playing on Missy's play equipment. Having changed out of their pajamas, Julia was swinging and Wyatt was climbing across the monkey bars. He looked kind of small to be hanging that high off the ground. Should he be doing that?

At a loss for determining the age appropriateness of the situation, she walked toward them. "Hey. Shouldn't you guys have let me know you were heading outside?"

"Why?" Julia muttered, glaring at Marin. "You don't care."

The girl continued swinging, the boy continued

across the bars, and Marin felt herself getting rather annoyed. "That wasn't very polite—"

The boy lost his grip and fell to the ground. Immediately, he cringed, gripped his ankle and started crying.

Just what Marin needed.

The little girl went to her brother. "Wyatt, are you okay?"

"Nooo," he wailed. "It hurts."

"Is it your ankle?" Marin asked.

"Yeeesss."

"All right. Let's get you inside." Marin bent to pick him up.

"Leave him alone," Julia said, holding Marin back.

"We need to ice his ankle."

"How do you know? You're not a very good babysitter," Julia said, sounding so mature for her seven years. "You're even worse than Phyllis. At least she watches us most of the time."

That stung, but the more Marin thought about it the more she realized that the kid was right. Marin had told her mother she'd babysit. The least she could do was do it right.

Marin took a deep breath. "You're right, Julia. I'm not very good at this, and I should've been watching both of you better. But I do know something about sports injuries and if we don't ice Wyatt's ankle, it'll swell up and hurt even more."

Julia's expression slowly cleared. "All right."

Marin picked up Wyatt, carried him inside and laid him on the couch. When she didn't find any ice packs in the freezer, she piled some ice into an air-tight storage bag, wrapped it in a thin towel and set it over Wyatt's ankle. Then she turned on the TV, thinking a kid's show might take his mind off the pain.

After a short while, Wyatt had not only dried his tears, he was smiling and laughing. Julia, on the other hand, sat stiffly on the couch. Marin removed the ice pack to look at his ankle. There was no swelling or bruising.

"Could it be broken?" Julia asked.

"That's what we're going to find out. Wyatt, can you move your foot?"

He wriggled it around without the slightest indication of pain. "It doesn't hurt anymore."

"Can you stand on it?"

He swung his feet down onto the ground and hopped off the couch. "Yep."

Crisis averted.

"Can I go back outside?" he asked.

Just then several men came around the side of the house hauling lumber and other supplies into the backyard. Then they started taking away the old metal swing set. "Maybe we should stay out of the backyard until those men are finished with the play equipment," Marin said. The last thing she needed was another injury. "Let's go somewhere else."

"Yeah! To the park!" Wyatt said.

"I don't wanna go to the park." Julia shook her head. "I want to do an art project."

"Park!"

"Project!"

Marin struggled to think of a compromise. "Hey." They ignored her.

"Hey, hey, hey. We have all day. We can do both, can't we?" Marin shrugged. "We'll go to the park this morning. Then we'll work on your art project this afternoon."

"Okay, let's go!" Wyatt said, and raced toward the front door.

"Julia, is that okay with you?"

"I suppose."

Marin stopped inside her own house to grab some money, just in case, and they headed down the hill toward the Mirabelle town center.

After a moment, Julia stopped. "I don't think this is a good idea. Daddy doesn't like us to come down to his work sites."

"We're not going there. We're going to the park."

"But the park is right by his office."

Marin studied the area. "That trailer? That's his office?"

Julia nodded. "He takes it wherever he goes."

"We won't bother him."

Wyatt skipped ahead, while Julia walked quietly, and Marin took in the sights and flavor of the island. These islanders were so lucky none of the big, stately elms, oaks and maples of this residential section of town got hit in the tornado. That kind of damage would've entirely changed the homey feel of this neighborhood.

When they reached the bottom of the hill, Marin noticed a couple of other women with kids at the park. One pushing a toddler in the baby swing and the other standing nearby a young girl about Wyatt's age who was scrambling around on a crisscrossing set of metal bars shaped like an igloo frame. While Wyatt raced to the same set of bars, Julia stopped and stared at a redheaded girl swinging by herself.

"That girl looks about your age," Marin said. "Don't you want to go play?"

"No." Julia crossed her arms and frowned.

"Doesn't she go to your school?"

"She's in my class." Julia nodded. "But I don't know her."

"Who do you play with at recess?"

"Wyatt."

Marin looked into Julia's little face and suddenly saw something other than self-sufficiency. Beneath that stubborn facade was a scared little girl. She'd lost her mom. She'd lost Carla. And she didn't even get to have Angelica today. Somehow the little girl acquiescing to Marin, the third caregiver in almost as many weeks, seemed even more sad than if she'd obstinately refused Marin as a babysitter. It was almost as if Julia had given up hope of any kind of permanence in her life. These kids deserved better than what Marin had given of herself that morning.

Marin bent down beside Julia. "I'll go with you to meet her," she whispered.

Uncertain, Julia glanced at Marin.

"Who knows?" Marin shrugged. "Maybe you two will hit it off and become best friends. Then you'll have someone else to play with at recess."

"Okay."

Shocking the hell out of Marin, Julia reached up, curled her hand inside Marin's and squeezed. Marin swallowed a sudden lump of apprehension. They walked toward the swings.

"Hi," Marin said to the other girl. "This is Julia. She just moved here to Mirabelle."

"Hey, you're in my class at school!" The other girl grinned. "I'm Kayla. Wanna swing?"

"Sure." Julia took the swing next to the other little girl.

The woman who'd been by the metal bars came toward Marin. "Hi, my name's Maddie. Kayla's my daughter."

"Marin. I'm just babysitting Julia and her brother, Wyatt." She pointed toward the slide Wyatt was climbing up backward.

"That's my other daughter, Abby, standing by the slide. You new on Mirabelle?"

"Visiting. My sister, Missy Abel, and her family live up the hill."

"Missy? The woman who owns Whimsy?"

"Yeah. What's left of it. So how long have you lived on Mirabelle?"

"Only a couple of months. I'm starting up a bed-and-breakfast inn." She frowned and crossed her arms as she kept an eye on Kayla. "At least I had been planning on that before all my construction workers left me to work on rebuilding the town."

"Oh, no."

"It's okay. I get it. We'll survive. We won't be having any guests until the island is up and running again anyway, so…"

They chatted for a while and Marin explained the babysitting situation with Adam's kids. They exchanged phone numbers and Marin promised that her mother would definitely want to get the kids together for playdates.

"Well, we've got to head home," Maddie said. "Get some lunch."

The kids all said goodbye and Maddie took off with her kids toward the other end of town.

"You guys hungry? Maybe we should go out for lunch."

Wyatt pointed toward his father's office trailer. "We should ask Daddy to come, too."

Dinner with Marin didn't work with his agenda. Maybe lunch with her and the kids would fit. "Good idea. Let's go talk to him."

CHAPTER TEN

"THAT'S NOT A GOOD IDEA," Julia said. "I've only been to Daddy's office twice my whole life."

"Oh, come on," Marin said. "If he's busy, he's busy."

After a brief knock on the trailer door, Marin stepped inside. With slide-out sections in both the front and rear, the trailer was roomier than she'd expected. The reception area, housing his assistant's desk, several file cabinets, a couple of chairs, and various pieces of office equipment, like copiers and fax machines, was empty.

"Adam?" she called. "You here?"

"Maybe he's in his office," Julia said. "Down the hall."

Marin moved tentatively through the small kitchen, past the bathroom and into his office. No Adam. But her curiosity was piqued. Offices often said so much about the person who occupied the space.

His large, wraparound desk was strewn with papers and files, not to mention architectural designs, floor plans and other types of schematics. A half-full cup of coffee sat next to his keyboard, and a light layer of dust clung to several flat surfaces. An organized neat freak he was not. Two framed photos sat on his desk next to his computer screen. The first was Julia standing beside a bike. She couldn't have been more than five. The photo of Wyatt, at about the age of two, appeared to be from approximately the same time period. The man clearly needed updated photos.

Just then the front door to the trailer opened and Phyllis came inside. She caught Marin's movements and glanced down the hall. "Can I help you guys?"

"We're looking for Adam." Marin walked toward the front.

"He's down on Main Street, and I'm sorry but you're not allowed in the construction zone." She smiled at the kids. "If it's an emergency, though, I can contact him on his radio."

"No. No emergency. We'll catch him some other time." She led the kids outside. "Maybe some other da—"

"Daddy!" Wyatt yelled, and, slipping under the construction tape, raced down the street.

Wearing a hard hat and speaking into his cell phone, a clipboard of paperwork under one arm, Adam walked from the main part of town toward his trailer. He looked up the moment he heard Wyatt's voice and frowned.

"See," Julia said, her voice resigned. "I told you we shouldn't have come down here."

"Wyatt, wait!" Marin called. "Your dad's on a call, and you're not supposed to be back there."

Wyatt pulled up just short of his father.

"No. No, that won't work," Adam spoke calmly into his phone. "I need those orders here tonight. If you have to charge me for a rush shipment, then fine, but my masons are sitting around twiddling their thumbs." He glanced at his kids, and then Marin. "Whatever you have to do, do it." Adam hung up his phone and directed Wyatt out of the construction zone. "No crossing the tape, Wyatt. Got it?"

"Sorry about that," Marin said, feeling very aware of him. There was something about that hard hat, coupled with Adam's lean, muscular frame that was, surprisingly, doing it for her.

"It's okay," he said. "How's it going?"

"We're doing fine, aren't we kids?"

"We just came down to play at the park, Daddy," Julia explained as if she was worried he might be upset.

"It's all right, honey. Don't worry."

"So where can we find some lunch around here?"

"There's the Mirabelle Island Inn. A good walk that way." He pointed east. "Rock Pointe Lodge." Then he pointed in the opposite direction. "And just a couple blocks away is Romeo's. Pizza and pasta."

"Pizza!" Wyatt said.

"Sound okay to you, Julia?"

The little girl nodded.

"Adam, can you join us?"

"Sorry." He shook his head and smiled at his kids. "I've got a conference call in ten minutes. Maybe some other day."

But Marin had the distinct impression that other day never managed to come around. Maybe these kids deserved better from their dad, too. "Okay, let's go." She took the kids' hands.

"Marin?" he called.

She was starting to love the way he said her name, his accent causing a sexy blurring of the last syllable. She turned, hoping he'd changed his mind.

"Stay away from the fencing, okay? We've surrounded the perimeter of the construction zone to keep people out of the dangerous areas."

"Will do."

ADAM'S HEART SANK AS HE watched Marin walk away holding hands with his kids. He could've taken a half hour away from the job. He had to eat, didn't he?

This was one of the reasons he didn't want Julia and Wyatt coming to his job sites. Safety wasn't the only concern. The distraction of the overwhelming emotions he felt every time he looked into their innocent faces was what, more than anything, had prompted the rule.

Guilt, sorrow and anxiety thrown together with intense feelings of love, protectiveness and pride, and Adam would get so confused he couldn't work. He couldn't make sense of anything he was feeling.

All he knew was that it hurt to be near them. It hurt to look into their big, sweet eyes and see Beth.

"Adam?" Phyllis called from the door to the trailer. "I've got the lumber supply company on the phone. They say they need to talk to you now for clarification on an order."

His feet didn't want to move. He couldn't believe Marin had asked him out to dinner. The thought came out of thin air. That had never happened to him before and he was still a bit shocked. The idea of a private, romantic meal with a woman was such a foreign concept, he simply couldn't imagine—

"Adam?"

He turned, took the phone from his assistant's hand. Kids and work. That was his life. "Harding, here." What was this about again? Oh, yeah. "Which order number is the problem..."

MY HEAVENS, but Missy has her hands full with these two.

Very gently, Angelica laid Nathan down in his crib. She softly caressed his stomach for a moment, covered him with a light blanket and tiptoed out of the room, being careful not to wake the already sleeping Michael.

Both of them down for a nap at the same time. She smiled. Now to put her feet up for a little while and relax. She'd no sooner hit the last step on the way to the family room than her cell phone rang from in the kitchen. Wanting to make sure the sound didn't wake her grandsons, she ran to pick up the phone. As soon as she saw Arthur's name on the display, her heart raced with uncertainty.

Had she acted too hastily in leaving D.C.? She and Art had been married more than thirty years. That was a damned lot of history to toss away. What if her choice took her from the frying pan into the fire?

No. She couldn't let fear immobilize her. She'd spent the past several years gathering the gumption to do this. Now was her time. *Her* time. If Arthur wasn't going to jump on her bandwagon, he was going to have to jump out of her way.

Determinedly she answered the call. "Hello, Arthur."

There was a moment of silence, as if he hadn't expected her to pick up. "How are you, Angie? The girls?" His voice sounded mild, nothing like the booming, powerful tone he used in campaign speeches or in interviews with the press.

"We're all fine."

"You settled in there okay?"

What was he up to with this uncharacteristic concern? Trying to catch her off her guard, more than likely. Well, it wasn't going to work. Not this time. "Why did you call?"

"I'm just trying to figure out what's going on here. This was all rather…sudden, wasn't it?"

"I don't think so. I think this is an entirely expected result of the conversation we had just before I left."

"But I thought you were going to think this over again…this job business."

"You weren't listening, Arthur. I said I wasn't certain if this was the right job and would be taking some time to think it over, but I am certain that I want a job."

"So that's it? You went to see a divorce attorney over a job?"

"In a nutshell."

Her marriage had come to a crossroads over her wanting a job. It wasn't a big important job and it didn't pay much, but that wasn't the point. She'd have something to do that she was sure she would enjoy. She'd have coworkers. Responsibilities. She'd have her own office. The thought was equally exciting and terrifying.

"Come home, Angie. We'll work this out. You gallivanting off like this is plain silly."

"It's exactly because you think it's silly that I'm ready to divorce you."

"If I have to I'll come to Mirabelle to talk some sense into you."

"Don't you dare come here, Art. I need time away from you to think. You stay in D.C. and you wait."

"Do you have a clue the strings I've had to pull to keep this quiet? Do you know what the press would do with a little tidbit like you going to see a divorce attorney?"

She knew very well, had pulled a few strings herself in days gone by with regard to their children's mishaps in their teenage years and early adult lives, but, for once in her life, she didn't care. "You're not pushing this under the rug for me, Arthur. It's for you."

"Angie, please," he said softly. "Don't do this—"

"Stop it!" He didn't do it on purpose. He wasn't a bad man. But he knew exactly what to say and how to say it to get her to cave in, to give him what he wanted. It wasn't his fault. It was hers. She needed to hold firm.

"Listen to me, Arthur, and listen well. I am not going to give in this time. I gave you—our children, our family—my youth. I supported you in your career every step of the way. Don't get me wrong, I have no regrets." Every step of the way, she'd chosen her own path. She'd never been coerced, or guilted into setting aside a career for her family, and she would not be coerced now. "But I am all done living for you."

CHAPTER ELEVEN

"I'M SO MAD RIGHT NOW I could spit bullets."

Marin paused in chopping red onions for a spinach and bacon salad to find Missy stalking into the kitchen from the backyard.

Marin had lost count of how long she'd been on Mirabelle, and her days had fallen into an easy, quiet, pattern. She ran errands, she helped Missy, she read, she ate and slept. She'd also been helping her mother here and there with Julia and Wyatt, but she'd managed to entirely avoid Adam. Still, she was no closer to a decision about her future. It was almost as if her body and mind had needed to shut down completely before rebooting.

Missy slid the patio door closed so hard the house seemed to rattle. "Sometimes I'm not sure if I want to kiss him or kill him."

"We talking about Jonas or one of the boys?" Marin asked.

Missy scrunched up her mouth and glared at Marin.

"What?" Marin shrugged. "Seems like a fair

question." At least to her, given those little boys could be downright terrors.

"What happened?" their mother asked.

"He planned a trip to go golfing someplace down south with his FBI buddies."

"What's so bad about that?"

"There wouldn't be anything bad about it if he didn't already travel so much. As it is, he's gone close to two weeks of every month. D.C., Minneapolis, Chicago, Quantico. I don't understand why he wants to be away from me even more."

"Oh, sweetheart." Angelica stood and hugged Missy. "If I know anything about Jonas, it's that he never wants to be away from you."

"I know." A tear slid down Missy's cheek. "But I think the only solution to this problem may be moving to D.C."

Given Missy's attachment to this island, a move like that might just break her little sister's heart. "Maybe Jonas should just quit consulting with the FBI."

"He loves his job."

"More than he loves you?"

Missy shook her head. "I couldn't ask him to do that."

"You know what?" Angelica said, slapping her hand on the table. "I think we need a girls' night out."

"Except with Duffy's gone there's no place to go *out*," Missy said, frowning.

"Then it's girls' night *in!*" For the first time since she'd come to Mirabelle this island had been closing in on her to some degree. She needed to cut loose a bit. Marin handed her sister the phone. "Call all your sisters and get them over here. Then you put your feet up and wait for the party to start. I'll make a run to the store."

Less than an hour later, Marin returned with a golf cart loaded down with an assortment of drinks and munchies and every form of chocolate known to womankind, including cake, cookies, ice cream, truffles and a liqueur, along with a few surprises. She found Sarah, Erica and Grace all in the kitchen ready to help unpack the evening's supplies.

When Missy got to the bottom of the first bag, she giggled. "What in the world are these for?"

Marin laughed. "For the hell of it." At the checkout counter, she'd grabbed a pack of cigars and cigarettes. "I've always wanted to try a cigarette. It looks so…so butch."

"Well, I for one won't be joining you," Sarah said with a smile. "Jesse probably wouldn't talk to me for a week if I picked up that habit again."

"You used to smoke?" Erica asked.

"I used to do a lot of stupid things." She patted the small bulge of baby at her belly. "But not anymore."

"Speaking of which." Marin produced a bottle of nonalcoholic wine. "This is for Sarah."

"And these, I take it," Missy said, pulling out a bottle of tequila and several limes, "are for me."

"Didn't your mother ever teach you to share?" Erica said, grabbing a couple limes.

"Well, apparently, I taught at least one of my daughters to share." Angelica produced a stack of shot glasses from one of the other bags and everyone laughed.

A few shots and wedges of lime later, the women lazed around the family room talking. "I'll make a pitcher of margaritas," Erica said, laughing. "To be on the safe side."

Marin felt suddenly melancholy. "Are all of you happy here on Mirabelle?" she asked, glancing from one woman to the other. "I mean, doing what you're doing?"

"I was happier before the tornado." Erica frowned. "But I love owning a restaurant and bar. Losing Duffy's Pub definitely put a damper on things."

"I've never been happier, except I do miss Duffy's," Sarah said with a smile. "I kind of fell into the wedding planning business, but I like it."

Grace was next in the circle, so all eyes turned toward her. "I just came home a couple months ago and went through a career crisis myself, so I'm probably not the best person to ask." She shrugged. "Right now, I can't imagine being anyplace else. Doing anything else."

The first time Marin had met Grace, she'd immediately recognized the woman as having been in the news sometime ago after a terrible car accident had ended her modeling career. From what Missy had said Grace was now designing her own line of clothes. Talk about turning lemons into lemonade.

"Why so curious?" Missy said, turning toward Marin. "Are you thinking of moving here?"

"God, no. I'm bordering on island fever as it is." Marin sighed. "I'm just trying to figure out what I want to be when I grow up. I might go back to Manhattan, but I won't return to Wall Street."

"What do you think you might do?" Grace asked.

"I have no idea."

"Missy should read your palm, or aura," Grace said. "Or whatever it is she does."

Marin raised her eyebrows. "What's this?"

"Oh, it's just a hobby. Silly stuff, really."

"Right." Sarah laughed. "She's only predicted every marriage here on Mirabelle since she moved here."

"Is that right?" Marin held out her palm. "Do me."

"It's not that easy. I have to be in the mood, and I'm not sure I can do my own sister."

"Warm up with me," Grace said, producing her hand.

Missy gulped down the rest of her margarita, poured some more from the pitcher, and took Grace's hand. A moment later, she rolled her eyes. "You're so easy, it's ridiculous."

"Sean." Grace smiled shyly.

"Forever."

"Would you like to try your mother?" Angelica grinned.

"No, I would not." Missy shook her head. "But I might be tempted if I knew how those eighteen holes with Doc and John went."

"Oh, that's right!" Grace laughed. "You went out with my dad. How'd it go?"

"What's this?" Marin asked. "You went out on a date?"

"Technically, it wasn't a date."

"So tell us, technically, what happened."

Angelica took another shot and grimaced as she sucked on the lime. "I don't kiss and tell."

Everyone laughed and Missy grabbed the bottle of tequila. "I need another shot."

"Mother!" Marin said. "You're still married."

"Oh, for crying out loud, Marin. We had a very nice time, and that's the extent of that. If I were available—which I made very clear to both of them I'm not—I'd certainly consider dating either one of them. Doc Welinski is a lot of fun, but John is very, very sweet." She glanced at Grace. "Although he is far from over the death of your mother."

"I know," Grace nodded. "But he'll get there."

"So what happened with Doc?" Missy pushed for more.

"Well, if you must know, he asked me out to dinner and I politely declined. End of story."

Imagining her mother dating threw Marin for a loop, but that was a definite possibility in the near future. Apparently, there'd be no shortage of men knocking on her door. At that somewhat disturbing thought, Marin grabbed the tequila bottle and poured herself another shot. "Okay, Missy's not getting off that easily. I still want my palm read." She flopped out her hand.

"Oh, all right, fine." Missy pointed to a couple of light lines on Marin's palm. "I'd guess that one's Greg. There's Phil."

Her high school and college boyfriends.

"And this heavy line? We know it's not Colin. Whoever it is, though, he's the last one."

Mumbo jumbo. "Does it say anything on there about jobs?"

"That, I can't help you with." She folded Marin's hand and smiled. "But I can read your hairline. It's clearly time for a change. Your roots are screaming for you to revert to your natural color."

"I know." Marin ran a hand through her long hair. "I'm not even sure they can be called roots anymore they're so long." She'd been in need of a color before she'd even come to Mirabelle.

"You're really blonde," Sarah said. After all the tequila being poured around, she was probably the only one in the room who could still see straight. "Why do you dye it such a dark shade when your natural one is so pretty?"

"Ever seen a blonde on Wall Street?" Marin cocked her head. "Me neither."

"No more Wall Street means no more need for a

power hairstyle," Missy said, a note of challenge in her voice.

"I need more than a cut. I need something drastic." She needed to slough off her old life and start all over again somewhere. Anywhere.

"Who knows where a haircut might lead," Erica said.

She had a point. "Okay." Marin sat up straighter. "Who can cut hair?"

"Don't look at me." Grace sipped on her drink.

"I cut the boys' hair all the time," Missy said, sipping on a margarita.

"You're hired."

"Wait a minute," Missy said. "I only cut short hair."

"Right. That's what I want. The shorter, the better. Cut all the fake brown stuff off. I'm going au naturel."

"Marin, that would be awfully short."

"Halle Berry short. Just what I need." Marin grabbed a bath towel, went to the kitchen sink and got her hair wet. While the other women stood by watching, she combed out her hair, draped the towel around her shoulders and sat in a chair in the kitchen.

Missy produced scissors and came to stand beside Marin. "You're sure about this?" Missy said. "And you're not going to hold me accountable for how this turns out, right?"

"Right."

"I have witnesses."

"Don't worry about it, Mel. Just cut."

Missy took a big sip of a margarita. "Here goes."

Marin closed her eyes. She opened them sometime later to find piles of dark hair had accumulated on the floor and a handheld mirror in front of her.

"There. How's that?" Missy said, not quite slurring her words.

Marin's initial reaction was to panic. Her hair had never, ever been this short. What the hell had she done? Was she insane? It was going to take forever for her hair to grow back, but then she turned her head this way and that and realized that the look wasn't half-bad. Missy had transformed Marin from Wall Street business executive into a hip-looking artist-type.

"Well?" Missy said nervously.

"I like it." Sarah shrugged.

"Me, too," Erica added.

"I love it," Angelica said.

"Fits *you*." Grace smiled. "But not that outfit."

Marin glanced down at her conservative sweater set. "You're right. But I do have a couple of things that might work." She ran upstairs, slipped on a casual, loose-fitting, short blue dress she'd bought months ago, but had never worn, and rejoined the group. Her new look was met with resounding approval.

"That works," Grace said.

"Okay, I'm next," Angelica said.

Everyone may have laughed, but Marin's mother was clearly serious. She sat in the chair and Missy snipped away.

"You know what?" Marin said. "I'm going outside to have a cigarette."

Missy laughed.

Their mother shook her head. "You'll be sorry tomorrow. Your throat will feel raw and your head will feel as if it's going to explode."

"That sounds like the voice of experience talking." Marin held up the pack of cigarettes. "Any takers?"

"You're on your own on this one," Missy said, chuckling.

Marin slid open the patio door. The moment she felt the brisk chill in the air, she grabbed a sweater hanging over the nearest chair.

"If you're not back in ten," Missy laughed, "we'll send out a search party."

CHAPTER TWELVE

IN WHAT WAS becoming at least a weekly habit, Adam sat in the dark in his backyard, sipping a beer. The kids had long since gone to sleep and his brain had not long ago shut down while working on his laptop, so he'd grabbed a beer and come outside for some fresh air, peace and quiet.

Next door, the patio door to Marin's house slid open and closed, and a woman in a flirty little dress with extremely short blond hair and a cigarette in her mouth walked outside. Apparently, Marin and her mother had a visitor. As the woman stepped out of the periphery of light and into the dark night, something about the way she moved seemed familiar to Adam.

That wasn't a guest. That was Marin. Since when did she smoke? Curious now, he walked into the other yard. "Wow. I almost didn't recognize you. What happened to your hair?"

"My roots were showing."

He chuckled. "Pretty drastic solution. Don't women usually dye their hair again to get rid of the roots?"

He'd never been very partial to short hair on women, but he liked the new style on Marin. Somehow it was softer, more feminine than her previous cut, and it suited the more relaxed personality that seemed to be emerging the longer she stayed on Mirabelle. The new haircut also bared her beautifully long and graceful—and very kissable—neck. A chunk of clipped hair clung to her skin just beneath her ear, and it was all he could do not to brush it away.

She flicked her thumb at a lighter, causing it to only spark.

"You don't want to smoke that," he said softly.

"Sure I do." She pursed her lips around the butt of the cigarette. "If I could just get this lighter going." She flicked it ineffectually a few more times.

"Want some help?"

"Adam to the rescue, is that it?"

"Do you want to smoke it or not?"

"You like to fix things, don't you?" she murmured around the filter in her mouth. "Too bad you can't fix yourself."

"Marin, what—"

"You never get mad, though, do you?" She snatched the cigarette out of her mouth and glared at him. "The always calm, always unflappable Adam Harding would never think of raising his voice. Do you even swear?"

"Marin—"

"I'm serious. Do you ever swear?"

"What's the point? Does swearing change anything? Does getting angry make one bit of difference?"

"No. But it sure as *hell* makes me feel better. To… feel…something…anything. See that's the problem with shutting yourself off. Shutting down. You're not only not feeling the lows, you're not feeling the highs, either. You end up with no passion in your life."

As she tossed the cigarette and lighter away, she moved toward him and he felt himself wanting to step back. Her unpredictable mood tonight set him even more on edge than he usually felt around her.

"But then maybe that's the way you like it? Maybe you like not feeling," she whispered, now only a foot away and closing. "You like being numb. Then you don't have to face anything. You can pretend everything is fine."

"Just because I don't show my emotions like you, like an open book for anyone to read, doesn't mean they don't exist." He felt himself getting riled up, his insides spinning and turning and getting tied up in knots. If she touched him, if she pushed this, she just might get more than she bargained for from him tonight. "Marin—"

"Adam?" She cocked an eyebrow at him and grinned.

God help him, but all he wanted was to bury his fingers in that flirty short hair and kiss that smirk right off her lips. "So I'm not passionate, is that it? Are you entirely sure about that?"

"Prove me wrong."

He hadn't even touched her and already a painful hard-on pressed against his jeans. For a man who'd been practically dead to the world for years, his libido sure was coming out swinging around this woman. He stepped toward her, bringing his chest to within inches of her breasts, his mouth within kissing distance of her lips. Then he wrapped his arms around her, leaning into her, his knee between her legs, his erection pressing against her hip. "Does that feel like I'm numb to you?"

"No," she breathed. "You feel so alive when you touch me."

She couldn't be more right about that, and at the moment he couldn't remember a single reason why he was supposed to walk away. All he wanted was to feel even more alive.

"You won't date me," she whispered. "But you'll kiss me again, won't you?"

"Yes." Slanting his head, he pressed his lips against hers, urged her mouth wider, thrust his tongue inside her mouth and tasted...alcohol. Tequila, if he wasn't mistaken. *Swell.* He drew back. "Marin, what have you been doing tonight?"

"What do you mean?" She looked dazed and her disorientation might've been from more than his kiss.

Curious, he glanced at her house. Light spilled

from the kitchen and family room out through the open windows and into the backyard, and he could just make out the murmur of laughter and loud voices. It sounded like a party.

"That explains it." He laughed. "You're drunk."

"No, just a little tipsy." She grinned. "That a problem?"

"Let's just say that I'd prefer you remember tonight." He dropped her hands and backed up, but even as he retreated, she advanced.

"Oh, I'll remember it, all right. I remember every look, every touch from you. How could I forget?"

He backed into a tree and was forced to stop.

She kept coming, though, until they were touching again at the hips. Reaching out, she flattened her hands on his chest and massaged her fingertips into his muscle. "How could I ever forget...anything about you?"

No, she wasn't drunk. Her gaze was clear, her hands steady. Still.... "You're going to be sorry for this in the morning."

"So far I haven't done anything warranting apology. Give me something to regret, Adam. I dare you."

"You dare me," he breathed.

As if she sensed the change in him, as if she understood that what was happening to him was much stronger and more volatile than what she could see, she stepped back.

He wasn't feeling all that magnanimous at the

moment and wasn't about to let her retreat, at least not that easily. He took her by the shoulders and turned them both around, backed her up against the tree and into the shadows, and drew her hands up and over her head. Then he kissed her soft neck. When he dragged his hand down the underside of her arm all the way to her breast, she groaned and her head fell to the side.

He cupped her breast and felt her nipple pebbling beneath the thin fabric of her bra. He groaned as their lips met again in a frantic, needy kiss. It'd been so long for him, so long since he'd felt anything close to what was happening now under his skin. Before he knew it, her hot hands were under his shirt, on his sides and back, and then working at the zipper of his jeans. Then he was free and her fingers gripped his erection.

"Marin, don't... Oh, God." His knees buckled and he slid to the ground behind the tree.

No one in the houses could see them, there in the dark as she slid to the ground with him, straddling him, mercilessly pulsing against him.

This wasn't going to go any further. It couldn't. But he wanted—needed—to feel her. Reaching between them, he slipped his fingers beneath her skimpy bikini panties and touched her swollen, slick center, and that was all she wrote. Any remaining resistance he might've been able to muster drowned in the wet, luscious feel of her.

His control completely gone, he moved her panties aside and she lifted her hips, poising herself over him. He slid into her quickly and easily, and she shuddered. Then she looked down at him, the moon highlighting her eyes, her hair, her smile and she pulsed against him, driving him wild.

"Marin," he whispered, and she covered his mouth with a kiss so full of passion that he thought he'd died and gone to heaven.

The feeling of her moving over him, so curvy and full, so erotic, was so different from Beth, startled him into awareness. What were they doing? This was wrong for both of them in so many ways. But it was too late. Even if he'd wanted to stop, he couldn't. He was too close, and she was too damned hot. Holding her hips steady and thrusting into her again and again, he came inside her with a violence he'd never felt.

"Marin," he groaned. "This is crazy."

The ripples of her own release shuddered through her as she pulsed against him and then, finally, stilled, collapsing against his chest like a rag doll. It was over within minutes.

Had that really just happened? Yeah, that had really happened. "Well, there you go," he whispered. "Now we both have something to regret."

GLARING, PAINFUL SUNLIGHT flooded Marin's bedroom. As if in a fog as thick as pea soup, she awoke with a hangover the likes of which she hadn't felt since her college days. Dry mouth. Queasy stomach. Head that felt clamped in a vise grip and repeatedly pounded upon by some monster with a rubber mallet.

Slowly, she sat up. What in the world had gotten into her last night? She ran her hands through her hair—very short hair—pulled out a chunk of tree bark, and the events of the previous night returned to her in one fell swoop.

"Oh, damn," she murmured, lying back down and closing her eyes. The haircut she could deal with, but Adam? How was she ever going to face him again? The things she'd said and done to him, the way she'd acted. Sensual. Brazen. Apparently, she could kiss a fervent goodbye to all the sexual insecurities that had gone along with her relationship with Colin. Marin had outright seduced Adam.

Colin had never, in all the years they'd been dating, turned her on the way Adam did. She'd wanted mind-blowing, blazing hot sex? She'd gotten it. Just thinking about him turned her thoughts to sex. Touching him, his erection, had lit her fuse. And she couldn't use the excuse of being drunk at the time, that's for sure. The aftersex shots were, without a doubt, the reason for this hangover.

"Marin?" her mother's voice sounded softly from the doorway. "Are you alive?"

"Barely."

"Adam called a little bit ago to tell me none of the nannies he interviewed panned out and he's starting from scratch."

Figures.

"And he asked how you were feeling."

Oh, God.

"Did you see him last night?"

"I don't want to talk about it, Mother." Marin buried her head under the pillow. She'd wanted regrets? She got 'em.

ADAM WAS SITTING AT HIS DESK when the office trailer door opened. Now what? The last thing he needed today was one more problem.

"Oh, hi," Phyllis said lightly. Maybe it wasn't a problem after all. "He's in his office. Go on back."

Adam glanced up from his computer screen just as Marin appeared at the threshold. *What the*— Immediately, he stood, but stayed where he was. A desk between him and Marin was probably a good idea, given the fact that the mere sight of her had just caused a semierection.

They both stood silently for a long and awkward moment. He would've thought that sex might've soothed any need that had built inside him through the years. Instead, having Marin once only made him want her again. And again.

Finally, unable to stand it another minute, he crossed the room, reached behind her and closed the door. "Spit it out, Marin."

"Um, I need to…I need to apologize for last night…the tequila…" She stopped.

Her gaze flew over every place she'd touched him

last night and it was all he could do not to pull her into his arms and pick up where they'd left off. He had to admit it was amazing what good sex could do for a man's outlook. Feeling right as rain for a change, he felt a slight smile tug on his lips.

"You're not going to make this easy for me, are you?" she whispered.

"You think I should?"

"That would be the gentlemanly thing to do."

"I think last night proved I'm not much of a gentleman." He sobered. "For which I should apologize."

"What happened was my fault."

"We both share the blame for what happened, Marin."

"Well, just so you know, I got tested for STDs right after I found out about Colin. I'm clean. And I'm still on birth control, so…"

"Well, I haven't been tested, but Beth was the only woman. Ever."

"See, that's what I'm talking about." Shaking her head, she turned away. "I'm sorry, Adam, but I think I really did take advantage of you last night. I used you, in a way, to prove something to myself and that wasn't fair."

"I'm not following. You're going to have to explain that."

"My relationship with Colin wasn't very…satisfying." As if she was feeling vulnerable, she crossed her arms. "I thought it was me. That I wasn't sexy or sensual enough. I used you, in a way, to prove to myself that I *could* turn on a man."

"That you could—" He stopped, things suddenly making sense. "Let me guess. Colin is either dead or he's gay."

Her silence was all the confirmation he needed. But she hadn't taken advantage of him any more than he had of her. It was kind of sweet, though, that she thought she'd used him.

"Let me ask you this," he said. "Did you kiss me last night with the intention of having sex?"

"No."

"Would you have seduced any man out there last night ready to light your cigarette for you?"

"No."

"Well, there you have it then." He smiled. "You didn't use me, Marin. We're both responsible for what happened, and I think it's safe to say you have nothing to worry about from a sexuality standpoint. Colin was the problem. Not you. Not by any stretch of the imagination." Just the thought of her worrying that she wasn't sexy enough had him shaking his head. "Marin, that was the best sex I've *ever* had, so you don't need to be too sorry."

"Really?"

"Really."

"Me, too. Actually."

"I think we're both in agreement, though. What happened last night? Never going to happen again, right?"

For a moment, she seemed to be debating. "Explain to me again why just sex is a problem."

He sobered. "There is no such thing as 'just sex,' Marin. Not with me, anyway."

"Okay then." She opened his office door. "It'll never happen again."

CHAPTER THIRTEEN

"CAN YOU WATCH JULIA and Wyatt this afternoon?" Marin's mother asked, coming into the house through the patio door.

Marin looked up from where she was sitting at the kitchen eating her lunch, a chicken salad sandwich, while reading a new book. "Why? What's up?"

"My cell phone died on me and I need to run to the mainland for a new one."

"Can't you wait until the weekend?"

"Would you go three days without your cell phone?"

A month ago, Marin wouldn't have gone three hours without one, but after all this time on Mirabelle she was unplugged, relatively speaking, and enjoying it. That didn't mean she wanted to babysit. "Mom, I—"

"What's the big deal, Marin?"

The big deal was that besides the quick apology in his office, she hadn't seen Adam since that disastrous tequila sex incident. Otherwise, she didn't have an excuse for not helping her mother out. After a surprisingly lazy morning, she'd gone for a run, had just finished with a shower and had nothing else on the agenda for the rest of the day.

"All right," Marin finally said. "I'll watch the kids."

"Great. They had an after-school snack, but you're going to need to feed them supper and help them with homework. Oh, and Adam's working late tonight. He won't be home until almost bedtime."

"What? I thought this would be just for an hour or so. What am I supposed to do with the kids for that long?"

"I'm sure you'll figure it out."

"Do they know I'm coming?"

"Yep. I told them."

"Awfully sure of me, aren't you, Mom?"

Her mother only grinned before grabbing her purse and taking off out the front door. Marin finished what was left of her sandwich and walked outside to find the kids climbing around on their new play equipment. It was a fairly elaborate system sporting a fully enclosed platform fort with a full roof and windows, a slide, three swings and monkey bars.

"Hi," she said, standing a short distance away.

Wyatt's head poked out through one of the fort windows. "Hi, Marin."

Julia came down the slide. "Hi."

"You okay with me babysitting?" Marin asked. "If I promise to do a better job than last time."

"Sure." Julia shrugged. "You got your hair cut."

Marin ran her hands through the short strands. "Yeah. Pretty short, huh?"

"It's pretty."

"Thanks."

Wyatt came through the door on the fort and reached for the monkey bars. What if he fell again? "Be careful up there." At a loss for what else to do, she went to stand beside him, just close enough so she could reach out on the chance he lost his grip.

"Okay!" he called as he reached the end. Then he let go of the bar.

Marin snatched him in midair. "Dude, careful."

"I do that all the time."

"Yeah, but the other day you got lucky. One of these times, you might really break an ankle." As Marin set him down, she caught Julia watching her. "Better?"

The little girl smiled.

The kids played for quite a while and Marin even remembered to bring them out something to drink. Later, she made dinner for them, grilled cheese sandwiches and apple slices. While she did a few dishes, they did homework. The evening went much better than she'd expected.

"I'm finished!" Julia exclaimed, putting her folders in her backpack.

"Me, too!"

Now what? "Did you guys ever finish your frames for Carla?"

"Yep. Last week with Angelica," Julia said. "But I'd like to make another frame for me."

"What are you going to frame?"

"A picture of my mom. That way I can remember my mom the way Carla can remember us."

Wyatt nodded. "I want one, too."

"Okay. Let's do it." Missy's craft box still happened to be at the Harding house, and it wasn't long after the kids had sat at the kitchen table to make more frames that Marin decided to join them. "Maybe I'll make one, too."

"What are you going to put in it?" Julia asked.

"I have no idea. This just looks fun."

Marin turned on some music and in no time they were talking and laughing as they worked on their projects. "How's school going?" she asked, sincerely curious.

"Okay," Julia said. "You were right about Kayla. She's my best friend now."

"That's great. So recess is going all right?"

"Most of the time," she said.

"When Cody isn't teasing us," Wyatt added.

"Who's Cody?"

"Just some stupid kid."

"Have you told your teacher about what's happening?"

"Yeah. But she can't make him stop."

"He's sneaky," Wyatt said.

"Maybe you should tell your dad."

"He's too busy."

"He never even took us school shopping. We just ordered some of what we needed on his computer."

Marin felt Julia's gaze on her.

"Would you take us shopping for everything else we need?" she asked softly as she looked down on her project.

Marin paused for a moment. She'd always loved back-to-school shopping even though she'd hated heading back to school. She needed some warmer clothes if she was going to be hanging around much longer, and these kids were easier to be around than she'd expected. "Why not? It sounds fun. As long as it's okay with your dad."

"I'll ask him. Sunday. We can go Sunday."

They returned to working on their frames and a short while later, they'd finished and were ready for pictures.

"I know where we can find some!" Julia said excitedly. "In Daddy's closet. I found a box of pictures one day when I was helping Carla clean."

"If it's private, we shouldn't be snooping."

"It's not private. I'll show you."

Marin followed the kids upstairs. It was already dark outside, so she flipped on lights as she hesitantly followed Julia and Wyatt into their father's bedroom. Snooping or not, she still felt as if she was invading someone's private space. Because she was.

That didn't stop her from glancing around the room in the hopes of gleaning some insight into the mind of their enigmatic father. Adam's bed, covered with a light geometrically patterned quilt in black and various shades of gray, was neatly made. Along with a coin jar and pen, electronic chargers for a phone and laptop sat on his bedside table, indicating he likely worked in bed. Just like his office, there was nothing remotely personal in this room, except for the faint masculine, spicy scent hanging in the air.

The kids had gone into the walk-in closet, and Julia was trying to get something down from the top shelf. "I'll get it." Marin grabbed the box, brought it out into the bedroom and set it on the floor. "You're sure this is all right?"

"Why wouldn't it be?" Julia asked.

"It's just pictures," Wyatt added.

Julia flipped open the top of the box to reveal stack after stack of photos that clearly spanned several years in the past. "We can find pictures of Mom in here," Julia said.

As the kids rifled through the lower layers, Marin picked up the photo lying right on top. It was Adam with both kids, albeit years younger, sitting on his lap. They hung on him like monkeys on a tree. The next one down was of a young woman in shorts and a T-shirt sitting on a large blanket in the grass. A toddler-aged Wyatt with fingers covered in cheesy chips sat next to her. Julia lay on her stomach next to them, her legs bent and her feet in the air, eating a sandwich.

"Looks like you were having a picnic in this one," Marin said, showing Julia the photo.

She smiled and nodded. "That's my mom. Isn't she pretty?"

Marin studied the woman's face. Big brown eyes, like Julia's. Long midnight-black hair. The kind of olive-colored skin of which Marin had always been envious. Who wouldn't want skin that tanned in a millisecond? "She's more than pretty." Marin smiled softly. "She's beautiful." Their mother looked a bit too skinny, though, and had dark circles under her eyes, making Marin wonder how she'd died. Had she been sick? For a long time or a short while?

Suddenly, she had this feeling they shouldn't be in Adam's room. They shouldn't be looking through these photos. "Come on, kids. Pick something out and let's go downstairs."

"No, THAT CAN'T BE RIGHT, Wayne." Adam was wrapping up his weekly phone meeting with his accounting manager as he walked home, juggling a bag of groceries. The update meeting with the islanders had gone well, but he had this one last thing to do before he could call it a day. "I looked at those financials you emailed and something's miscoded between jobs."

"You're probably right. The numbers looked a little funky to me, too. I'll take another look at the individual accounts and get back to you tomorrow. Anything else, Adam?"

"No, I think that'll do it."

"I took a look at the Mirabelle progress reports. You got a mixed bag going on there, don't you?"

"Yeah. We had some late shipments. The library and Setterbergs' buildings, Duffy's, Whimsy, and the wedding shop are still giving us trouble, but The Rusty Nail is finished along with the other shops on that block."

"You know it'd be a hell of a lot easier for you and I to put our heads together on this stuff if you were here in St. Louis."

"I know." Adam did not want to be having this conversation, but Wayne needed to vent every once in a while.

"You hire the right project managers and they can be onsite running the jobs. You can manage from here."

"I know that."

"Did you hear about the late season tornado that hit Kansas last week?" He paused. "Well, it's our type of business. We could expand this company if we're not limited by what you can handle. Double, triple the number of jobs."

"I know that, too." They could hire several operations managers and expand, and he could still be out managing the most challenging projects.

"In other words, you don't want to talk about it."

"Something like that. I gotta run, Wayne, I'm home."

"Okay. Think about focusing your efforts at corporate, all right?"

"Will do," he said, just to end the discussion. There was no way he was moving back to St. Louis. He disconnected the call and walked into his house.

"I like this one," he heard Wyatt say.

"You can have that one," Julia added. "I like mine better."

"Okay, that's it then." That sounded like Marin. "You both like the ones you picked the best."

The sounds of the voices, the children talking with Marin, carried from upstairs as Adam hung up his jacket. Immediately, he was suffused with a sense of belonging he hadn't felt in a long while. After a tough day at work, there was something about coming home to his family that had always been soothing to him. But it was more than that. Barely a moment had gone by since they'd had sex in the backyard that he hadn't thought of Marin, of wanting to touch her again.

Quietly, as they continued talking, he set the groceries down on the kitchen table and climbed the steps. That was odd. Their voices came from the direction of his bedroom. He walked down the hall and saw Marin sitting on the floor, her back to him, and the kids on her either side.

"What are you guys—" He stopped in his tracks as Bethany's smiling face stared out at him from a photo lying on the carpet. Sunshine overhead caused silvery highlights in her dark black hair as she hiked in the foothills near their hometown. He remembered taking that picture of her as if it was yesterday. That was the day she'd told him she was pregnant with Julia.

Marin spun around. "Oh. Hi." She faltered, as if she'd been caught in the act of something. "We were just… The kids made more frames. This time for themselves," she explained. "They each wanted a picture of their mother to put on their bedside tables. I hope it's—I hope it's okay."

"Yeah, it's fine." He bent down, picked up the photos and tossed them into the box. "You two can keep the ones you picked out, but the rest go back."

"But, Daddy—"

"I brought some ice cream home." Adam felt as if he'd been punched in the gut. "It's in the grocery bag on the kitchen table. You guys go down and scoop up a bowl for yourselves. I'll be down in a minute."

"Can Marin stay?" Julia's eyes lit up. "Can she, Daddy, please!"

"Please, please, please," Wyatt begged.

"I think Marin needs to go," Adam said, barely controlling the anger suddenly boiling up inside him like a geyser. "Don't you, Marin?"

Marin seemed to sense his emotions. "Sorry, kids. Some other time. Maybe."

The kids ran out of the room and down the stairs. "I appreciate you watching my kids tonight," he whispered. "But I'd also appreciate it if you'd leave now."

"Is it so bad they remember their mother?"

"Stay out of it, Marin." He jammed the photos in the box. "It's none of your business."

"She's their moth—"

"Who just happened to have killed herself." He shut the door to his bedroom. "Slit her wrists. Right in the tub at our home outside St. Louis."

"Oh, my God," Marin murmured.

"Now you know." He held her horrified gaze. "Satisfied?"

"I didn't—I—oh, God, did Julia find her?"

"No. The kids were at a friend's house for the day. I found her when I got home from work."

Adam turned away from Marin, hoping to keep the memories at bay, but there was no point. They ripped through him as if someone was drawing a dull hacksaw down his back. Beth pregnant or nursing. Beth laughing or making love to him. Beth... dead. Her skin more pale than Adam could've ever imagined skin could be. And blood everywhere. Beth's blood. Everywhere.

"I'm sorry," Marin whispered.

"You have nothing to be sorry for." He turned and opened the door, sending her the message loud and clear it was time for her to leave. "It's my fault it happened. No one else is to blame. No one."

"DADDY?" JULIA CALLED from her and Wyatt's bedroom later that night.

On the way downstairs from his own room, Adam

stopped in the hall, and stuck his head through the open door, keeping his gaze averted from the photos of Beth on the tables on either side of their bed. The house was big enough for them each to have their own room, but they weren't interested in privacy. In every house they'd rented since leaving Missouri they'd wanted to share a room. Tonight, like every night, they were both piled into Julia's queen-size bed with a book and a small light illuminating the pages. "You two are supposed to be asleep."

"We're not tired," Julia whispered.

"We're sorry," Wyatt said.

"There's nothing to be sorry about." He turned to go.

"Daddy?" Julia said softly. "Will you read to us?"

Adam went completely still. Reading to the kids had always been a special thing for Beth. She'd never known that watching her read had been one of his favorite things, too. Her voice had been the most soothing sound in his world. He used to sit and watch them when she hadn't a clue she was on center stage. He couldn't imagine trying to take her place any more than he could imagine being so close to those photos of Beth.

"I'm pretty tired," he murmured. "Maybe another time."

"You said you'd take us shopping. Can we go this weekend?"

He had state and federal people coming on

Monday to do some inspections. "That's bad timing for me, honey. Let's wait and see."

"That means no."

"It means let's wait and see."

CHAPTER FOURTEEN

"I'M EXHAUSTED," MARIN'S mother said late that night. "I'm going to bed."

"Okay," Marin murmured. "See you in the morning."

Marin's mother had gotten home from the mainland only a little while before Marin had come home from Adam's house. They'd each had a piece of fresh apple pie that Angelica had made using the apples they'd bought from the orchard on Mirabelle, and Angelica had pumped Marin for information about the hours she'd spent with Julia and Wyatt. Marin hadn't been able to bring herself to explain what had happened with the pictures of Adam's wife, so as far as Angelica knew things had gone off again without a hitch.

Her mother turned in the hall on the way to her room. "You seem preoccupied. You all right?"

"Sure. I'm fine."

"And everything went well with the Harding kids?"

"Yeah. We had fun."

"Did you? Did you really have fun?"

"Yes, Mother. I had fun."

"Does that mean you're rethink—"

"No, it doesn't." Marin laughed. "I still don't want kids. Not every woman is born with the mothering gene like you and Missy."

"They're awfully sweet, though, aren't they?"

Marin turned away. "Go to bed, Mom."

After her mother closed the door to her bedroom, Marin walked through the house, switching off lights and leaving only a lamp on in the living room and a light over the sink in the kitchen. Adam's house was completely dark. He wasn't in his office, but he wasn't asleep, either. She could feel it. Strange, but it was almost as if she could feel him.

Glancing outside into the backyard, she saw his silhouette in the moonlight. He was leaning up against that tree again, sipping on a beer. Knowing it would more than likely be a mistake, but feeling as if she should apologize again for what happened earlier, Marin went outside and quietly walked toward him. "Care if I join you?"

"You sure you want to do that?"

"Yes." She grabbed a beer without asking and popped the top. It was impossible to not think of the last time they'd been together at night in this backyard, of how it had felt to be in his strong, warm arms, but she had a feeling neither had to be worried about a repeat performance tonight.

A soft rustling sound came from the nearby bushes and Slim walked cautiously toward them.

Marin reached out to pet him. The cat purred, arched his back and rubbed against Adam.

"He comes around every night I'm out here," Adam said, petting him. "Wonder who he belongs to."

"Missy. His name's Slim." She scratched his neck and smiled as he closed his eyes and leaned into her touch. "I've always wanted cats."

"Why don't you get one?"

"Too much of a commitment." She took a drink of her beer as the cat wandered away. "I'm really sorry for what happened earlier tonight."

"Don't be. I should apologize for the way I reacted. Those were Beth's favorite photos from throughout the years. She'd always intended on putting them in albums, but it never got done. You couldn't know."

"Still, I can't help but wonder...is it so wrong for Julia and Wyatt to want to remember her with pictures beside their beds?"

"Not at all. It's only hard for me to see her face."

"Maybe if you saw her more it wouldn't be so difficult."

"Oh, so now you're a therapist?"

"Sorry. You're right," she murmured. "Do the kids know? About how she died?"

He nodded.

"Afterward...is that when you started traveling from one town to the next?"

"Yeah. Beth and I were born and raised in the same small town outside of St. Louis. She was the only woman I ever dated." He smiled. "We went to the same college. Got married after we graduated, and ended up settling in our hometown. Her family. Mine. Everyone was there, and everyone, relative or not, knew what had happened."

She tried to imagine what that had been like for him and couldn't, but she wasn't imagining the painful memories etched in every line on his face. He'd gone through hell and back. "That had to have been difficult. Facing them."

"People's reactions, strangely enough, ranged from compassion to outright disdain to denial. Her parents tried not to blame me, but it was always there. When they looked at me." He glanced out over at the lake as if the memories were almost too painful. "Some of her friends came out and accused me of pushing her into it. Rightly so."

"How could it be your fault?"

"She'd been suffering from a postpartum depression. After Wyatt was born, she just seemed to get more and more sad. More and more withdrawn."

"Did she get help?"

"She was seeing a doctor for it. I thought she was on an antidepressant, but we found out later that she hadn't been taking the medicine."

"But how could you have known?" The unfairness of it hit her. "What could you have done differently?"

"She'd gone through the same thing with Julia, only she seemed to have snapped out of it after a while. With Wyatt, though, something was different. I should've known she was worse. I should've paid more attention."

"It doesn't make sense that you blame yourself."

"You have to understand. Beth wasn't a depressed person by nature. She was extremely outgoing and happy. Homecoming queen. First flute in band. Captain of the cheerleading squad."

"And you were the quarterback?"

"No, defensive line." He smiled slightly. "My point is that she was constantly busy. Always planning or doing something. Then after the babies were born, that all came to a standstill. I didn't even notice the changes in her after Julia. Too wrapped up, I suppose, in my own stuff and freaked out about supporting a family and becoming a dad.

"I came home from work one night, and she told me she'd gone to the doctor. Explained very matter-of-factly that she was in a postpartum depression and was going to be taking antidepressants. That was that."

"You never talked about it again?"

"I asked her about it every once in a while, but she didn't like to talk about it. I think, in hindsight, she was ashamed, in a way. I remember her once saying that she felt as though her body had betrayed her, so I paid more attention when Wyatt was born. Not enough, though. I should've…been there for her."

"Did you travel at all back then, too?"

"No, but I owned a commercial construction business in the city and spent a lot of time commuting. We were behind on a big project, so I was working long hours and coming home late. She was alone a lot with the kids."

"Still. It's not your fault, Adam."

"Fault is a funny thing to try and wrap your arms around. Did I draw the razor over her wrist? No. But was I there to listen, to help with the kids when she was feeling run-down? No. To rub her feet or give her a back rub? To care for her the way she cared for all of us? If I had been, then maybe, just maybe, she'd still be alive."

"And maybe she'd still be gone." Marin turned the bottle of beer in her hand. "You can't read minds. If she never told you how desperate she was feeling how could you expect to have known?"

"Ever been married, Marin?"

"No." And at the rate she was going, she probably never would be.

"Well, the way I see it, Beth killed herself because she lost hope. She couldn't see any other way to end her pain." Steady and clear, Adam held her gaze. "When a man makes a vow to love and cherish a woman, he's vowing to make sure she feels that way. Every day. I don't need to read minds to know a wife needs to feel loved. If Beth had felt the depth of my love for her, she would've also felt the hope that comes with love. She would've had the hope she needed to carry on that day. She never would've ended her life."

Try as she might, Marin could find no argument against his logic. All she could do was respect this man for his deep level of commitment. How different he was from Colin, a man who had been ready to go through with a marriage based on a lie.

No wonder Adam wasn't up for a casual relationship. It all made so much more sense now that she knew the details surrounding Beth's death. Unfortunately, Marin only wanted this man all the more. "I have this feeling, Adam," she whispered. "Your wife knew very well that you loved her."

IN HER BEDROOM, ANGELICA took out her new phone and plugged it in. She really hadn't needed a new one, but it seemed like a reasonable excuse to get Marin over to the Harding house. She'd just turned away when the darned thing vibrated with an incoming text.

I need to talk to you. ASAP

Arthur. She couldn't keep avoiding him. Well, she could, but that wasn't going to make him go away.

Sighing, she dialed his number. "Yes, Arthur. What is it?"

"It's good to hear your voice."

"That it? That's why it was so important for me to call?"

"No. I called because I know you don't read the newspapers."

She'd stopped watching the news and reading papers a long time ago, after reading lies published about Arthur and their family one too many times. That was one part of public life she'd never gotten used to.

"I wanted to let you know that they're saying we're separated."

"Well, at least the media got something right for a change."

"We are not separated, Angie. You're just taking some well-deserved time to yourself. Visiting your daughter and grandchildren."

"If you say so."

"That's what I have to believe."

"Believe what you want, but I'll be staying here on Mirabelle for a little while longer." Not only would that give Arthur time to stew, but it also gave Marin more time to figure things out with Adam.

"How long?"

"However long it takes."

"THESE ARE ACTUALLY QUITE good."

Marin stuck a marker in her book. "What are you talking about, Mom?"

"Missy's children's stories." She looked at Marin over the tops of her reading glasses. "I assumed she had talent. All of you kids are creative in your own way, but I had no idea she could write this well."

Missy's spiral notebook lay open in her mother's lap.

"If I take that editorial job, Missy's going to be my first author. Haven't you read them?"

"No."

"You should." Her mother tossed the notebook onto the coffee table. "By the way, I talked to your father."

"And?"

"Apparently, it's all over the news that he and I are separated. I've decided to stay on Mirabelle at least until things die down, and I might just stay until I decide about the job."

Marin considered her options. She still wasn't ready to go back to Manhattan. "Mind if I stay with you?"

Her mother smiled. "I would love nothing better." She stood and walked toward the kitchen. "I'm going to make dinner. Found a new recipe for chicken *piccata* that I'd like to try."

"Sounds delicious." Marin picked up the notebook, thumbed through the beginning pages that looked like a bunch of notes, and finally came to the first story and started reading. Each story was about one of the Great Lakes. With the use of lyrical and descriptive phrases that were at once poetic and yet completely accessible, Missy managed to breathe life into each lake, giving each of them individual personalities. As Marin read, visions of loons and bald eagles, white pines and both rocky and sandy shores, sailboats, ferries, great ships, locks and canals, fish, fowl, and other wildlife filled her mind.

Before stopping to think, she flipped to the end

of Missy's notebook, found several empty pages and sketched out several ideas for illustrations as quickly as possible. As soon as she finished one, another was ready at the tip of her pencil. Then another. And another.

"Missy, you devil, you." Marin chuckled. She couldn't wait to start painting, and this time maybe she'd get something right.

"Yes, I know it's late and I do appreciate you returning my call tonight," Adam said over the phone to the nanny agency. "I'm sorry, but after phone interviews, I don't think any of these candidates will fit with our family."

She countered with some talk of matching up profiles and how they had the highest compatibility scores. The bottom line for Adam, though, was that one was too old and another too young. The third wouldn't be able to start until after Thanksgiving, the fourth was a man and, call him sexist, but with their mom gone he felt the kids needed feminine influence, and the final of the five candidates had taken another job offer a day after the agency had sent him the name.

"I would appreciate it if you would send me another list."

"All right, but that'll delay the process."

So be it. "Thank you." He hung up the phone to find Julia standing in his office doorway.

"Daddy, I don't feel good." Her hair was mussed and her eyes red as if she'd been crying.

He hopped up from his desk and knelt down in front of her. "What's the matter?"

"I feel icky. Like I might throw up. And I have a fever." She held out a thermometer. "I got it out of the upstairs bathroom."

The digital display showed a temperature of over one hundred. He felt her forehead. She was a little warm, but she wasn't burning up. "Let's get you some medicine for that fever."

"But my tummy's upset."

"You need to take something." But what? He had to admit he was feeling a little out of his league. The kids didn't get sick all that often and when they had Beth and then Carla had taken care of them. "There's got to be something upstairs."

He lifted her up into his arms and carried her up the steps and into the bathroom. She wrapped her arms around his neck and hung on him like a limp noodle, and for the first time in a long, long while he was scared, scared something might happen to his precious little girl. But kids got sick all the time and didn't die, he thought, calming himself. She'd be fine. He just had to get her fever down.

He looked through the child-aged medications Carla had kept stocked in the cabinet and found a fever reducer, quickly read the directions for her age and weight and shook out the proper dosage. "Chew these up, honey."

"I don't wanna, Daddy. I might throw up," she cried. "I want...Marin."

"Marin? What about Angelica?"

"Marin. Please, Daddy?"

It wasn't that late, not even ten, yet, so she'd be awake. Would she mind? Hard to say. "All right. I'll go see if she can come over for a little bit." If Marin objected, maybe Angelica would help out. He carried Julia down the hall to his bedroom, folded back the sheets and comforter, and tucked her in. "You stay in here, okay, so we don't wake up Wyatt. I'll be right back."

"Okay," she said, smiling weakly.

Adam ran next door. Lights were on in the kitchen and living area, so he knocked on the front door.

On seeing him, Angelica quickly swung the door wide. "What is it? What's wrong?"

"Sorry for bothering you." He glanced past her into the house.

Marin was coming down the stairs. God, she looked good even in flannel pajama pants and a T-shirt, her face fresh from clearly just having been washed, and the moment the thought crossed his mind he felt terrible thinking about a woman when his daughter was lying sick in bed.

"What do you need, Adam?" Angelica asked.

"Julia's sick. Tummy upset. High fever—"

"I'll come right over," Angelica said, grabbing a coat.

"Actually..." He looked from mother to daughter. "She asked for Marin."

Surprise registered on Angelica's face. "Really?"

"Me?" Marin looked shocked. "I don't know anything about sick kids. Why me?"

"I don't know. Do you mind—"

"Of course she doesn't." Angelica shoved a sweatshirt in Marin's hands. "Go."

Marin glared at her mother. "But—"

"That's okay." He stepped away from the door. "I can handle it."

"Marin Elizabeth—"

"Oh, all right." Marin grabbed the sweatshirt, came outside and closed the door. "Has she been sick all night?"

"She seemed fine when they went to bed, but she woke up and came downstairs just now." He let her in through the front and she tossed her sweatshirt on the nearest chair. "She's up in my room." He followed her up the stairs.

The minute Julia saw Marin she rubbed her eyes dry. Marin sat on the side of the bed and felt Julia's forehead. "So you don't feel good, huh?"

Julia shook her head.

Marin turned on the digital thermometer, displaying the last reading. "Is this your temperature?"

Julia nodded. "Will you stay here with us tonight?"

Marin turned toward him. "Adam, will you get Julia a glass of water? I think that might help her feel better."

"Sure. I'll be right back." He heard them talking

to each other as he walked downstairs. By the time he returned, Julia was smiling and looked as if she felt much better.

"You're going to be fine," Marin said as she kissed Julia's forehead. "See you this weekend." Then she stood.

He handed Julia the water and Marin took him by the arm. "Can I talk to you for a second?"

Wary suddenly, he followed her down into the kitchen. "What's going on?"

"Julia's not really sick."

"But she has a fever."

"No." Marin showed him the reading on the thermometer. "You can't have a fever that high and still be alive, Adam. I know at least that much about kids."

"But...what..."

"While you were getting her a glass of water, she admitted she'd put the thermometer up to the light-bulb in the lamp. She wanted me to come over and stay the night. She said she had fun with me the other day and she missed me. You should know, too, that things aren't going the best at school. She told me the other day that there's a boy who sometimes teases her and Wyatt at recess."

He ran his hands over his face. "I'm sorry, Marin. That you had to get involved."

"Don't be. She's so sweet and such a great kid."

"Who lied to me and to you." Frowning, he turned.

"Adam, don't be angry with her." She reached out and ran her hand along his arm. "She's in even more pain than you are. She's not only lost her mother, she's lost her father, too."

"What's that supposed to mean?" He did his best to rein in the anger he could feel building inside him. "I'm here every day for my kids. I would give my life for them. Drop anything to take care of them."

"I know that, but there's a part of you that you don't let anyone touch. Even Julia and Wyatt. A piece of you in so much pain—"

"That's enough," he said softly.

"You said you're a man who honors his commitments. What about your commitment as a fath—"

"Thank you for coming over here so late," he said, interrupting before she went too far. "I'll walk you home."

"Don't bother." She grabbed her sweatshirt. "I'll be fine."

Adam watched Marin stalk across their yards. The moment she'd gotten safely inside her own house, he closed his front door and leaned against it. What did she know about being a single parent? It wasn't easy. Yes, he worked god-awful hours, but every morning and every night he made an effort to spend one-on-one time with his kids. No doubt he made mistakes, but he was doing the best he could.

Or was he? Sighing, he went upstairs and peeked in on Julia.

She was still wide-awake. "Are you mad at me?"

"No, honey. I'm not mad." He sat on the bed and pulled her into his arms.

"It's just that…I like Marin. She's fun and nice. You like her, too, don't you, Daddy?"

Yeah, he liked her all right. "Sure, I do. But she's not our nanny. She's our neighbor." A neighbor who just might be seeing the trees for the forest better than he was these days. "Marin said you were having some problems with a boy at school. Do you want to talk about it?"

"It's not important. I can take care of myself."

"You know what?" he said. This was going to wreak havoc with his work schedule, but he needed to do this. "How 'bout we do that shopping this weekend. Take a whole day with it and have some fun, too."

She smiled hopefully. "On Sunday?"

"Sure. On Sunday." He held her until she was sound asleep and then carried her to her own bed. Then he went down to his office and got back to work.

CHAPTER FIFTEEN

"YOU GUYS READY?" ADAM PUT his coffee cup in the sink.

"Yep," Julia and Wyatt both said excitedly.

"Then let's hit it." On the way to the front door, he double-checked to make sure he had everything, various shopping lists, jackets for later in the day, and the keys for the car he had stored in Bayfield for just such an occasion. They stepped outside, and he turned to lock the door.

"Wait a minute, Daddy," Julia said. "I have to go to the bathroom."

"You just went."

"I have to go again."

"Okay. It's a long drive." He and Wyatt waited on the porch.

It was mid-October and summer was long over, but that didn't mean they couldn't do some summer-time-type activities. Since they were heading to the mainland to do some shopping, he'd figured they'd make a day of it by going into Duluth. They could get their shopping done, go out to lunch, maybe even dinner, and check out a couple of the sights he'd heard about in the waterfront district. The forecast called for an unseasonably warm autumn day, so at least the weather was cooperating.

Julia came outside a few minutes later. "Okay, I'm ready. Wyatt, did you go to the bathroom?"

"Huh?"

"You know? The bathroom."

"Oh, yeah. I have to go, too, Daddy." He took off into the house.

The kids had been excited about the day, so they had to be stalling for some reason. "Julia, what's going—"

"Hey, sorry I'm late." Marin jogged toward them across her front lawn.

Dressed in jeans and a black printed blouse, a sweater over her arm and a wallet-type purse angled over her shoulder, she looked as if she were prepared for something other than the usual. She was wearing makeup, lipstick even.

"We were just heading out for the day," he explained, feeling a bit confused. "Some shopping and other activities. What's up?"

"Oh, sorry." She stopped in the grass. "I thought I was taking the kids."

Adam threw a questioning glance at Julia just as Wyatt came outside.

"Sorry, Daddy." She frowned. "But you're bad at picking out girl's clothes."

Marin laughed. "So that's why you asked me?"

Julia glanced hopefully up at him. "Is it okay if she comes?"

Adam honestly wasn't sure how he felt about spending the day with Marin. On one hand, he'd shared more of himself with her in the past month than he had with anyone, friends or family, in the past three years, a testament to the fact that he felt more than at ease around her. On the other hand, that comfort level coupled with his obvious attraction to her carried the risk of adding up to something so much more.

"Can she, Daddy?" Wyatt asked.

This was their day. How could he start it off on the wrong foot? "It's all right with me if Marin doesn't mind. We're planning on heading into Duluth and taking in some sightseeing. That okay with you? Being gone the entire day?"

Marin considered it for a moment. "It sounds nice to get off the island and see more of the area." She looked from him to the kids. "I'd love to come."

The general mood was festive as the four of them took the ferry to Bayfield and then drove on to Duluth. During the couple hours it took them to get to Minnesota, Marin taught Julia and Wyatt several travel games. Twenty Questions, I Spy and the Alphabet Game. It reminded him of his own childhood, driving from St. Louis to his grandparents' house in Kansas City.

While Marin kept the kids entertained, he found himself, rather than listening to the words she was saying, letting the sound of her voice roll over him. Her voice had a surprisingly soothing effect, on him at least. He could almost feel the tension that had been building inside him since coming to Mirabelle roll off him in waves.

"Where'd you learn all those games?" he asked during a pause in play.

"Two brothers and a sister," she said. "Spending a lot of time on the train or in the car from D.C. to Manhattan. Manhattan to Long Island. It was either fight or play games."

"Did your mom play them with you?" Julia asked.

Marin turned to look into the backseat. "She did."

"She plays games with us, too, when she baby-sits," Wyatt said.

"You're lucky," Julia murmured.

"You know, you're right." Marin cocked her head. "She was a good mom."

"Here we are, guys," Adam said as they approached the harbor city located at the very south-westernmost point of Lake Superior. "Look out into the harbor. See the big red ships? Some of them come all the way here from the ocean, through all the Great Lakes. This is as far as they can go."

"Why do they come here?" Wyatt asked, his nose almost pressing against the glass.

"They're carrying cargo coming and going. All kinds of stuff."

"This is a big city," Julia said.

Bigger than Adam had expected. The town had

built up around the hills surrounding the harbor and it seemed to stretch on as far as the eye could see.

"It's rather picturesque," Marin added. "With the lake. The hills."

It was a warm autumn morning and there wasn't a cloud in the sky, but there was a slight wind. The deep blue lake was choppy with white caps. They went over bridges and along a crisscrossing, confusing freeway system.

"Let's get the shopping done first," he said, and they drove into town. "Then we play."

The first stop was a superstore where he pulled out a list to replenish school supplies. The aisles were overflowing with shoppers and more than once Adam had inadvertently brushed up against Marin, but they'd soon managed to get everything the kids needed as well as a few special treats.

When they'd finished, Marin carefully navigated the cart through the crowds. "I could use some shampoo and a few other things if we have time for a detour."

"Us, too." He pulled out another shopping list. They headed to the health and beauty aids section and stocked up on a variety of items. Next, they found a mall nearby with a fairly large department store. "If we split up, we can get to the fun stuff quicker," Adam said, glancing at Marin. "Would you mind taking off with Julia to get her the clothes she needs?"

"That okay with you?" Marin asked, glancing at his daughter.

Julia grinned. "Definitely."

Adam handed Marin the list he'd put together earlier that morning of all the things Julia needed.

She smiled. "Oh, you're good."

"Been doing this for a while now," he said, walking through the crowded parking lot, although he'd always shopped alone with the kids. Having Marin along not only made the excursion more efficient, it also added an enjoyable dimension to an otherwise mundane task.

"If in doubt, get it," he said to Marin as he grabbed two carts, wheeling one off toward her. "I'm not sure I'll have time to make it here again, so I'd rather have too much for her than not enough."

"Will do." Marin smiled down at Julia. "Let's go!"

Adam and Wyatt took off for the boys' section. Less than an hour later, they'd managed to find everything on Wyatt's list, sweatpants, jeans and khakis, shirts, sweatshirts, socks and underwear. Adam had even grabbed a sweatshirt and fleece jacket for himself. Everyone had been warning him how chilly the fall evenings could get on Mirabelle, so he thought it best to be prepared. All they needed was to decide on a couple pairs of shoes for Wyatt.

Wyatt sat on the floor as Adam fitted him with tennis shoes. "When do we get to the fun stuff?" he asked, his patience all but gone.

"As soon as we're done here."

"Then can we be done?"

Adam checked the fit, then tossed the shoes in the cart. "Okay, we're done. Let's go find Julia and Marin. If the girls are finished we can go."

The girls. It seemed like such a natural thing to say, as if Marin and Julia belonged together. *Don't do that. Do not get used to this.* He saw Marin and Julia outside the girls' dressing room. As he and Wyatt approached, the conversation he overheard had him pausing.

"I really think pink is your color," Marin said. "Or turquoise. Brights look best on you."

"One of these is for Kayla's birthday party," Julia said, apparently debating two different outfits. "I just don't know which one."

"How did school go this week?" Marin asked.

"Better," Julia said.

"That's good."

They might not be mother and daughter, but they sure looked and sounded the part.

Julia's eyes suddenly widened and she pulled a black outfit off the rack. "What about this one?"

Adam took in the too-short black skirt and a suggestive screen print T-shirt and realized he'd forgotten to remind Marin that his daughter was tall for her age. So many clothes that fit her were inappropriate for her age, and he was almost afraid to see what had accumulated in Marin and Julia's shopping cart. He pushed his and Wyatt's cart forward. "Hey, how's it going?"

Marin held out the two outfits. "Black or pink?"

"Which one, Daddy?" Julia said.

"Pink," he said decisively.

"Told you! It's your color." Marin grinned and held up a beaded necklace. "And it goes with this."

In truth either one of the outfits went with the necklace Marin was holding up and Julia looked good in black, but as he looked in the cart to peruse their selections, he could see Marin understood, as if she'd read his mind. And he was glad to see that Marin had apparently gotten some shopping done for herself.

"Okay!" Julia tossed the pink outfit in the cart.

"Are we done yet?" Wyatt groaned.

"That was the last thing on our list," Marin said.

"Finally!" Wyatt whipped around. "Let's get out of here before I die."

The kids ran ahead while he and Marin turned the carts around. "Thanks for remembering she's only seven."

"Tall for her age, though," Marin said, glancing up at him. "But she is your daughter."

"She gets it from Beth, too."

"Oh, no!" Wyatt groaned again as they reached the front registers. The lines seemed to stretch for miles. It looked as if the entire town was out shopping this weekend.

A store clerk signaled to Marin. "I can help you check out." She scooted behind a free register. "If you and your husband come over here."

Husband.

Julia and Wyatt giggled.

"I'm not…we're not… Oh, never mind." Marin wouldn't look at Adam as she piled Julia's clothes onto the counter.

And Adam was hit with the sad realization that he'd never be a husband again.

CHAPTER SIXTEEN

I CANNOT BELIEVE I'm doing this. First shopping for kids' clothes and now children's museums.

Marin chuckled to herself as the four of them strolled down the boardwalk at Canal Park, an old warehouse district converted into a touristy waterfront area jutting out into Duluth Harbor.

Adam had thrown out all the activities in the area and let the kids pick. Rather than perusing the trendy clothing, gift shops and galleries, Marin had joined everyone at the children's museum, the aquarium and the Maritime Visitor Center where they were able to watch giant ships, both foreign and domestic, pass under Duluth's famous Aerial Lift Bridge. Even more amazing than joining in all the family-oriented activities was the fact that she'd actually enjoyed herself.

More than anything, though, Marin had enjoyed watching Adam interacting with his kids. In spite of how busy he was with his job, he clearly adored them both. She couldn't help but feel a bit remorseful over confronting him the night Julia faked being sick.

"How 'bout a couple pictures," Adam said, pulling out his camera as they walked the sidewalks of Canal Park. "You three go stand right over there. By that ship's anchor."

"Me?" Marin pointed to herself. "You want me in it, too?"

"Yeah!" Julia and Wyatt each grabbed one of her hands and tugged her toward the giant anchor sitting near the edge of the rocky shore. They stood next to her and Adam clicked off several shots. Then Marin took some photos of Adam with his kids. He looked good, relaxed and calm.

"Do you want a picture of your whole family?" a young woman said as she walked by. "I'd be glad to take a shot."

"Yeah, Marin!"

"Come on, Marin."

She hesitated.

"Ah, come on, Marin," Adam called, a slight smile on his face.

Marin handed the woman the camera and then joined the three Hardings. Wyatt climbing onto her lap she could tolerate. When her arm brushed up against Adam's all she could think about was the way he'd touched her on Tequila Night.

"Smile," Adam said softly. "It's just a picture."

The woman snapped off several shots. "Nice-looking family," she said, handing the camera to Adam.

"Thanks."

"I'm hungry," Wyatt said.

"Me, too," Julia added.

They headed toward the shops and restaurants. "Let's let Marin pick where we're going." Adam handed her a pamphlet listing the various restaurants. There were a few fast food alternatives, but most of the establishments were geared toward adult entertainment. He pointed to one. "What do you think? You game?"

A kids' pizza arcade. She grinned. "In for a penny, in for a pound." Her decision was worth it just to hear the kids scream with excitement when they found out what was next.

The pizza, it turned out, wasn't too bad. The beer was ice-cold and the arcade games, batting cages and minigolf course were a hit with the kids and, surprisingly, Marin.

"I've never played laser tag," she said after they'd finished eating. "Who's game?"

"Me!" Both kids called in unison.

In no time, they had their laser guns in hand and their vests on, complete with electronic scorekeepers. Wyatt wanted a picture of himself, and that led to pictures of the entire group. Adam gave Marin a quick tutorial. "It's every man for himself out there," he whispered into her ear only a moment before the game began.

Marin followed the others into the arena. While her eyes adjusted to the dark lights, Adam shot her.

Another whisper in her ear, "Bang, bang, you're dead for thirty seconds."

"No fair."

"So come and get me." He grinned before disappearing into the darkness.

It took her a few minutes to get used to how the gun worked, but in no time, she was shooting targets and the kids. Adam, though, had clearly done this on several occasions. She couldn't get near him. Finally, she caught sight of him, followed him for a moment, and predicting his next move, went the other way around an obstacle. She was waiting for him when he turned the corner.

"Gotcha!" Marin exclaimed, firing. Then she ran off.

"I'm coming for you, Marin."

"That's supposed to scare me?" she called.

They chased each other and the kids. Marin hid in a corner. A moment later, Adam backed into her dark hiding place, obviously unaware she was behind him. As he moved close, and closer still, playtime turned serious. She felt too stunned to say anything. Then he turned, bumping into her and knocking her off balance.

"Whoa!" Putting his hands on her waist, he steadied her. "You okay?" he asked, but his hands never left her as they stood in the dark only inches away from each other.

"I'm fine." Her gaze flew from his eyes to his lips. This was crazy. This day hadn't been a date, but it had, in a way, felt like one, and she found herself wanting to kiss him to make it real.

His smile disappeared as his mouth parted. As his gaze slipped to her lips, it was obvious his thoughts were tracking along the same lines as hers. One breath. Two. His head seemed to angle toward her. Were his hands tightening around her, his thumbs moving to caress her abdomen? Then, abruptly, the arena lights blinked on as their time ran out on the laser tag game.

"Dad?" Wyatt called. "I hit the jackpot!"

"Game over," he whispered, his accent suddenly heavy and deep. Then he spun away from her.

Not a moment too soon.

BY THE TIME THEY DROVE into Bayfield, it was late and the kids had long been asleep in the rear seat of Adam's SUV. He and Marin had talked most of the way home about everything including favorite foods and restaurants, the towns and cities he and kids had lived in while his company did restoration work, and the pros and cons of living in D.C. and Manhattan.

"I think I'm ready to live someplace else," she said softly as they drove into Bayfield. "I'm just not sure where that someplace might be."

"What about staying on Mirabelle?"

"I like being close to Missy, but I'm fairly certain I'm not a small town girl," she said, laughing.

"What about you? Do you think you'll ever go back to St. Louis?"

He didn't know what to say.

Her features, illuminated by the dashboard panel, turned pensive. "Too many memories?" she asked softly.

"I guess. I still haven't sold the house Beth and I bought when we first got married."

"So you do think about moving back."

"More out of necessity than anything." At the thought of work, he tensed. "My company has more business than I can handle on my own. I've decided to put a couple operations officers in place to manage the smaller projects, but there's some sense in me being centrally located at our corporate headquarters in Missouri."

"I shouldn't have brought up work. I'm sorry."

Hoping the sight of her might relax him again, he glanced over at Marin. It worked. "I had a nice day. A much needed break. Thank you for coming with us."

"I think I'm the one who should be thanking you for letting me come along." She grinned. "I had no idea arcade pizza places could be so much fun."

Adam pulled his car into the garage he was renting near the Bayfield marina and gently woke the kids. "We're almost home, guys." He helped them put on their jackets.

"Daddy," Julia murmured sleepily. "Will you carry me?"

"Sorry, sweetie, but I'm going to need you both to walk. I've got too many packages."

"I'll help with the bags." Marin took as many as she could in each hand and Adam grabbed the rest.

Rather than wait for the ferry, Adam hired a water taxi and they were docking at Mirabelle's marina in no time. A few minutes later, the kids trudged groggily into the house.

"I'm so tired," Julia moaned. "I can't go up the stairs."

"All right, I'll carry you the rest of the way." Adam set the bags down in the living room and lifted Julia into his arms.

"What about me?" Wyatt groaned.

"I got you." Marin set down her bags, lifted him and followed Adam up the steps.

"They sleep together," he whispered as he went into Julia's room. He drew back the bedcovers, laid Julia down and eased off her shoes. Marin followed suit with Wyatt. A moment later, he'd closed their bedroom door and was following Marin down the stairs. He reached around her to flick on the outdoor light, bringing them to within inches of each other, and Marin went utterly still. For a moment, he looked into her eyes, felt her leaning toward him.

"Thanks again for coming today," he whispered.

"I had a nice day," she said, almost breathless.

Kissing her at that moment seemed like the most natural thing in the world. This time, he was the one who moved toward her. Her mouth parted as their lips touched. Their tongues danced softly, slowly and before he knew it he gripped her shoulders and pulled her close, but that didn't seem to bring her nearly close enough. He tried wrapping his arms around her and, slanting his head, dared to let his tongue slip through her lips for a better taste.

That did it. Almost.

She drew in a shuddering breath and melted against him. Her arms flew around his neck, her fingers dug into his hair, his shoulders. He wanted to sink into her, her into him. He kissed her neck, breathed in her scent, soap and the fresh lake air.

This is going too far again, a tiny corner of his brain whispered. *In another minute, you're not going to want to stop.*

Reluctantly, he drew back, ran his hands down her cheeks and drew a thumb over her mouth. A few inches lower and he could feel her neck, her chest. Lower still and he would feel her breasts heavy in the palms of his hands, but he wouldn't want to stop there. Neither would she.

You know you want this.

Quickly, he pulled his hands away from her.

"Remind me again why this is wrong," she whispered.

"Daddy?"

Julia. At the top of the steps. Looking right at them. Adam held Marin's gaze. She looked as drugged as he felt. "What do you need, Julia?" he called over his shoulder.

"I'm thirsty."

"I'll be right there with a glass of water. Go back to bed, honey." The moment Julia disappeared, he whispered, "That's why." He rested his forehead against Marin's. "Wait here. Please. We need to talk." As quickly as he could, he filled a glass with water and ran up the stairs to Julia.

"Why is Marin here?" she asked.

"She helped carry in all our shopping bags."

Her sleepy expression was tinged with hope. "Is she staying the night?"

"No, honey, she's leav—"

"But she could stay, couldn't she?"

Adam wasn't sure how to respond to the question that seemed to have come out of left field. "She has to go home. Now go back to sleep."

Quietly, he left the bedroom. By the time he got downstairs, Marin was gone. That's when he saw her outside running to her house, running to safety. That was one smart woman, much smarter than him, that was for sure.

TALK? TALK ABOUT WHAT?

Marin raced into her house, quickly locked the patio door and leaned against it, catching her breath. She wasn't fool enough to believe she wouldn't unlock it if he came after her, but he wouldn't come. Would he?

Keeping the lights off, she studied Adam's house. The rooms were still dark, but he was there in his kitchen. She could feel him. Hurting. Wanting. Needing.

Who was he trying to kid? If she'd stayed there in his house waiting for him to come back to her, they wouldn't have talked. There was nothing to talk about. There would've been only one outcome to her staying at the Harding house tonight, and it wouldn't have been merely getting a glass of water for Julia.

It wouldn't have been just sex, either. Adam was right. Marin had made one crucial mistake. She was starting to care for Adam. Even worse, she was starting to care for his kids.

ANGELICA STOOD IN THE BATHROOM off her main floor bedroom brushing her teeth when the patio door quickly opened and just as quickly slammed shut. She wiped off her mouth and cocked an ear, listening. There was no other sound other than the lock clicking into place.

Had she been in Manhattan or D.C. she might've had cause to be alarmed, but this was Mirabelle. Already in pajamas, she tiptoed through the dark house and found Marin standing at the door looking out toward the Harding house. "Marin, are you all right?"

Her daughter spun around, looking for all the world as if she were a five-year-old caught with her hand in the cookie jar. "Yeah," she said, a bit on the breathless side. "Yeah, I'm fine. Why wouldn't I be?" Her cheeks were flushed, her lips cherry-red and what was that on her neck?

Good, Lord! If that wasn't a whisker rub on her skin, Angelica was a monkey's uncle. But how—?

Adam. Good for him. Angelica should've expected as much. With the way those two had been making eyes at each other every chance they got, she should've been surprised her daughter had come home at all after spending the day with them in Duluth.

"I'm going to bed," Marin said, rushing past Angelica. "Good night, Mom."

"Night, sweetheart."

With a smile on her face, Angelica returned to her bathroom. As she washed her face, she considered the possibilities of a real romance between her daughter and Adam Harding. That man probably didn't even know it yet, but he needed someone exactly like her daughter, someone strong, generous and loving. And Marin? No doubt she was struggling to see past those two children, no matter how lovely they were, to the attractive, honorable and very lonely man standing behind them.

Oh, to feel that kind of passion and angst again. Hard to believe she was once that young. With a long heavy sigh, she gently brushed night cream over her face and neck, smoothing the heavy emollient into her wrinkles, and studied herself in the mirror. The color of her eyes was still a bright blue. Her thick, chin-length hair was more gray than blond these days, but the silvery sections were, thank heavens, manageable and blended well with her natural color. She was, she supposed, maturing well, but this body had seen better days.

Where had the time gone? How had she gotten to be so old? It was as if one day she'd been in college having the time of her life and the next she'd been raising babies. Then before she'd known it, her children were all grown and living their own lives and she was a damned empty-nester. What had happened to that energetic and determined young woman who had looked forward to her future with hope and fearlessness?

Angelica sighed. That bold woman was still there, hiding, deep under all those wrinkles. She just needed a little TLC before drumming up the courage to show her face again, but show her face, she would. Very soon.

CHAPTER SEVENTEEN

"THEY SAID OUR DOCUMENTATION wasn't complete."

"I talked to the new supervisor this morning." Adam sat at his office desk talking on his cell phone to a very worried Carl Andersen, Mirabelle's mayor. The federal and state funding for the Mirabelle project was getting held up over a couple of invoices. "Phyllis already refaxed everything to their offices in Madison. We should be set."

"Do you think the money will fall through?"

"No, don't worry about it, Carl."

"But what if…"

Adam had a meeting in two minutes down at Setterberg's building, but he couldn't very well cut the man off. While Carl continued talking, he pushed away from his desk and headed out of his office. "I'll be down on Main if you need me," he mouthed to Phyllis before stepping outside.

"Carl, we're doing everything we're supposed to be doing. They're just having transition problems with new staffing. Give them time to work through the wrinkles."

He'd gotten less than a block away from his office,

when Phyllis came out of the trailer. "Adam!" He turned to find her running toward him carrying the phone. By the look on her face, it was urgent. "You're going to want to take this."

"Carl, I have to go. I'll let you know when I hear back from Madison." He shut off his cell phone and took the office phone from Phyllis. "Harding here."

"Adam Harding?"

"This is." Adam held the phone up to his ear, but could barely hear the voice on the other end of the line over the sound of a truck backing up less than a block away. "Could you hold on a minute, please?" Unable to hear the response, he ran across the road and snuck into Newman's grocery. "Okay, I'm here. Sorry about that."

"No problem," the woman said. "This is Peg Ackerman, principal at Mirabelle Elementary."

"Are Wyatt and Julia okay?"

"They're fine, but we had a...situation over recess."

Adam held his breath. Other than calls from nurses the few times Julia had gotten sick through the years, he'd never been contacted before by a school. A principal calling could be nothing but bad news.

"Apparently," she went on, "one of the boys was teasing Wyatt. There was a fight on the playground. A fairly nasty one from all accounts. We have a couple of split lips here and a possible black eye."

Wyatt. The boy had a temper, but Adam never would've expected this.

"Can you come to my office to talk?"

"Absolutely. When?"

"I think it's best you come as soon as you can."

"I'll be right there." Adam hung up the phone, told Phyllis he'd be unavailable for the next two hours and walked swiftly toward school.

The administrative offices were just inside the main entrance to the building. Before Adam made it to the receptionist's desk, the principal had come out of her office and introduced herself. Then she led Adam into her office. He stepped through the door and stopped dead in his tracks.

Julia, not Wyatt, sat in the corner chair sniffling. Her cheeks were blotchy, her eyes red and puffy, her lower lip swollen and caked with a bit of dried blood, and at the sight of her a fury like nothing Adam had ever known coursed through him.

He knew it was sexist, he knew it was inappropriate on many levels, but Wyatt getting into a fight, either defending himself or starting one, seemed, while not acceptable, at least more predictable. Boys were physical. They tended to fight more. But this was Julia. His daughter. Someone had hit his little girl.

"I'm sorry, Daddy," Julia cried, and ran to him.

As he wrapped his arms around her and hugged her tightly, he did his best to defuse the anger building inside him. "It's all right, Julia. You're all right."

Then he glared at the principal. "Who hit my daughter?"

"Why don't you take a seat, Mr. Harding, and we can—"

"I want to know who hit my daughter."

"Another second grade boy pushed her. She fell and hit her mouth on the edge of a slide."

"Where is he? Have you talked to his parents?"

"Mr. Harding, please sit down."

"Is he still here—"

"Mr. Harding. While the other boy is not blameless, he did not hit Julia. Julia hit him."

More than a little shocked, Adam held the principal's even gaze. "You're trying to tell me that my daughter threw the first punch?"

"That's the account that has been given by all involved parties."

Adam turned to his daughter. "Is that the truth? Did you start this fight?"

"He asked for it."

"What happened, Julia?"

"I'm sorry, Daddy."

"Just tell me what happened."

"He was teasing Wyatt. Cody was. He's been teasing Wyatt since the first day of school when Wyatt threw up in the hall." Suddenly, her tears dried and her brow furrowed with anger. "I kept asking him to stop, but he wouldn't. So I told the playground monitor, and she gave him a couple time-outs. But as soon as he came back to the swings he'd go right after Wyatt again."

"Every day?"

"Just some days."

"Honey, why didn't you or Wyatt say anything to me?"

"You're always so busy, Daddy, so I took care of it myself." She frowned. "I know I'm not supposed to hit, but I just...I just got so...mad."

She clenched her jaw shut. He'd never seen her like this. Her hands were curled into fists. Her eyes piercing and intimidating. She was a mass of emotion, seething and out of control.

"And Wyatt? Was he involved in what happened today?"

"I told him to stay back. That I'd take care of him."

Her actions were wrong, but Adam was just a little bit proud of his daughter for standing up for her brother.

"I think it's best if Julia spends the rest of the afternoon with you, Mr. Harding, to discuss alternatives to what happened today." The principal said to Julia, "Why don't you go get your things from your locker and wait in the hall while your dad and I talk?"

His daughter nodded and left the room. Once Julia was in the hall, he and the principal discussed the school's disciplinary policy. Julia as well as the other boy involved would both be required to spend two recesses inside in a type of detention, and that sounded reasonable.

"Who's the boy she hit?" Adam asked.

"Cody Stall."

Bud Stall was the community center manager and, as far as Adam could tell, a good man. Adam felt sure the other father would do his best to handle his side of this situation.

"Maybe it would be best if we could talk a little bit about what's going on with Julia," the principal said.

"She's a good girl." Adam shook his head. "I've never had any problems at any of the other schools with her lashing out like this."

"You move a lot?"

"It's my job. It's what I do."

"I understand, but that kind of constant change can be stressful on children. How are things at home?"

"No family is perfect," Adam said, feeling defensive, but he wasn't going to pull the widower card looking for sympathy. "We have our shares of ups and downs, but we manage. Now if there isn't anything else—"

"I don't mean to pry, but Julia's mother? I understand she passed away some time ago?"

Okay, that's it. "Julia's mother is none of your business. Julia was protecting her little brother from, it sounds like, a bully. I'm not condoning her actions. I don't hit anyone at my house, so you can rest assured that I won't tolerate my kids hitting other kids. The fact remains that if you didn't have this bully on the playground, we wouldn't be having this discussion now, would we?"

"No." She sighed. "But if Julia, or for that matter Wyatt, ever need to talk, we have different counseling options avail—"

"Julia's fine. So is Wyatt." Adam stood. "Now are we finished here?"

"Apparently."

He stalked out of the room. "You ready, Julia? We're going home." Unaccustomed as Adam was to anger, it took him most of the distance to their house to calm himself.

"I'm really, really sorry to cause a problem, Daddy," Julia said, running up the stairs. Then the door to her bedroom slammed shut and all was quiet.

His first impulse was to go into his office and check his emails and voice messages. To work. He told himself it would do Julia some good to let her settle down some before they talked, but that was a lie. Work would be Adam's escape, not Julia's.

He paced through the house and the truth slowly but surely sunk in. He'd changed since Beth's death. Changing as a man was one thing, but what kind of father had he become? This father, this man who kept his distance, who let nannies and babysitters take care of more than just the everyday tasks, wasn't the Adam he knew. This man he'd become wasn't the father Julia and Wyatt deserved.

What would Beth do?

She'd be there. She'd listen. Adam climbed the steps and knocked softly on Julia's bedroom door. "Julia, can we talk?" He turned the knob and found his daughter curled up on her bed. He crossed the room and sat on the edge of the mattress. "I'm not mad at you, honey."

"You looked mad."

"I wasn't mad at you." Admitting he was mad at the principal, at the situation, at the little boy teasing Wyatt would stir up a whole other can of worms. "You know you're not supposed to hit. You made a mistake. Are you going to do it again?"

His daughter shook her head.

"Even if that boy teases Wyatt again?"

"No."

"Well, there you go." They talked about options for how to handle Cody in the future. Adam brushed Julia's hair away from her forehead and his daughter's shoulders shook as a new round of tears flowed. He pulled Julia into his arms, held her and rocked her. "I want you to know that no matter how busy I am, I always, always have time for you and Wyatt. So if you have a problem at school, I will drop whatever I'm doing and you can talk to me about it, okay?"

"Okay."

"My job here on Mirabelle is important, but not as important as you and Wyatt."

She shuddered in his arms and a fresh round of tears started.

"I love you, Julia, and there is nothing you could do that will make me stop loving you. One way or another, we're going to get through this."

They sat there for a long, long while as Julia poured out her heart and soul. Adam couldn't remember having ever held his daughter like this, but he wouldn't be waiting for a crisis to hold her this way again.

PROPPED UP IN BED, MARIN finished the last line in the book she'd been reading and snapped the cover closed. Since she'd come to Mirabelle, when she hadn't been painting, she'd burned through her sister's bookcase full of romances and women's fiction and then some. She was relaxed enough. She needed to do something. Exactly what, she wasn't sure. Knowing some exercise might clear her head and allow for some direction, she put on her running gear and bounded downstairs.

"Going for a run?" her mother asked. "Would you mind walking Wyatt home from school today?"

"I'll stop on my way home. Why just Wyatt?"

"I don't know. Adam called a little while ago and said he was home with Julia. He said he wouldn't need me this afternoon, but wondered if we could still pick up Wyatt."

"Maybe Julia's sick."

"Could be."

"Whatever. I'll get Wyatt."

Pacing herself, she went out the door and took off toward Island Drive. It felt good to be outside. Mirabelle was a pretty place even with the trees bare and the colorful garden mums withering from the chilly nights of late autumn. Before she knew it, she'd passed the picturesque Mirabelle Island Inn, its white gazebo down by the shore now fully restored, compliments of Adam's work crews. At the golf course more of Adam's crews were laying sod and planting trees, work that most likely needed to be finished before the first snow flew and the ground froze. And at Mirabelle Stable and Livery, even more of Adam's men were rebuilding a barn that the tornado had apparently decimated. Evidence of Adam's impact on Mirabelle appeared to be everywhere she looked.

What would Mirabelle do without Adam Harding?

Suddenly, she felt horrible for the things she said to him about being an absent father. It wasn't as simple as him being a workaholic. He had an incredibly important and demanding job that touched a lot of people's lives. If he failed, Mirabelle's businesses failed. This island would wither and die. No wonder he took his work so seriously. She ran a little faster, trying to puzzle out a solution. There wasn't one. He needed a nanny. Or a wife. The idea of Adam with another woman settled like a rock in the pit of her stomach.

Feeling her body just about running out of steam, she turned around and headed toward the elementary school. She ran up the entrance to the little school and managed to get in a few stretches before Maddie showed up. They chatted while other parents arrived. Then the bell rang, the doors opened and general mayhem ensued. The older kids, kids who didn't need escorts, took off across the school lawn toward home. The younger kids all seemed to be looking for a familiar face.

Marin spotted Wyatt right away. "Wyatt!" she called.

He grinned and ran at her, his backpack looking way too big for his little body.

"So." She smiled. "How'd your day go?"

"I got to sit next to Abby during the sixth and seventh grader's play today."

"That's cool. Julia's already home with your dad, right?"

"Yeah. My teacher said he came to pick her up and take her home."

Marin waved at Maddie, and she and Wyatt headed down the sidewalk toward their houses. "Why? What happened?"

He frowned and told her there'd been a fight at recess. "Cody was teasing me about throwing up on my first day of school."

"I did that, too, on my first day," Marin said, chuckling. "I think that happens to a lot of kids."

"Yeah, well, he's been bugging me about it ever

since. Julia couldn't stand it anymore. She punched him."

"What!"

"You should've seen it." His eyes lit up with pride. "She told him to knock it off. He said 'make me.' And bam! She punched him right in the face. Twice!"

Oh, no. "Is she okay?"

"Yeah. Cody pushed her back, and she hit the slide. Her mouth started bleeding."

By this time they'd arrived at their houses. Wyatt ran up the sidewalk and raced through the front door. "Julia!"

"She's up here." Adam's voice sounded from inside.

Marin came to the door in time to see Wyatt drop his backpack and race upstairs just as Adam was coming down the stairs. He gave her a slight smile. "I suppose you heard what happened."

"Wyatt told me. Is she okay?"

"She's fine."

"Are you okay?" she whispered.

"I need to apologize to you." He held her gaze. "Wyatt's been getting teased since the first day of school and they never told me because I'm too busy. You were right that other night. About me not being—"

She held up her hand. "I was out of line. I grew up with an absent father. He did his best when he was around, but that wasn't very often. And I know what it's like to be a workaholic. I've been in a ten-, twelve-hour workday job. So I guess a little of my own issues got tossed into that mix. Your job is different than mine was. Other people's livelihoods are at stake. I get—"

"Marin." He took her hand in his, making her immediately snap her mouth closed. "My job is demanding, but at the end of the day, it's a job. Julia and Wyatt are my life. I'd lost sight of that, so thank you for reminding me."

"Can I see her?"

"Sure."

Marin went up the steps and down the hall to Julia's room. Julia's lower lip was slightly swollen, but her eyes were worse. She'd probably been crying the entire afternoon. "Hey," Marin said as she stepped into the room and went to sit on the bed. "How you doing?"

"Okay."

Wyatt was sitting next to her with a book in his lap. "Marin threw up, too," he said. "On her first day of school."

"You did?"

"Yeah. Got teased, too, of course."

"I'll bet you didn't hit anyone."

"No, but I wanted to. Joel Strathmore. I wanted to punch him good." She smiled at Julia. "If he'd been teasing my little brother, Max, I just might've hit him."

Tears welled anew in Julia's eyes.

"It's going to be all right," Marin said, hugging her.

"No. It's not," she whispered. "Because I miss Mommy, and she's never coming back."

At that, Wyatt started crying, too. Both kids ended up in her arms, and she was completely at a loss as to what to do.

Adam came into the room and stood watching them for a moment. Then he came forward. "I got this," he said, taking her hand and disentangling her from the kids. Then he sat, taking her place and wrapping his arms around both kids. "We all miss Mommy," he whispered. "Some days are worse than others, and that's okay because it shows we loved her…"

As Marin slipped away, Adam caught her gaze. His eyes were clear, his demeanor filled with purpose, and there was no doubt in her mind that Julia and Wyatt's dad was back.

ANGELICA CONTEMPLATED the Harding house through the side window. Marin had come home with Wyatt some time ago and had, surprisingly, gone inside the house. Maybe Angelica's tactics were finally paying off.

She wasn't playing matchmaker. She was just ensuring that Marin and Adam were forced to deal with one another. If those two were meant to be together, and Angelica had the distinct feeling they were, they'd figure it out on their own.

The front doorbell rang, abruptly putting an end to the silence and Angelica's musings.

A man stood on the porch, his body casting a distinctive shadow over the front door sheers. That height. Those shoulders. Anger flashed through her and she embraced that emotion with everything in her. She was going to need that edge for this conversation. She yanked open the door. "Arthur, what in the world are you doing here?"

"That's it?" He stood there in black dress pants and a golf shirt, overnight bag in hand, looking distinctly irritated. "No hello? No hug? Nothing?"

"You shouldn't have come."

For a moment, he only studied her, as if deciding his best plan of attack. "Did you really expect me to just roll over? To let you have your way?"

"Expect? No. Hope? Yes."

"You're acting like a child."

At that, she stepped out onto the porch and shut the door behind her. "The only children around here are our two grandbabies sleeping next door." There was no way this man was going to be invited into her house, rental or not.

"Angie, stop this nonsense and come home."

"You are the most stubborn, the most arrogant man I've ever known. These traits have served you well in congress, but they get you absolutely nowhere with me."

"Listen to—"

"No." She held firm. "I've told you what I need

from you. If it's not something you can provide gracefully, then there's no point in us…there's no point in us being together."

He pressed his lips together as if he was holding in his emotions. That's when she noticed his skin was just a bit sallow and his eyes looked bloodshot. Hangover? No, damn him, it was possible he'd been crying.

For a moment, she softened. She'd spent so many years with this man. Two-thirds of her life. They'd cried and laughed together as they'd raised four children. And here he was, bent low, looking broken and alone. But had he changed? Did he understand? No. If she gave in, everything would go back to the way it had always been and she could not live like that. Not anymore. "Goodbye, Arthur." She turned.

"You can't get rid of me this easily, Angie," he said. "I'm not going back to D.C. I'll be staying here as long as it takes."

"Suit yourself. There are several inns and hotels on the island. Good luck finding a room." Without looking back, she went into the house and firmly locked the door.

CHAPTER EIGHTEEN

"I DON'T KNOW IF IT'S FALL allergies or a cold, but I feel awful." Marin's mother loudly blew her already red nose. "Achy all over. My head feels as if it's going to explode."

Marin put her hand on her mother's forehead. "You don't have a fever, but maybe you should take something and go back to bed."

"Can't. Need to watch the Harding kids."

"But it's Saturday."

"Adam has some critical meetings down at the site with some state and federal officials, so he asked if I could watch them for a few hours." Still in her pajamas, she moved slowly toward her bedroom. "Be a dear and make me some tea while I change, would you?" she said, her voice sounding extremely nasally.

Marin watched her mother shuffle away. She would've offered right then and there to watch Julia and Wyatt, but she was trying as hard as possible to stay away from their father. The sound of her mother blowing her nose came through her closed bedroom door.

"Oh, all right." Her shoulders sagged. Knocking on her mother's door, she said, "I can watch the kids today, Mom. You go back to bed."

The door opened. "Really? You don't mind?"

Suddenly her mother's nose didn't sound quite so stuffy, her eyes not as tired. Would her mom— No. She wouldn't do that.

"It's okay. You get better. Oh, and, Mom, one more thing. I know this isn't the best time to tell you this, but Dad's here on the island. He just called my cell to tell me he's staying at the Mirabelle Island Inn."

"I know. He came by the house the other day."

"You've seen him?"

Her mother nodded.

"I'll talk to him." Sometimes, oddly enough, Marin and her father often spoke the same language. "Maybe I can knock some sense into him."

"Good luck with that."

Marin went upstairs, quickly washed her face, dressed in jeans and a T-shirt, and fingered her hair into a ponytail. Then she made some tea for both her and her mom and took off for Adam's house. After knocking lightly and finding the door open, she let herself into the house. Adam was on the phone in his office. She gave him an awkward wave. Never missing a beat in his conversation, he nodded. Although he never seemed to raise his voice, his word choices and the brevity of his sentences indicated this conversation was serious. She went into the family room and found both it and the kitchen empty.

A moment later, Adam joined her in the kitchen. "The kids are still asleep."

Dressed in a black shirt and tan khakis his big frame filled the little kitchen, making her feel a bit closed in. His hair was wet and his cheeks cleanly shaven. His face looked so soft in the morning, so rugged in the evening. "Um, that's fine."

"So what—" he cocked his head at her "—what are you doing here, anyway?"

"My mom's sick. I told her I'd watch Julia and Wyatt again. That okay?"

"Yeah, sure, anytime. They like you. Which is amazing."

She felt herself stiffening. "Why is it amazing?"

"Don't look so insulted." He laughed as he poured a cup of coffee into a travel mug, coming a little too close to her. "I didn't mean the fact that they like you was amazing. I meant the fact that they were okay with someone your age is amazing."

"Oh."

"That's why I need a middle-aged or older nanny. Julia hadn't accepted any of the younger babysitters I've tried through the years. I think they've reminded her too much of her mother. Anyway, thanks for coming." He glanced at his watch. "I have to meet some state and federal officials down at the pier in ten minutes. Okay, if I…"

"Go. Yeah." She swung her arms awkwardly. "I'll get the kids breakfast and stuff."

He shoved his laptop and a stack of files into a bag, grabbed several rolls of blueprints from his desk and glanced at her as if he had something more to say. Then, as if thinking better of it, he suddenly took off out the front door.

"You'd better go," she whispered, her heart aching just a bit for him, his kids, herself. "There's nothing to say."

She went into the kitchen, put away the clean dishes in the dishwasher and then wandered around the house, picking up this or that, straightening things. Next thing she knew, she was in his office.

The room looked like any other office, phone, computer, desk light, calculator. Stacks of mail and invoices. The only thing uniquely Adam in the room was the lingering scent of his aftershave. Situated in the front corner of the house, the room had two large windows, one facing the front and the other the side yard. She glanced out the side window. Her bedroom was only thirty, maybe forty feet away from his desk. Did he know that?

"Daddy doesn't like anyone in his office." Wyatt stood at the base of the steps looking into the room.

"No, I supposed not." She smiled. "Wouldn't want to mess up his paperwork, right?"

Wyatt yawned sleepily.

She went toward him. "Want to watch some cartoons and wake up?" As she walked past him, he reached up and grabbed her hand.

Marin's heart skipped a beat as his fingers curled around hers. Suddenly, all she wanted to do was pull that little boy into her arms and snuggle with him, so that's exactly what she did.

Immediately, his head dropped to her shoulder and his face was in her neck. "You smell good."

"Oh, yeah?" She settled on the couch with him in her lap. "What do I smell like?"

"Soap."

She smiled and the TV stayed off.

Light footsteps sounded down the stairs and Julia appeared in the room. Without a word, she sat close to Marin and snuggled into her side.

Oh, God. Marin closed her eyes and she wrapped her arm around Julia. *How could this be happening?*

"You guys hungry?"

"No," Julia whispered. "I just want to sit here."

"Me, too," Wyatt agreed.

Marin wasn't sure, but it was entirely possible they all fell back to sleep.

Adam came home several hours later, and as she walked down to the Mirabelle Island Inn Marin did her best to slough off the softness that had settled over her after the quiet morning with Julia and Wyatt. Now, she stood outside the door to her father's suite and prepared herself for the inevitable confrontation. His voice, loud and authoritative, emanated through the thick door in a one-sided conversation. Apparently, he was on the phone.

"Reschedule the subcommittee meeting." Pause. "No, tomorrow won't work. Give me two days." Pause. "On second thought, dammit, you'd better wait until next week."

Interesting. He was considering a week away from D.C. for this issue with her mother. The man didn't sound nearly desperate enough, but it was a start. She knocked, and a moment later, the door swung open.

A cell phone pressed to his ear, her father gestured for her to enter. Marin stepped through the doorway and immediately the richness of the room with its heavy antique Baroque furniture and navy blue carpet and textured wallpaper enveloped her like a cocoon.

"Yes, yes," her father said impatiently to the person on the other end of the line. "We'll deal with that later. I'll call you back." He clicked off the call and turned to Marin. "Thank God you're here. Maybe you can talk some sense into your mother."

"Dad—"

"She's got this crazy idea in her head that she needs a job. As if she doesn't have enough to do already with all the entertaining we do. The correspondence she's been handling for years. Charity events. State functions—"

"Dad—"

"If there's one thing she cannot fault me for it's

taking her for granted through the years. I have always, always respected how busy she's been raising you kids, managing the household and juggling my career needs—"

"That's the point, Dad," Marin said as forcefully as she could manage without yelling. "They're *your* career needs."

"But she's been with me every step of the way. It's as much her career—"

"You're not listening. She does not want your career. She wants her own."

"I thought she enjoyed being a part of it. I thought she wanted..." He fell silent, reconsidering things for the first time since Marin had walked into the room.

"She dealt with it all these years, but she's shared some things with Missy and I. She's never been comfortable in the public eye."

"Well, that's the silliest thing I've ever heard. She's the model senator's wife."

"She did it for you, Dad. Her needs and wants have changed. You need to change as well, or your marriage is over."

He looked at her as if she'd just told him he had an inoperable brain tumor. "Change what?" he asked softly. "Change how?"

"I'm not exactly sure, Dad, but for once in your life try to let go and give in."

"GET YOUR TRUCK OFF the cobblestone!" Adam called to the driver who was just pulling up in front of Duffy's to deliver a load of lumber.

"Ray Worley told me to park it here."

"Well, I'm Ray's boss." Looks like he and Mr. Worley were going to have to have another talk. "Move it two blocks inland onto the asphalt." Adam pointed. "Then use a forklift to unload down here."

"That's going to take three times as long."

"Which is why there's a higher delivery charge," Adam said patiently. "Take a look at your invoice and then move your truck."

His cell phone rang. The nanny agency. "Hello."

"Mr. Harding. You called."

"Yes, ma'am. I wanted to let you know that we can drop the age level. I think my kids are ready for someone younger."

"Well, that will certainly open up the possibilities. I'll send you a new listing. Anything else?"

"No, ma'am. Thank you." He disconnected the call.

"Adam?" Jesse Taylor was coming toward him from the interior of Duffy's.

Adam had been keeping an eye on this man's work since the day he'd shown up for a job after that first town meeting. He'd quickly realized this was one local who knew what he was doing. Within a week, after having found out that Jesse had previously managed construction projects, Adam had moved him from a day laborer position into a supervisory role and had no regrets. "What can I do for you, Jesse?"

"I don't know how to say this." He looked around

uncomfortably. "Oh, hell. I'm just coming out with it. Worley's cutting corners. Corners I don't think, from what I know of you and your reputation, you'd want cut."

"Give me an example."

He flicked his thumb behind him. "Right here at Duffy's, for one."

This was his brother and sister-in-law's pub, so it wasn't surprising that Jesse might be extra critical. "Yeah? What's going on?"

"The replacement windows upstairs were installed improperly." They went up to the second floor apartment, and Jesse pointed to the untrimmed and exposed area around the first window. "He told his men not to bother with shims on the interior. Said they didn't have time."

Which meant the windows not being properly leveled and stabilized would, over time, shift or warp. Adam studied the workmanship. Jesse was right.

"And this isn't the only problem I've noticed. Down the block at the art gallery, it's not windows. It's the roof."

The gallery was located in an old Victorian that had been turned into a commercial property. "What's happening there?"

"Your man's only replacing the shingles, but I was up in the attic yesterday, fixing the gable. The toe-nailed connections where the rafters are attached to the top roof plates have been pulled apart. That roof was lifted up in the storm. It has to be replaced."

This he had to see for himself. As they walked down the block and entered the building, Adam asked, "How do you know so much about tornado damage?"

"I did a few months of repair work down in Kansas one year. A couple farmhouses hit by a tornado."

Adam followed Jesse into the attic, pulled a flashlight from his pocket and flashed the strong beam up at the roof plates. Sure enough, the nails, pounded in at ninety-degree angles to secure the roof, had very definitely pulled free. He walked the length of the building. Some spots had resettled, but there was no doubt the high winds had lifted this roof right off its rafters, causing irreparable damage.

Adam snapped off his light. "Thanks for bringing all this to my attention." They climbed down from the attic and walked outside. "How would you like a promotion, Jesse?"

"Heck, yeah," Jesse said, shrugging.

"It might be a bit above your qualifications, but I need your help."

"If I'm not qualified to do the job, I'll let you know."

"Head to my office. I'll be there in five minutes to get you up to speed."

As Jesse took off toward Adam's trailer, Adam found Ray talking to one of the roofing crews. "I need to talk to you."

Ray came toward Adam. "Yeah. What's up?"

Adam explained what Jesse had just shown him.

"Oh, hell, Adam. What does one of them locals know about storm damage? I've been doing this for years. Those connections weren't that bad. It'd take another tornado coming through here to take the roof off, and what's the likelihood of that happening?"

"It doesn't matter. That wasn't your call."

"I'm saving you money," he said angrily, his breath tinged with the scent of alcohol. "You should be happy."

"Have you been drinking?"

"Had a beer at lunch. What's the big deal?"

That was it. "You're fired."

"I have a contract. You can't fire me."

"Without cause," Adam said calmly. "I'd say I have plenty."

"You son of a bitch!" Ray took a swing at Adam.

Adam quickly ducked, saw another fist coming at him and deflected it. Instinct took over and he punched Ray in the gut, knocking the wind out of him. Then he kicked the other man's feet out from under him, knocking him flat on his back. "I'm not going to fight you." He'd win, but it wouldn't solve anything.

"Need some help there?"

Adam spotted Garrett walking toward them. "This man needs to gather his things and leave the island. Now."

"You heard the man," Garrett said. "I'm your escort, so get up. Let's go."

"I'll mail your last check," Adam said.

Ray stood and pushed Adam as he walked past him.

Adam felt his fingers curl into fists, and he barely managed to contain himself.

"Ray, just so you don't get any stupid ideas," Garrett said. "I spent a lot of years as a Chicago cop, and I kind of miss discharging my weapon. Go ahead. Give me a reason."

Glaring at the two of them, Ray stalked away.

Adam turned to Garrett. "How did you—"

"Jesse called, thinking there might be trouble."

"Thank you, Garrett."

"No, Adam, thank you, for caring enough about the job you're doing to do it right." He took off after Ray.

Today, Garrett was happy the job was getting done properly, but when he realized all this was going to mess with the timetable, he wasn't going to be so happy. Having to fire Ray meant Duffy's just might not get finished by Christmas.

CHAPTER NINETEEN

November 6.

ALL DAY, Adam had been in an ugly mood, so much so that his men began scattering when they saw him coming through the construction site. Adam ignored the messages left on his cell phone early in the day from Beth's mom and his own parents and went about his business as if it was any other day of the year, even though it wasn't, even though it never could be ever again.

None of his employees, either at the corporate office or here on Mirabelle, including his assistant, remembered, and he was thankful for at least that. The kids had been too young to remember dates, and he'd never told any of the new people he'd met here on the island. As far as the rest of his world was concerned, this day was like any other. And just like most other days, he worked late and got home after supper. He walked through the front door and found Angelica out in the backyard with Julia and Wyatt.

She noticed him at the patio door and came toward

him. "Sorry, but the kids were too hungry to wait for you," she said. "They've already eaten dinner."

For a few minutes, Adam watched his kids playing outside with some neighbors.

"There are some leftovers in the refrigerator for you," Angelica said.

"Thank you." He turned. "I finally found a nanny today."

"That's good, isn't it?"

"She's much younger than Carla, but I'm hopeful it'll work out. I'm not sure exactly when she'll be able to start, but I'll let you know." He tried smiling, but his heart wasn't in it. "I can't tell you, Angelica, how much I appreciate all your help these last couple of months."

She held his eyes for a moment. "Something's wrong. What happened, Adam?"

He slipped past her, turning his back on her inquisitive gaze. "Everything's fine."

"Is it work?" She paused. "No, it isn't. Work problems don't tie you up in a knot. This is something much worse."

He grabbed a beer out of the fridge, popped the top and chugged a good third of the frosty cold liquid down, hoping to take the edge off.

"That's not going to fix it, you know? Whatever it is will still be there later tonight, in the morning, next year."

"Why can you Camden women never leave well enough alone?" he said, chuckling.

"Probably because things are seldom well enough."

Would it kill him to talk with someone? Someone as levelheaded as Angelica? Was he afraid? Of what? That he might actually be able to let this go and move on? That wasn't going to happen. That was never going to happen. That he might let off some steam? Was that so bad?

"This is the anniversary of Beth's death," he whispered.

"Marin told me she…" Angelica paused. "That Beth committed suicide. We weren't gossiping. She just felt—"

"It's all right. I get it. No explanation necessary."

"You know there's been something I've wanted to share with you all this time, but the right moment never seemed to pop up. And now that I'm getting ready to leave Mirabelle…well…" Angelica pulled out a chair. "For what it's worth, I went through a postpartum depression, too. After Max, my youngest."

"It happens more than people realize."

"Yes. It's not something my generation talks about, and when you're a senator's wife, well, that kind of thing is kept quiet." She sighed heavily. "Four kids under the age of six. A baby that didn't sleep through the night for close to a year. A husband busy in a very demanding job." She held his gaze. "It can happen to anyone, Adam. It's not your fault."

"You don't know that."

"Yes, I do. I've gotten to know you, and I know you're a caring, loving man. I also know what it's like to be in Beth's shoes. I know the kind of thoughts that were going through her mind."

"How could you know what she was thinking?"

"I don't need to know the specifics to get an inkling of what she was feeling. Depression, postpartum or otherwise, affects people in very similar ways."

He'd heard it all before in the support group, grief counseling meetings his mother had convinced him to attempt years ago, but he'd only been able to stomach a couple of the sessions. Between the experts laying down the facts of the physiological symptoms of depression and listening to the families of suicide victims trying to explain and justify to assuage their guilt, it had all been a nightmare.

"I've never told anyone this, but..." Angelica looked away. "I thought about killing myself several times during that very dark period in my life."

"Why?" he asked, desperate for answers. "Why would you do that?"

"Because I was so miserable that death seemed preferable to life."

"How could death ever be an answer?"

"It puts a stop to all the problems that seem insurmountable at the time. It ends the pain."

He wasn't going to kid himself into thinking he understood. He didn't. He probably never would.

But he was beginning to understand that sometimes there were no answers. Sometimes things just were. "What stopped you?" he whispered.

"I'm not sure, but I can tell you that there was no one in my life who could've made a difference. I was alone in my own mind, and I didn't realize how skewed my thoughts had become. Had I slipped just a step or two further down that slope, I might not be here today. Short of locking up your wife, there was nothing you could've done to stop her from hurting herself. And I'd bet anything that you had no clue she was feeling so desperate that she might need to be hospitalized."

"But I should have known, shouldn't I have? I was her husband. If I didn't know how badly she was feeling, if I didn't know how sick she was, who could know?"

"That's the point, Adam. She didn't do it to you. She didn't do it because of you. She did it because she was sick." Angelica reached out and put her hand over his. "Forgive Beth. Forgive yourself." She pushed away from the table and headed toward the door. "Do yourself and your kids a favor and do something today to remember something good about Beth."

A moment later she was gone.

The phone rang and Adam stared at the number displayed. A telemarketer this time, but this morning he'd gotten calls from both his parents and Beth's and returned neither. Running a hand over his face, he debated. His parents he might be able to stomach calling, but Beth's? Not today. Talking to them would have to wait a few weeks. He picked up the house phone and dialed his parents. As the call was about to go through, he quickly disconnected.

Forgive Beth. Forgive yourself.

He called another number.

Beth's mother picked up on the first ring as if she'd been waiting next to the phone all day hoping to hear from him. "Adam," she said, a smile in her voice. "It's so good you called."

"Hello, Sandra. How have you been?"

"As well as can be expected."

They chatted for several minutes, catching up on a year's worth of news. He couldn't believe it'd been that long since he'd last called.

As they wound down, she paused. "We had a memorial service for Beth today, you know, after the fundraiser. We had a good turnout for the walk. Close to five hundred registered. Lots of your old friends asked how you were doing." She paused. "How are you doing, Adam?"

"I'm getting there." Oddly enough, he found himself wanting to tell her about Marin, of all people. "Want to talk to the kids?"

"I thought you'd never ask."

"Julia! Wyatt!" he called outside. "Come talk to Grandma Sandra."

They raced toward him and he handed them each a house phone. Then he listened to them jabber away.

He didn't yet know what town he was going to end up rebuilding after Mirabelle, but one thing was for sure. They were going to spend some time back in Missouri reconnecting. For the first time in three years, he wanted his kids to know their families.

FEELING PENSIVE, ANGELICA left the Harding house and walked next door. Talking about that dark phase in her life after Max's birth always made Angelica sad. It'd been the only time in all those years with young children that she'd ever regretted the choices she'd made. Giving up her job, her freedom, what had felt at the time like the rest of her life, to raise a family.

She smiled, though, remembering Art coming home one night and surprising her with a long weekend away at a spa with her closest friends. He'd planned the entire thing himself. Well, more than likely, his administrative assistant had been the one to call all her friends and make travel arrangements, but Art had thought of it. He'd set the plan in motion and he'd taken time away from his busy D.C. schedule to take care of the kids while she was away.

The flowers. The meals he'd brought home. The late night trips to the store for diapers or formula or ice cream, just because she'd been in the mood. More than once, she'd looked back at that year after Max had been born thankful that Art had been there. If he hadn't stepped up to the plate, let his own career take the back burner for a short while, there's no telling what might've happened to her, their family.

That didn't mean that Adam could've changed what happened with Beth. Angelica had been quite vocal with Arthur as to what she needed from him, but Art had come through for her. In so many ways, he'd been a good husband, and he still needed her. Did she really need to take that job in Manhattan? Maybe there was an editorial job in D.C.

Her head down, her thoughts racing, she didn't see Arthur sitting on the front porch until she reached the steps. "Oh," she said. "How long have you been here?"

"A while." He stood and paced. "Angie, I don't want a divorce. Do you?"

"I don't know."

"Will you at least come out to dinner with me so we can talk?"

After all they'd been through together, didn't she owe him at least that much? "I'll think about it."

"THEY EAT AT FIVE-THIRTY. Adam's usually not home until six-thirty," Angelica said hurriedly. "They might need help with their schoolwork, but you'll have to double-check with Wyatt. He has a tendency to forget homework. They've already had a snack. They're—"

"Mom, it's okay," Marin said, interrupting her as they walked through the backyard to the Harding house. "If anything comes up you're next door and you'll be back soon, right?"

Her mother had come over to their house a moment ago and begged Marin to watch Julia and Wyatt. She'd gotten a voice mail from her publisher friend and needed to return the call right away to discuss specifics about the possible editor position. Marin had been a bit skeptical at first, thinking her mother was using this as just another excuse to get Marin over to the Hardings, but her mother's obvious excitement tipped the scales.

"I don't know how long the call will take," Angelica said.

"The kids are kind of used to me, so I'm guessing I can handle it."

Angelica headed to their house. "I'll be back when I'm through with the call."

Marin found Julia and Wyatt chilling in front of the TV. "Hey, guys," she said. "How are you doing?"

"Marin!" Immediately, the TV show was forgotten and Julia and Wyatt raced toward her for a hug. They sat in her lap and held her hand as she asked questions about school and friends and, in general, caught up. They showed her art projects, starred homework assignments and midterm report cards. She had to admit, she loved being appreciated and hated to put an end to it, but it was almost dinnertime.

"My mom said you guys had homework."

"A little."

"So how do you usually do this?"

"We get out our backpacks and sit at the kitchen table," Julia said.

"Sounds good to me. I'll get dinner going."

While the kids sat at the table to do their work, Marin looked through the refrigerator and kitchen cabinets. Angelica liked experimenting with recipes, so most of the groceries were staples with a few surprises. Marin, on the other hand, rarely cooked. She grabbed a couple boxes of macaroni and cheese.

While the macaroni boiled on the stove, she sliced apples and cucumbers. Missy had made some comment about kids liking finger foods and this was the best Marin could come up with at such short notice. Once or twice, she walked over to the table. Julia was concentrating on a packet of math worksheets, and Wyatt, his tongue sticking out the edge of his little mouth, was tracing letters, learning cursive.

"Looks good," she said, patting his back. A moment later, he finished. "Is that it?"

He nodded.

"You sure?"

"Yep."

"Wyatt, you have to look at your assignment notebook," Julia said, rolling her eyes. "Remember?"

At least someone around here knew the ropes. It turned out Wyatt had one more thing to do, a simple math sheet. As Marin grabbed plates and cups, she noticed Adam pacing on the sidewalk in front of the house. His head down, he spoke into his cell phone, apparently needing to get one last call completed before dinner. She walked across the room for a better look at him.

Wearing a tan canvas jacket and faded jeans, his dark hair ruffling in the breeze, he looked good enough to make Marin almost wish she got to watch him come home every day. What if he was hers? What if she walked out and met him on the sidewalk, took that phone out of his hand and slipped her hands inside his jacket and around his waist? That'd take his mind off work and her mind off everything.

He turned toward the house then and noticed her through the window. His reaction went instantaneously from surprise to awareness to something she didn't want to name.

What was she doing? Cooking meals and chatting with the kids as if she belonged here? Imagining her and Adam in domestic bliss? What was next? Volunteering up at school? Meeting Adam at the door with a martini? Great sex was not worth losing herself.

With that sobering thought, she returned to the kitchen, got out silverware and then dumped the noodles into the colander and melted some butter and cheese.

"Daddy!"

Julia and Wyatt ran to the front door and a moment later Adam came into the kitchen, Wyatt in his arms. "Hi, Marin."

"Hi," she said, hoping for light. "My mom had an important call to make, so—"

"You're filling in for her." He wouldn't take his eyes off her face, making her zing again. "Thanks."

"You're home early."

"I've been trying to make it home for dinner a couple times a week."

Good for him. "I didn't know you were going to be here for dinner, so you're stuck with macaroni and cheese." She shrugged and scooped up three plates. "A gourmet, I'm not."

"It looks great. Thank you." He set Wyatt down. "Aren't you staying to eat with us?"

"Well, I…"

"Just wondering. Your mom does sometimes."

"Yeah, Marin, stay."

"Please!"

Once. Just once. "Okay." She grabbed another plate and sat at the table across from Adam. Adam talked and laughed with his kids, managed to get them to tell him even more about their day than they'd told her. Once or twice her gaze caught with Adam's over forkfuls of noodles or a slice of apple, and they both seemed to get caught up in some flow of awareness and emotion. The third time, she couldn't take it anymore. The moment her plate was empty, she stood and walked to the sink.

Then he was behind her, setting his own dishes next to hers. "I'll clean up," he said, his hand brushing lightly against hers, his mouth inches from her cheek.

She closed her eyes as her body keyed into his closeness. If not for the kids' presence ten feet away, there's no telling what might've happened between them.

"The new nanny's coming tomorrow," he whispered, his sleeve slipping over her arm. He knew what he was doing to her. He knew, and he didn't care.

"Good. That's good."

"I'll call your mom to let her know."

"I have to go." She made to brush past him, but he didn't move out of her way, bringing her arm in direct contact with his chest, her hand with his thigh. "Adam." She looked up at him, saw his tortured gaze mirroring her own thoughts and she understood she'd been wrong. He did care. And what she was apparently doing to him looked just as painful.

The kids finished eating and brought their plates to the sink, oblivious to the tension building between Marin and Adam.

"Why don't you kids go get a little fresh air before we settle down for the night?" Adam said, his voice raspy.

"Okay!" They pulled on their jackets and ran outside.

She should go. Now. But her feet wouldn't move. Adam closed his eyes and leaned toward her, brushed his cheeks alongside hers. "I've missed you."

"Don't say that." His lips were on her neck, making it difficult to think straight. "This can't happen between us. You've made that very clear."

"That doesn't stop me from wanting you. Needing you. Thinking about you every minute of every day."

"Well, I'll make it easy for you, then." She pushed him away. "I don't think this should happen between us, either."

SEEMED LIKE ADAM WAS ALWAYS watching Marin leave him. One of these days very soon, she was going to leave Mirabelle and him for good, and then what? Nothing. How could he, in good conscience, bring any woman into his mess of a life? He couldn't. That meant, no matter what, he'd have to let her go. That didn't mean he'd ever forget her, though.

He turned away from the window and went to clean the supper dishes off the table. Then he went outside. "Did you guys remember the new nanny is coming tomorrow?"

"Yeah," Wyatt said.

Julia only frowned.

"I'd like to do something nice for Angelica and Marin. For all they've done for us these last couple of months." He'd ordered them both bronze sculptures of children at play by a famous artist and they'd be arriving by courier any day now. The statues had been expensive, probably more than he would've paid a nanny for the same period of time they'd helped out, but, as far as he was concerned, their help had been priceless. The statues, though, didn't seem personal enough.

Julia's eyes brightened. "Let's make picture frames. Just like we did for Carla."

"Yeah!" Wyatt said.

"Okay. What are we framing?"

"Pictures of us with them."

They'd taken some photos in Duluth with Marin. He'd find some way to get some of Angelica in the next few days. "So how do we make the frames?" he asked, feeling clueless.

"Missy has a big box of supplies," Julia said.

He went to Missy's and asked if he could use her craft supplies. With a smile, she handed it to him, and he and the kids set about making frames. As the glue was drying, he flipped through the photos of Marin in Duluth after loading them on his computer.

"I like that one," Wyatt said, as he and Julia came into his office. He pointed to one of him and Julia with Marin decked out in laser tag gear. "Will you print that one out?"

"Sure," he said, sending it to his printer.

"I like that one," Julia said, pointing to one of all four of them together at the anchor.

The young woman who'd taken the photo had

been right. They did look like a family. A happy one. "Wouldn't you rather have one of just you and Wyatt with Marin?"

"No," she said, leaning up against his arm. "I want her to remember you, too. Always."

CHAPTER TWENTY

"WHAT IF SHE'S MEAN?"

"What if she's ugly?"

"I want Marin."

"Or Angelica."

"Or Carla back."

Sitting between his two kids on a bench down by the marina the next morning, Adam waited for the ferry to dock. "Look." He put one arm around each child. "I know this is hard, but we need to give her a chance, okay?"

Neither said anything.

"You'll be in school all day and I'll be home right after supper, so at most you'll be spending a couple hours a day with the new nanny."

"Except for weekends," Julia muttered.

"I do have to work Saturdays, but I promise to spend every Sunday with you."

"You really promise?"

From now on he was keeping his promises. "I can't promise that I won't have to do some work, but I can promise it'll be just us three on Sundays."

Stephanie Moore, the new nanny, had requested

Sundays off and if she was like Carla, she'd spend any free time she had during the evenings and on weekends to herself in her own quarters. They'd likely see neither hide nor hair of her at least one day each week, giving everyone a break.

The ferry docked, and given Mirabelle's current state of flux there were no tourists disembarking, only a few locals returning from the mainland. Spotting the new nanny was easy. A medium height young woman with a pleasant, somewhat broad face and long, sandy-brown hair, she came off the ferry toting two rolling suitcases behind her. Dressed in tan wool pants and a belted brown plaid jacket with a hood, she looked well prepared for the cold autumn day and awfully mature for her age.

"Stephanie?" Adam approached her.

"Yes."

"I'm Adam Harding." He held out his hand. "It's a pleasure to meet you."

"Good to meet you, too."

Adam put his hands on his children's backs, but didn't urge them forward. They'd advance at their own pace. "This is Julia and Wyatt."

Julia's brow furrowed and Wyatt frowned. This was worse than the first day of school.

"Well, I for one can't wait to get to know you both." Stephanie gave them a big smile. "I've heard so many wonderful things about you two from Carla."

Mentioning Carla. Good move.

"You talked to her?" Julia asked.

"I most certainly did. On the phone. She assured me that I would love being your new nanny."

"How is she?"

"She sounded all right, but her mother isn't well. She needs Carla now more than ever."

Ice officially broken. "Well, should we go home?" Adam asked. He took the young woman's suitcases and held back, letting her get acquainted with the kids as they walked up the hill. The entire time, she kept the kids talking, answering questions about school. Carla had been quiet. Stephanie, on the other hand, seemed quite talkative. Maybe this wouldn't be such a difficult adjustment, after all.

"WELL, THERE SHE IS," Angelica murmured as she stood at the patio door glancing outside. "The new nanny."

"That so?" Feigning disinterest, Marin kept her hand on her paintbrush and the brush on the paper in an attempt to keep her focus on her latest illustration for Missy's book. The Harding children were no concern of hers. Absolutely no concern whatsoever.

"She's younger than I expected."

Marin pulled more color onto her brush, deepening a few shadows of the trees on a shoreline scene.

"She looks so...stern."

Determinedly, Marin rinsed out her brush and

loaded up with another color. Red. She needed red on the sail of the boat on the water.

"Oh, for heaven's sake," her mother said, clearly exasperated. "Let the boy do it himself."

At that, Marin glanced up. "Do what? What are you talking about?"

"Oh, it doesn't matter." Angelica waved Marin's concern away. "I'm sure you couldn't care less."

"All right, I'll bite." Marin dropped her brush into the water and stalked into the kitchen. "What's going on?"

She went to stand next to her mother and together they looked out into the backyard, analyzing the scene. The new nanny, a surprisingly young woman, was playing some sort of a game with the kids that seemed to combine memorizing with calisthenics.

"They've been in school all day." Marin couldn't seem to take her eyes off what was happening. "You'd think she could give them a bit of a break."

"I'm sure she's perfectly capable."

Marin turned away from the backyard and returned to her painting. Maybe now was the time to start that stormy scene she'd been putting off since she first started Missy's Lake Superior book. Capable was one thing. Loving and caring was quite another.

"MARIN, CAN I COME IN?" That was Missy at the door.

"Yeah," Marin said, straightening. She stretched

her stiff back. She'd been bent over this painting for hours, and it was almost time for the kids to get out of school. She still hadn't gotten used to not having to walk down to pick them up.

Missy stood in the doorway. "Looks like you set up an art studio in here."

"Yeah. Basically." She'd pushed the dining room table against the wall, covered it with several drop cloths to protect the wood, and moved all of the chairs into the basement. Then she'd put up make-shift shelving along one wall with all of her supplies.

"Can I see what you're working on?"

Fairly happy with the way this picture was turning out, Marin shrugged.

Missy stepped into the room and within seconds she was grinning. "Oh, my God, you've captured the stormy chapter perfectly."

"You think?"

"Marin, it's beautiful."

"Thanks." But her mind wasn't on her painting.

"You don't like it?"

"No, I like it. I just…" Marin dropped her brush into the water. "How did you know you wanted children?" She blurted the question out before giving it a second thought.

Missy raised her eyebrows. "Hmm. I don't remember ever not wanting them."

"Oh, come on. You always knew you were going to be a mother?"

"It's not that. I simply didn't think much about

it at all. Until I met Jonas." At that, her expression softened. "Having children with him seemed like the most natural thing in the world. I never questioned it." She sat in the only chair in the room and frowned. "And then when I miscarried that first time and I thought I'd lost Jonas, too, having children was the *only* thing I wanted. A family. I missed you. Artie, Max, Mom. Even Dad sometimes."

"Why didn't you come home?"

"I didn't know how, and I was already here on Mirabelle by then. Everyone here became my new family." She reached out for Marin's hand. "It wasn't you, you know. I just didn't know how to be me around our family."

Missy always had been different from the rest of them. Soft-spoken, kind and generous, not a competitive bone in her body. Marin, on the other hand, had been assertive enough for both of them. She'd had to be first in everything. Second just hadn't been good enough.

"I used to think you were a sissy," Marin said, smiling. "Now I know you're stronger than any of the rest of us."

"Well, that's not true. We're just different."

If nothing else came of her extended stay here on Mirabelle, Marin would be more than satisfied at having forged a new, adult relationship with Missy.

"So do these questions have anything to do with you and a certain neighbor?" Missy asked.

"You know I'd be lying if I said no. If Adam didn't

have children, I think I'd be all over him. But he does." She sighed and decided to come right out with it. "Weren't you ever afraid that by focusing so much of your life around kids that you would lose yourself?"

"How do you mean?"

"The way Mom did. While we were growing up, she seemed to live solely for us. She was our chauffeur, cook, laundress, counselor, tutor, coach and secretary all rolled into one. I don't ever remember her not being there if I needed something. What does that say about her life?"

"That she had pride in being a mother. That she took her job very seriously."

"Or that she had no life of her own."

"Marin, that's unfair."

"Why? What was the point in her getting an English degree, anyway? Of ever working for that publishing house to begin with, if she was just going to throw it all away to stay home with us? She lost her career. Her life. For us."

"We were her life by her choice. She didn't *lose* herself. She *gave* herself. There's a difference."

"The end result is the same."

"Maybe so, but not the attitude. I would drop anything if my boys needed me. If one of them was sick, I'd stay up all night caring for him. I'd stay home from the shop. I'd cook his favorite foods. I'd do whatever he needed to get well. Because it's what I've *chosen* to do. Taking care of them makes me happy. But I've also chosen to keep Whimsy, my gift shop, because it's important to me. I've continued to make jewelry because I enjoy the process. And I've picked up writing children's books because it's fun. Do I seem like I've lost myself to you?"

Unconvinced, Marin grunted. "Look what Mom is going through right now with Dad. How do you know that won't be you twenty years from now?"

"Because Jonas is not our father." Missy smiled. "And there's no doubt in my mind that if you choose to become a mother, you'll put everything you have into being the best mother possible because you never do anything halfway."

"Maybe that's exactly what I'm afraid of."

"I'M TIRED," WYATT GROANED. "Do I have to vacuum?"

"At least you don't have to clean the bathroom," Julia muttered. "Like me."

The office door wide-open, Adam sat behind his desk listening to the Saturday afternoon goings-on in the main part of the house. He was uncertain as to what exactly amounted to age-appropriate chores for a five- and seven-year-old, but the duties Stephanie had them doing seemed a bit of a stretch.

"As soon as we're finished with Saturday cleaning," Stephanie said, "we can go outside and play."

It was an unseasonably warm November day with the temperature hitting close to fifty degrees, so Adam would've rather they skipped cleaning entirely in favor of enjoying the weather, but a little time outside was better than nothing.

"Play by ourselves or with you?" Julia grumbled under her breath.

"Excuse me? Did you have something to say to me, Julia?"

"You make us play your games, and I don't like them. I wish you'd just...I wish you'd die."

Adam closed his eyes and sighed. *Oh, Julia, baby.*

"That comment, young lady, was out of line. You may go to your room until suppertime."

That was at least three hours from now. Julia's feet pounded sullenly up the steps and a moment later her bedroom door slammed shut.

"I wish you'd die, too," Wyatt said. Obviously, the kid was no dummy. Get out of chores? Why not?

"To your room, too, Wyatt."

More pounding. More slamming.

Adam stood and went out into the kitchen where Stephanie was scrubbing the kitchen sink. "Stephanie?"

She turned toward him.

"Can I talk to you a minute?"

CHAPTER TWENTY-ONE

STEPHANIE RINSED OFF her hands and turned toward Adam, her face a mask.

"I couldn't help but overhear what just happened," Adam said.

"No kids like chores, Adam. Yours are no exception."

Odd, but she was much less formal when speaking with him than the kids. "I understand you're trying to instill some discipline in Julia and Wyatt's lives and I appreciate that, but I'm not entirely sure the type of chores and the number of chores you're having them do is for the best."

"They're not doing anything I wasn't doing at Julia's age."

"You were the oldest of four, Steph, and older than Julia—"

"Stephanie."

"Stephanie. As I was saying, you were several years older than Julia when your mother passed away, and you weren't lucky enough to have a nanny. Don't you think your situation may have been a bit different?"

"I suppose."

"Think about it, would you? Then let's the two of us talk later and come to an agreement on exactly what chores Julia and Wyatt should be doing and when."

"That's fair."

"One other thing." He paused and rubbed his neck. "I know what Julia and Wyatt just said to you was wrong, and I'm sorry, but I don't entirely agree with your response."

"They needed to be disciplined."

"Absolutely, but three hours alone in their rooms isn't what I had in mind when we talked about discipline before you even came to Mirabelle."

She crossed her arms. "What do you think is appropriate?"

"A time-out in their rooms for a short while to let them cool down followed up with an explanation as to why what they said was wrong and what they should do differently the next time they're angry or frustrated."

"Well, it's possible I did overreact. What they said was very hurtful."

"I'm sure it was, and again I'm sorry. We're all still dealing with Beth's death."

"That's no excuse."

"No. I didn't intend it that way, but it helps to understand why us Hardings do what we do."

She looked entirely unsatisfied.

"Why don't you take the rest of the day off along

with tomorrow, okay? We'll manage without you for the rest of the afternoon."

She shrugged. "I've been wanting to get some shopping done, so I'll be heading to the mainland and won't be home until late Sunday night. I'll see you Monday morning."

"Enjoy the rest of your weekend."

As she disappeared into her quarters, Adam went upstairs and knocked on Julia's door.

"What?" she snapped.

"Julia, it's Dad." He opened the door and found her sitting on her bed brushing her favorite doll's hair. Wyatt was sitting on the floor flipping through a book. "Can I come in?"

"If you want."

"We need to talk."

"I don't wanna talk," Julia mumbled as she worked the brush even harder.

"Okay. Then you can listen." He leaned against the wall. "What you both said to Stephanie was wrong. It was mean, and you hurt her feelings."

"She doesn't have any feelings."

"Oh, yes, she does." He explained more appropriate ways of expressing their anger. "There's always a period of adjustment when families get new nannies. We just need to give Stephanie some time. Okay?"

"How much time?"

That was a fair question. Too bad he didn't have an answer for her. "I don't know, Julia, but we'll figure it out."

She put down her brush and hugged her doll.

"I gave Stephanie the rest of the afternoon off." As if to prove his point, the front door opened and closed. "She won't be back until tomorrow night."

"Yes!" Julia and Wyatt smiled at each other.

"I still have a little more work to do, so you guys are on your own for a while, then we'll do something together later on." He returned to his office and got back to work. He checked on them a few times and made sure they got a snack and got their homework finished, but, in truth, having to monitor what was happening with the nanny had been more of a distraction.

He was on the phone with Wayne discussing potential problems with federal aid payments and their bid on a job in Mississippi when he heard Julia call for him. "Daddy?" She stood in the doorway. "Oh," she murmured, the sound of her disappointment evident in that one small word.

Adam waved her into the room. "I'm almost done, Julia. Come on in."

"Have a good weekend, Adam. What's left of it, anyway."

"You, too, Wayne." He disconnected the call. "What's up, honey?"

"How much longer are you going to be working?" she asked, frowning.

"I'm all done for the day." He closed out all his screens, shut his computers off and turned toward his daughter. "How would you and Wyatt like to…

go out for pizza?" They found Wyatt in the family room playing a video game. "Wyatt, time to get off the game, buddy."

"In a minute."

"He's been playing that all day."

Technically, that wasn't true. Adam had made sure the kids had played outside for a long while and gotten them both going on some homework and reading, but his son quite likely had been on the game long enough.

"I'm declaring tonight a no-electronic-device night," Adam said.

"Ah! No fair," Wyatt groaned as he exited out of his game.

"We can't even watch TV?" Julia asked.

"Nope."

"Well, then you can't be on your computer," Julia said.

"Or talk on your phone," Wyatt added.

"You two strike a hard bargain." Adam took his cell phone out of his pocket, switched it off and set it on the counter. "I'm in."

A child's squeal of delight sounded from outside and Julia and Wyatt both ran to the patio doors. "Nate and Michael are outside," Julia said.

So were Angelica, Missy, Jonas and Marin. Dressed in jeans and a long-sleeved sweater, Marin looked comfortable despite the early evening chill that had settled in the air. She looked toward their house, almost as if she could feel them—him—

watching her. Since that night she'd made macaroni and cheese for him and his kids, he'd been doing a pretty good job of avoiding her. He had to focus on his kids and this Mirabelle project, and she had a way about her that was damned unsettling.

"Can we go play?" Wyatt asked.

"I thought we were going to get pizza."

"I'm not hungry yet," he said, opening the door and heading outside.

"Me neither." Julia followed him across the yard.

Adam followed his kids, hoping to find a way to extricate them all from this situation. One thing led to another, though, and before he knew it they'd been invited to stay for a barbecue at Jonas and Missy's. He couldn't say no without dealing with major disappointment from the kids.

"Good day for a barbecue," he said to Missy.

"Probably the last hurrah before the snow flies."

In no time, several of the Abels' friends had joined the get-together, including the Taylor brothers, Garrett and Jesse, along with their wives, Erica and Sarah, and kids, Zach, David and Brian. Zach and Brian were a little bit older than Julia, but they seemed like nice boys and went out of their way to include both Julia and Wyatt in their play.

Marin's father, Arthur, had also been invited. Angelica and her husband seemed to get along fine, but even Adam sensed some underlying tension. The last couple to wander into the Abels' backyard were Sean Griffin, the new island stable and livery owner as well as the doctor, and Grace Andersen, who looked very familiar to Adam for some reason.

Adam contributed some sodas and cookies he'd picked up at the store the previous day, along with some beer and a bottle of wine. Someone had brought hot dogs, brats and veggie burgers, someone else a fruit salad, and someone else chips and potato salad. They were nice folks, and he enjoyed everyone's company. It was only Marin who was difficult to be around, but he managed to keep his distance. That is, until she cornered him at the grill after he'd offered to cook.

"You're doing a pretty good job of avoiding me," she whispered, coming to stand next to him.

"Who said I was avoiding you?" He flipped several beef patties.

She chuckled. "It's almost as if you're purposefully trying to keep exactly eight feet between us."

Actually, it was ten feet, but who was counting? "I'm sorry. I didn't mean to hurt your feelings."

She nodded as she watched the kids play. "How's it going with the new nanny?"

"It's an adjustment. I'd be lying if I said the kids didn't miss you and Angelica." The look of longing on her face suggested she just might miss them, too, but there was no point going down that road. He stepped away from her. "The grilling's done."

"Time to eat, everyone!" Jonas called.

"Hey, Adam?" Sarah Taylor got his attention from

across the table. "Thanks for getting my flower shop open."

"You're welcome. Everything okay?"

"Better than okay. It's perfect."

"Hey, Whimsy, too!" Missy said, excited. "I opened yesterday."

"Good," he said.

"Now if you could just get Duffy's open for Erica, everyone would be happy," Garrett said.

"No pressure, though," Erica said with a grin.

"Right." Adam smiled and added, "We're catching up on things, thanks to Jesse." In fact, Adam didn't know what he would've done without the younger Taylor brother. The man was proving to be the best foreman Adam had on his team. "If all goes according to plan, you will be open for Christmas."

"That'd be good," Erica said. "Very good."

A long while later, stomachs were full, the leftovers had been put away and the sun was setting. Wyatt was kicking a soccer ball around with Brian, Zach and Julia. For a little squirt, he managed to maneuver around the older kids fairly well.

Adam interrupted the play. "I think it's time we head home, kids."

"No, Daddy, I want to stay," Wyatt said, kicking the ball to Brian.

"Let's have a campfire!" Julia exclaimed.

"Yeah!" Brian added.

Adam picked up the ball. "Great idea, except I don't have any wood."

"We have a bunch of it over by the fire pit." Jonas pointed at several cords of split logs lined up alongside the shed in the corner of their yard.

"And it's a perfect night for a fire," Missy added, smiling. "Could be the last one of the season."

"Can we stay, Daddy?" Julia asked, smiling sweetly up at him.

His initial reaction was to turn her down. With all the couples here tonight, holding hands and making eyes at each other, it had turned into one of the most awkward nights of his life. The kids, though, were having so much fun he didn't have the heart to break it up. Besides, this was a big group. He wasn't likely to find himself alone with Marin. On top of that, the bronze statues he'd planned on giving to Angelica and Marin had been delivered the other day, and he and the kids had wrapped all the gifts. They'd been waiting for an opportune moment to give them to the Camden women, and now seemed as good a time as any.

"All right, we can stay." Then he leaned down and whispered in Julia's ear, "Maybe now's a good time to give Marin and Angelica the gifts from you and Wyatt."

CURIOUSLY, MARIN WATCHED Julia and Wyatt run off to their house while Adam stacked up kindling in the fire pit. Grace and Sean, as well as Jesse and Sarah, had called it a night and gone home, while several of the other adults lined up lawn chairs around the fire. Marin's dad and mom stood next to one another, each holding one of Missy and Jonas's two boys in their arms. All night, they'd been smiling and laughing with each other as if there'd never been a problem, as if Angelica hadn't just spent the past couple months separated from him while contemplating a divorce.

"What's with Mom and Dad?" Marin whispered to Missy.

"You got me. All I know is that he's been extremely attentive tonight. All casual conversation and no politics. He even dished up dessert for Mom."

"Got her a couple beers."

"And have you noticed him with my kids?"

"Yeah," Marin muttered.

"Can you believe he changed their diapers?"

"And he's been playing with them. Either he's trying to impress Mom, or he's really enjoying having grandkids."

"I don't think he's sucking up, Mar. I think he really likes being a part of this. He's mellowed since I lived at home."

"But has he mellowed enough for Mom?"

"I don't know." Missy smiled. "Might be enough for me, though, to let bygones be bygones."

That was saying something.

"What's up with you and Adam?" Missy asked.

"He's doing his best to steer clear of me."

"Why?"

"Because he can. His new nanny is here."

"Hmm. You ready to let him off the hook so easily?"

"What do you mean?"

"Marin, it's obvious you've developed feelings for him and his kids. What are you going to do about it?"

Wasn't that the million-dollar question?

As everyone sat around the fire, Julia and Wyatt returned from their house holding several wrapped and bagged gifts. They went first to Angelica and handed her three packages.

"Thank you, Angelica, for taking care of us," Julia said, hugging her.

"Me, too," Wyatt grinned and kissed Angelica's cheek.

Then they came to Marin and handed her three packages, as well. "Thanks, Marin."

She leaned down and hugged them both.

"We can't thank you enough, Angelica. And Marin," Adam said from his position by the fire. "For everything you did for our family."

"Adam, it was truly my pleasure," Angelica said.

"Do you want us to open these now?" Marin asked.

The kids both nodded vehemently.

Marin opened the heavy package first and found a lovely bronze statue by an artist she recognized of a tall, lithe figure of a woman holding a child's hand.

"We helped pick it out," Julia said.

"It's beautiful." The moment her gaze connected with Adam's, he looked away.

Angelica's statue was from the same artist, a woman sitting and reading to the child sitting in her lap. "It's gorgeous. I love it."

The next packages were colorful and inventive frames the kids had made, but it was the photos inside that had Marin swallowing down her emotions. The pictures were from the day she'd spent with their family in Duluth, the day she'd inadvertently let the Hardings into her heart.

She set the gifts aside and hugged the kids. "I'd never forget either one of you even without these pictures, but I will treasure them forever. I promise."

Adam kept his focus on the fire, as if the moment was almost too much for him. Then the gifts were set aside, and the group was sitting around a blazing fire telling stories and making s'mores. Adam sat almost directly opposite of Marin. She couldn't seem to keep her eyes off his face, the way the flames of the fire flickered in his eyes and highlighted his hair. Once or twice, she caught his gaze, only to have him look quickly away.

As it got late, Garrett and Erica left with their kids, and Angelica headed off to say good-night to Arthur. Soon, all the kids left around the fire were fast asleep. Nate sat snuggled in Missy's lap, Michael in Jonas's. Wyatt had fallen asleep in Marin's lap, and Julia had climbed into Adam's lap a short while ago. The sight of Julia peacefully asleep in his arms about stopped Marin's heart. He and his kids were going to be all right.

"Well, what do you think, Miss?" Jonas whispered. "Time to get these rascals up to bed?"

"I think so, but the rest of you don't need to leave on our account." Missy stood. "Good night."

"Thanks for having us over," Adam whispered.

"Don't worry about the fire," Jonas said. "I'll take care of it later." They carried their boys into the house.

"If you don't mind waiting here with Wyatt," Adam whispered to Marin. "I'll carry Julia in and then come back out for him."

"He's not that heavy. I can carry him and follow you."

"I don't think—"

"It's fine, Adam, I can carry him."

Without another word, he carried Julia to the house, slid the door closed behind Marin, and then climbed the steps in the dark. Marin followed him into Julia's room and took Wyatt to the other side of the bed. As she settled Wyatt, Adam laid Julia down, and then he took off her shoes and drew the covers over her.

They straightened from the bed at the same time, caught each other's gazes and seemed to both be paralyzed by the intimacy of the moment. He was the first to break the spell by moving toward the hallway. He closed the door behind Marin and followed her down the stairs. By the time she made it to the bottom step, her heart was beating so fast, she could barely catch her breath. It was all she could do to not turn around and walk into his arms.

"I'm trying to stay away from you," he whispered, coming behind her. He couldn't have been more than an inch or two away. "I'm trying not to touch you, but I... Marin..."

"I love the way you say my name." She felt his heat on her back a moment before his arm came around her waist, drawing her against his chest. She closed her eyes and reveled in the sensation of being in his arms. If they were so wrong for each other, then why did this feel so right?

"I can't stop wanting you." His palm pressed against her belly and he curled his other hand around her neck, easing her head to one side. What was he—oh, God. His warm breath buffeted her cheek only a moment before his lips pressed against the sensitive skin of her neck. He dragged his mouth down to her collarbone.

His growing erection pressed against her backside and she groaned, letting her head fall against his shoulder. Then he dipped his fingers beneath the waistband of her jeans and she couldn't take it any longer.

She spun around and ran her hands through his hair, pulling him toward her for a crushing kiss.

He groaned and pulled her into a dark room. "You taste like chocolate," he breathed, clearly trying to hold himself together.

"You taste like...everything I've ever wanted." She was only marginally aware they were in his office until he lifted her onto his desk, pushed all his paperwork to the floor and laid her back, kissing her.

She wrapped her legs around his waist, and they were face-to-face, his erection pressing against her. All instinct and no reason now, she ran her fingers under his shirt and dragged her hands up his back. Caressing muscles, lean and hot. She moaned and arched to meet him. Then he was trailing kisses along her cheek and down her neck, only to bury his face in her hair, breathing her in.

"Marin." He left a trail of kisses all the way to her lips. "What are we doing to each other?"

"Don't ask. Don't think. Just feel."

He ran his hand up under her sweater, along her sides. When his hand reached her breasts, he groaned, cupping her in his palms, with reverence and passion. Then his mouth claimed hers again in a long, luxurious kiss.

Marin heard it then. A creak on the steps. She went completely still.

Lost in their embrace, Adam was oblivious.

"Adam," she whispered. "I think...the kids..."

Instantly, he pulled away, drawing her up with him. He straightened out her sweater, smoothed her hair and glanced at the open door to his office. They listened for a moment, but there wasn't a sound. Even so, he pulled her to her feet. "That shouldn't have happened. I'm sorry. You said yourself I'm all wrong for you."

"Maybe I've changed my mind."

"Your mind isn't doing the thinking right now."

"I don't want to think."

"Well, I *have* to think, so I'll do it for both of us." He stepped away from her. "I have two kids to worry about, and they come first. I can't—I won't— ever have another woman in my life. Ever. I won't risk their hearts again." He swallowed. "Go home, Marin. Forget about me. Forget about the kids. Forget about us."

What could she say to refute that? Could she promise to never break Julia's and Wyatt's hearts? No. He was right. Without a word, she made herself leave, made herself walk away from the family she'd never known she wanted.

As THE FRONT DOOR CLOSED, Adam dropped into the chair at his desk and put his head in his hands. He could smell Marin on him, the scent of her, a clean, soapy smell mixed with the smoke from tonight's fire. His body was on fire, his brain like jelly.

Beth wasn't just the only woman he'd ever kissed. She was the only woman he'd ever touched intimately, the only woman with whom he'd ever made love. Every time he touched Marin, and he wanted to touch her every moment she was near, a part of him felt as if he was betraying Beth, her memory, their marriage, their children.

When he'd married Beth, he assumed, believed, hoped that she was it, the only woman he'd be with for the rest of his life. He'd never thought past Beth, never wanted to think past her. Until now. Until Marin.

But he'd done the right thing in stopping what was happening between them tonight, in sending her home. What he'd said about protecting the kids was true, but there was more. While his kids might be healing, Adam wasn't. Marin deserved so much more than half a man, but half a man was all he had to give.

CHAPTER TWENTY-TWO

THE FRONT DOORBELL RANG, and Angelica couldn't stop the nervousness fluttering through her stomach. When Arthur had asked her again the night of the campfire at Missy's to have dinner with him, she'd been prepared to turn him down, but after seeing him with Nathan and Michael, after watching him at the fire, she'd known their marriage wasn't over yet, not by a long shot. Maybe a quiet, romantic dinner would be the turning point for them. Maybe tonight he'd get it and, once and for all, they could put this behind them and get on with their lives, their marriage.

With a hopeful heart, she went downstairs and opened the door. Arthur stood on the porch holding a gorgeous arrangement of orchids, lilies and roses in brilliant pinks and oranges with a splash of white. He held out the cut flowers. "I didn't know if you'd have a vase, so…"

"Thank you." She took the flowers from him and set them on the sofa table in the living room. "They're surprisingly unique for a little place like Mirabelle."

"The flower shop downtown just opened, apparently, the other day. Did you know it's Sarah's place? The Sarah who was at Missy's barbecue the other night?"

They talked about Mirabelle, about nothing and everything as they walked down to the Mirabelle Island Inn, each of them doing their best to keep the conversation light. Arthur had reserved a table for two near the fireplace in the inn's cozy French restaurant. More often than not for them, dinner out would've included some other member of congress and his or her spouse, one of Arthur's staff members or other political couple.

As they were leaving the restaurant, Arthur put his hand on her neck and massaged her stiff muscles. Quite suddenly, he drew her off into a quiet and dark hallway, pulled her up against the wall and kissed her. "My hotel room is much, much closer than that house you're renting up by Melissa's."

"Is that right?" She kissed him.

"Stay with me tonight, Ang."

His hand was warm on her neck. His other hand inched up her side, coming tantalizingly close to her breast, and she felt like a young woman in love all over again. "Yes."

He kissed her, whispering against her lips, "Guess we all need a little attention every once in a while."

Attention? That one little word had the hair at the back of her neck standing on end and she pulled abruptly away.

"What?" he said. "What is it?"

"Is that what you think this is about?" She put her hands on his chest and pushed him away. "That I needed you to pay attention to me?"

A confused look passed over his features. "Well… wasn't it? In a way?"

"No, Arthur." A part of her felt terrible for him. He looked so confused. So clueless. "This didn't have anything to do with me wanting attention."

"I feel as though I'm jumping through hoops to try and make you happy. But nothing's working. I'm not sure I can do this anymore, Angie."

"Can you hear yourself? You can't step outside yourself for one minute and see me as a living, breathing person who has her own needs. Who wants her own life. Separate from you. I don't need your attention. Your neck rubs. Your flowers. Apparently, what I need is simply something you're incapable of giving." She backed up. "I'm calling Donna tomorrow and accepting the job. I'll be living in Manhattan full-time."

"So that's it."

"That's it, Arthur. They wanted me as soon as possible, so I'll no doubt be starting next week. I'm leaving tomorrow. We can either find a way to make this work for both of us, or we can end it right here and now."

"I've never been good with ultimatums."

"Maybe that's because you've never *had* to get good at it." She turned and left the inn. He wouldn't follow. He was too proud, too stubborn. As she walked as quickly as she could up the hill, her eyes welled with tears and finally, finally, she cried for the first time since this had all started. The anger was gone and in its place was nothing but an overwhelming sadness over what they had let slip away.

THIS HOUSE WAS ALMOST TOO quiet now that Marin's mother had gone back east. After a few days of solitude, Marin found herself spending more and more time at Missy's for the company and, when she was honest with herself, to hear the sound of little voices. This morning, though, Missy and her kids just wouldn't be enough. Marin missed Julia and Wyatt.

The kids would be getting out of school in a few minutes. If she hurried, she could walk home with them. She'd have to tolerate that battle-ax who called herself a nanny, but she'd be able to completely avoid Adam.

Grabbing a jacket, she raced out of the house and down the street toward the elementary school. Stephanie was standing at the front of the school waiting, keeping to herself. Another mom smiled at Stephanie, but the young woman didn't bother acknowledging the greeting, let alone try visiting with the other moms. When she saw Marin approaching, she merely nodded.

"Is it all right if I walk home with you and the children?" Marin asked.

"Sure."

While they waited, Marin attempted a conversation, but after several one- or two-word answers, she gave up.

Wyatt came outside first. The moment he noticed Marin, he grinned and ran toward them. "Hi!"

"Hey, you. How have you been?"

"Okay." Immediately, he jabbered with her about his day.

Stephanie seemed to be only half listening.

"Can I go to Abby's house now?" Wyatt asked Marin.

"I don't know," Marin said. "You have to ask Stephanie."

He glanced up at the nanny. "Can I go to Abby's house?"

"Do you have homework?"

"A little, but I can do it after supper."

"We do homework after school. No exceptions. You can play with Abby after you finish homework."

"But she can't play later. She said she can only play now."

"Then you'll have to plan another day."

Marin glared at the woman, but kept her mouth shut. She didn't have a right to intrude in front of Wyatt.

Julia came outside then and hugged Marin. "I've missed you."

"I've missed you, too."

As the four of them walked toward their houses,

Stephanie in front and Marin and the two kids trailing behind, Julia caught Marin up on things that had been happening in her life.

"How's it going with Cody?"

"Bad. Now he's teasing Kayla."

"Have you talked to your teacher again?"

"Yeah. He's okay for a few days, but then he starts up again. The only time he was nice was after I punched him. I feel like pu—"

"Girls do not fight," Stephanie said, turning around.

"I know." Julia looked down, as if ashamed.

So it was okay for boys to fight? Marin didn't take issue with a no fighting rule, rather the way the woman had singled out girls.

Julia said, "I was just saying how I get so mad that sometimes I feel—"

"Any more talk about fighting and you'll be grounded."

For talking about her day, about what she was feeling? The woman wasn't just strict, she was repressive. Marin said her goodbyes to the kids at their house and then marched down the hill, straight toward Adam's office. Resolute, she went inside. Phyllis was on the phone at her desk, but glanced up the moment Marin entered the trailer.

"I need to see Adam," Marin mouthed. Unable to tell whether or not he was in his office, Marin went down the hall. He was gone, probably out on the job site.

She returned to the reception area to find Phyllis studying her. "He's down at Duffy's," she said.

Marin reached for the doorknob.

"Wait a minute, Marin."

"I know, I know." Frustrated, Marin turned. "I'm not allowed past the tape."

"Actually, what I was about to say is that if you're going into the construction zone, you'll need this." She tossed Marin a hard hat.

"Thanks, but I don't…" Suddenly, Marin felt quite out of her league.

The other woman raised her eyebrows. "Or you can always leave a message with me."

"No, this is too important."

"All right, then." Phyllis smiled. "Be careful out there."

"Thanks." Marin crammed the hat onto her head and took off out the door. Two blocks later, under the scrutiny of Adam's all-male crews, she reached Main and the bulk of the construction activity. Dodging several pieces of heavy equipment moving up and down a side street, Marin crossed over to Duffy's Pub and stepped carefully inside.

The sounds of pounding and electric saws permeated the air. Adam was so focused he didn't notice Marin's approach. "Make sure you're careful around that antique bar," he said to one of the men. "I don't want it damaged."

"Yes, sir."

"Hey, you shouldn't be in here," said one of the other men, coming toward her.

Adam's gaze narrowed at the sight of her. "That's all right. I got this." He handed his clipboard to Jesse. "Go ahead and finish this up. I'll be back in a bit." Moving around a sawhorse, he took her by the arm and led her outside. "You shouldn't be here. It's dangerous."

"Phyllis gave me a hard hat," she said, tapping the hat.

"I see that, but she's not supposed to let anyone in here." He didn't look happy. "What's going on?"

She opened her mouth to complain about the nanny he'd hired, and stopped. She had no right to complain. They weren't her kids. The nanny wasn't working for Marin, and short of the woman abusing the Harding children Marin had no right to interfere. So why was it she felt compelled to butt her nose where it surely didn't belong?

"Marin?" He paused, studied her gaze. "Did something happen at home?"

"No. I…well, yes. It's that new nanny. I just don't like her, Adam."

Surprisingly, he didn't dismiss her. He actually looked as if he was taking her opinion quite seriously. "Why? What happened?"

"It's not any one thing, in particular. It's a lot of little things. Where did she come from?"

"Through the agency I've been working with. She came with the highest recommendations."

"Well, if she's so wonderful, why was she available?"

"I asked the very same question only a bit more diplomatically." He smiled slightly. "Her previous charges, a family of four between six and twelve that she'd been with for several years, moved to Russia. The father was transferred with his company. She's moved four different times with this family within the U.S., but refused to move out of the country. The family was so heartsick, the father offered to double her salary."

"That's what they all say."

"Marin—"

"She just doesn't fit with your family." She explained what had happened earlier after school.

"I hear what you're saying, but I'm not sure it's worth firing her over."

"But, Adam—"

"I appreciate your concern for my children, but I already know Stephanie isn't perfect. She's not Carla. She's not your mother." He paused and swallowed. "And she's not you, but she's had experience with the death of a parent. Her own mother died when she was fairly young. She started working for this last family when the mom got cancer, and Stephanie stayed on after the mother died."

It felt as if a hand had sunk into Marin's chest and was ripping out her heart.

"We need a nanny," he continued. "Someone who can stick with us for the long haul. Someone who's willing to move from Mirabelle to wherever we end up next because I'd like some stability in my children's lives."

"I know."

"You offering your services, Marin?"

God help her, but she actually entertained the notion for a very long and conflicting moment. This was crazy, absolutely insane. She had to get the hell off this island. "No," she said suddenly. "I think it's time for me to go home to Manhattan."

He looked away, seemed to be absorbing the news. "Then that's that, isn't it?" He turned.

"Adam, wait!"

He stopped, but wouldn't look at her.

Her heart racing, she whispered, "What if I stayed on Mirabelle? Give me a reason to stay. One reason and I'll stay."

Slowly, he turned. "What are you saying?"

"I'm saying if you and I…if we—"

"That's not going to happen, Marin."

"You won't even give us a chance?" Didn't he see that they deserved a chance, that what was happening between them simply didn't happen every day? "You won't even try for some kind of normal relationship? Why the hell not?"

"Because I can't give you what you need, Marin. I'm not the same man as before. Beth's death did me in. You deserve better than I can give."

"It's my choice! Don't you dare make this decision for me!"

"It's already made. You're right about going back to Manhattan. Forget about me." He walked away.

CHAPTER TWENTY-THREE

HAVING SCHEDULED A LATE status update meeting with his foreman, it was well past supper and dark as midnight outside by the time Adam arrived home. A light, fluffy snow was falling as he reached the porch. Taking a long, deep breath, he sloughed off the day as best he could and opened the front door.

"Oh, no, Julia!" Stephanie was in the kitchen, and she didn't sound happy. "What in the world are you doing?"

"I'm making a painting of my mom and the house where I was born," Julia said.

Quietly, he closed the front door and listened.

"No. What you've done is make a mess. You, too, Wyatt." Sounding exasperated, she blew out a puff of air. "I step into my room for ten minutes and look at this kitchen, and I just finished cleaning up after supper."

Adam went into his office and hung his coat over his desk chair, debating. Stephanie had been here less than a month, and while they seemed to be working through some of their differences of opinions, he had a feeling they might never be a good fit.

"Let's clean this up, so we can get ready for bed."

"But I'm not done yet," Julia said, sounding a bit frantic, as if she almost expected Stephanie to take the painting.

"Me, neither," Wyatt said.

That's it. Adam had to put a stop to this.

"Both of you can finish them another time."

"No, that's mine! Give it back—"

The sound of tearing paper filled the air just as Adam reached the kitchen. Stephanie held two large paintings in her hands, one of them ripped in half. The kitchen was, indeed, a mess with paint spilled everywhere, cups of dirty paint water making rings on the table, and brushes scattered on the floor.

"I can't believe you did that! Now it's ruined!" Julia cried as she swung her fist back.

"Hey, hey," Adam said softly as he reached for Julia's hand and gently, but firmly held her. "It's okay."

"She ruined my painting of Mommy!"

"You can make another one." He kneeled down to be eye level with her. "Right?"

"But, Daddy—"

"I know that picture was important to you, but it's not okay to hit. You know that."

She frowned, her lower lip trembled and she fell into his arms, sobbing. A moment later, Wyatt was crying, too, and hugging him. Adam clearly hadn't done the best job he could've in helping Julia grieve, and Wyatt for that matter, which might account for why Beth's death was still so fresh, but it was never too late to try. He closed his eyes and held both his kids for a long while. In the meantime, Stephanie went about cleaning up the paintbrushes and spilled paint as if nothing had happened.

"It's okay," Adam said after a while. "We're not always going to be sad about Mommy." Therapists had warned him that a child's grief over a parent committing suicide would come and go, and that children sometimes needed the permission to move on with their lives. Maybe it was time to take their advice. "Right now, we have some bad days," he went on. "But it'll get better. We'll be happy again."

Julia sniffled and pulled away. "You promise?" she asked, drying her tears.

"I promise." He kissed both of their foreheads. "Why don't you guys go upstairs and get ready for bed and I'll be up in a few minutes. Okay?"

Julia glared at Stephanie, but she went upstairs. Wyatt followed. The moment he heard them in Julia's room, he said to Stephanie, "I don't at all like the way you handled that situation."

"Your daughter needs more discipline in her life. For the way she just behaved, she should be grounded, or assigned several chores, or have her TV privileges taken away."

"That painting was important to her and you not

only failed to acknowledge that, you ruined the painting."

"Well, I think it's time everyone quits indulging these children." Seemingly unperturbed, she continued to clean as she talked. "Parents die every day. It is what it is. They've had time to adjust to their mom being gone. Now it's time to move on."

God help him, but there was a time when he'd thought, believed, what she'd just said, almost verbatim. Now he finally understood just how wrong he'd been. If he were to guess, he'd say Stephanie's own issues with her mother's death were coming into play here more than she realized.

Marin had been right about him all along. She'd seen what he'd not wanted to look at for years. True, he was a relatively attentive single father. He wasn't perfect by any means, but for the most part, he did what he needed to do when he was supposed to do it. But he did hold a piece of himself back from his children in the same way he held a large chunk of himself back from the world. The world didn't really matter, but his children deserved better from him.

"Stephanie, I know you've only been here a few weeks, but…it's just not working out between you and my kids. I think it's best if you find another family. Immediately."

"Excuse me?"

"I'm letting you go." Adam held her gaze. He had no clue how he was going to care for his kids and still manage to get this Mirabelle project finished, but something had to give and it wasn't going to be his kids. "I'll pay for you to stay at the Mirabelle Island Inn, the Rock Pointe Lodge or Mrs. Gilbert's bed-and-breakfast for the night. Wherever you would prefer, but I want you out of our house within the hour."

"Well, that's a little extreme. I understand you being protective of your children, but don't you think you're overreacting a bit?"

"No. In fact, I think I've been underreacting for a very long time." He stood and held open the door to her private quarters. "I'll pay double the agency's normal severance agreement as long as you pack your things without incident and are gone before the children return. I'll call for a carriage to pick you up."

"All right, but can I say—"

"No. Thank you. You've said more than enough since you arrived on Mirabelle."

While she collected her things, he went into his office and called a carriage to take the woman anyplace but here. By the time she came out of her rooms, her driver had arrived. He carried her luggage out to the road, and they exchanged curt farewells. He returned to the house and climbed the stairs, thoroughly exhausted, but knowing he had to make this right.

He found the kids in Julia's room, sitting on her bed. "Stephanie's left," he said. "She's not going to be your nanny anymore."

"Yes!" Wyatt fist-punched the air.

"Did you fire her?" Julia asked.

"She and I disagreed on too many things, so it's best she finds another family." He sat on the edge of the mattress.

"You did fire her." Julia scooted over to hug him. "Thank you, Daddy."

He kicked off his shoes and rested against the headboard. "I want to talk to you guys for a bit. About your mom. Any questions you have," he said, "I want to answer."

Both kids stared at him, their eyes widening as if he'd grown two heads. Wyatt shifted to face Adam, tucking his feet under him. Immediately, Julia asked, "Why did she kill herself?"

Adam closed his eyes. He didn't want to do this, but he had to do this. "I'm not sure I can answer that completely. Because she's really the only one who knows for sure, but I think she got really sad."

"I get sad. So does Wyatt. And you. Does that mean you might—"

"No, Julia. Never. I would never do that." He swallowed. He was screwing this up. Making things worse. But then how could he possibly make things worse than they already were?

Try again, Adam.

"The kind of sad your mom felt was different than what we feel when…say, a kid says something at school that hurts your feelings. Or you cut your finger. Or a friend can't have a sleepover. That's normal kind of sad.

"Mom's sadness was the kind that didn't go away. It went on for days and weeks. Months, probably. She began to think that her sadness would never end. She forgot what it was like to be happy."

"Did I do something?" Julia asked. "To make her sad?"

"Or me?" Wyatt added.

"Absolutely not. Neither one of you did anything. It's no one's fault that Mom died. She loved you more than anything, and I know that if she'd understood how much it was going to hurt all of us to have her gone, she never would've taken her own life. But there was something wrong with Mom's body. Something that doesn't just go away like a cold or the stomach flu without help. And I didn't know. No one knew she was so sick."

"Can I catch suicide?" Wyatt asked.

"No, Wyatt. It's not the kind of sick that you get from germs, and you won't inherit it from Mom, either, like your hair and eye color. I promise." He sighed as he looked from one to the other. "Anything else you want to talk about?"

Wyatt shook his head, but Julia frowned.

"Julia, ask me anything."

Tears in her eyes, she said, "Sometimes, kids ask me at school why I don't have a mom. When I tell them she died, they always ask how. I don't know what to say, Daddy."

"Me neither," Wyatt said.

What should they say? What was right for their age? "You could say that your mom got really sick and died. That's the truth. As you get older, you might want to talk about it with your best friends, but you might not. You can tell people it's something you don't want to talk about, and that's okay." He smiled gently. "But I want you to talk about your mom with me, okay? We should've been talking about Beth all this time, but I didn't think it was important. I was wrong. We need to remember your mom. We need to talk about her. Both the good and the bad. Okay?"

They both nodded.

"So if you ever, ever have any more questions, no matter how silly they seem or hard they are to ask, I want you to come to me."

This wouldn't be the end of their questions, in fact, he *hoped* it wasn't. They were going to need to talk about this for a long time, and some day they might just want answers to things that they didn't want to talk about now.

"You guys go brush your teeth, and I'll be right back." He went into his closet and pulled out the box of family photos from his closet. Surprisingly, he found two photo albums sitting atop the box, most likely courtesy of Marin.

Julia and Wyatt came out of the bathroom and they all climbed onto Julia's bed. "Let's put these pictures in these photo albums. One for Julia. One for Wyatt."

"What about for you, Daddy?"

Adam's gaze landed on one of his favorite pictures of Beth. He picked it up and smiled. "I'll just take this one. We were on vacation. All four of us." They'd taken a spring break somewhere down in Florida and were on a beach. She was lying on a chaise longue, a floppy hat shading her face. "You and I were building a sandcastle, Julia, and Wyatt was sound asleep under an umbrella." She'd looked up at him and without a word simply blown him a kiss. "She was happy this day," he whispered.

"Tell me more about her, Daddy?" Julia said as she flipped through pictures.

"Like what?"

"I don't know," Julia said. "Everything."

"Everything when she was happy." Wyatt smiled.

Adam took a deep breath and did his best to remember. "Your mom, Bethany Sandra Druett, was born in St. Louis, Missouri. Grandma Sandra always says she was the best baby…"

"THEY'RE TALKING ABOUT stopping the payments of state and federal aid." Carl Andersen paced the length of Adam's office.

"What?"

"I got a call from the office in Madison. They're not satisfied with our documentation."

"It's got to be the new administrator," Adam said.

"He doesn't know me or my company. I have to go down there and meet with him."

"Can you make it right?"

"I can only promise that I'll do my best."

Carl left Adam's office and Adam gave Phyllis instructions to set up appointments for as soon as possible with the federal and state officials in Madison. She came back with something he hadn't expected. They had time to meet with him tomorrow. The appointments were spread out through the day, but he could take care of all the problems at once. He called Carl to let him know.

"I'm going with you," Carl said. "Marty's going to want to come, too."

"All right, but I won't be able to leave until late tonight."

"Carl and I are ready now. How 'bout we just meet you down there."

"Fine by me."

They discussed hotel arrangements, but as Adam hung up the phone another problem arose front and center. He'd been managing to take care of Julia and Wyatt on his own since he'd fired Stephanie, but he couldn't take the kids with him to Madison. Missing a day of school wasn't that big of a deal, but who would take care of them while he was in meetings? Phyllis had a more than full schedule tomorrow, and he couldn't leave his office unmanned. There was only one thing he could do. It wasn't right. It wasn't fair, but he didn't have a choice.

IN THE KITCHEN, A SPOT that offered the best natural light in the house, Marin leaned over the table to put the finishing touches on her latest watercolor. The focal point of the picture was a lighthouse on Lake Superior's rocky shore. To date, it was her best work, having captured the turbulence of the morning with white-capped waves rolling in and crashing against the rocks and the gulls fighting the wind as the sun rose on a reddish sky.

But the point where the bright yellow sunrise met the pink tinted clouds was too abrupt. She was adding an orange tint to transition from one color to the next when a shadow passed over her work.

A light tap sounded on the glass panel behind her only a moment before Adam slid open the door. "Morning."

She hadn't seen him in several days and, with so much unsettled between them, wasn't exactly sure how to be around him. "Hi."

For a moment, he just looked into her face, as if he'd actually missed her then his gaze moved to her painting and he slanted his head for a better look. "Marin, that's beautiful. Amazing."

"Thank you."

"Another one for Missy's books?"

"Yeah."

"I always thought watercolors were for kids. Pale and washed out. Blurry. Hard to believe that bright, vibrant, defined picture is a watercolor."

"It's all about how much water you use and how you apply the paint."

He smiled slightly. "From a Wall Street suit to a world-class painter."

"I wouldn't go that far." She was surprised by how much it hurt simply being in the same room with him. She should've left immediately after that discussion about his nanny when he'd shut the door on her and any future they might have. It had been a mistake to try and wrap up these paintings for Missy before leaving. Tomorrow. Tomorrow, she'd leave.

She prepped her paintbrush with more pale orange and bent again toward the paper, sending the signal that she wanted to get this over with. "Adam, what can I do for you?"

"I need a favor and it's a lot to ask." He paused. "But it's important."

Stephanie was probably busy with something, making it impossible for her to care for Julia and Wyatt, and he had some big meeting, so he was going to ask her to watch the kids. She stilled her brush and waited for the inevitable.

"I fired Stephanie last week."

That she hadn't expected. She straightened. "You did? Why?" She tossed the brush in the water.

"Because you were right. She didn't fit with our family."

She held his gaze, not sure what to think.

"We've been managing okay without her, but I'm having problems with the federal disaster relief people and have to go to Madison and iron things out for Mirabelle's sake. I have to leave tonight, so I can be there for meetings in the morning." He took a deep breath. "I know it's a lot to ask, especially with everything going on between us, but could you stay overnight with the kids? Tonight and tomorrow ni—"

"Yes," she said. God help her, but she had to suppress the urge to rub his neck and shoulders to ease the tension she could see building inside him.

"Are you sure?" he asked. "I have to go pack a bag and leave right now."

"Yes." She glared at him. "I'm not going to punish your kids just because their father's an asshole."

He held her gaze.

"I'll pick the kids up at school. I'll stay overnight at your house. And when you get back, I'm leaving for Manhattan."

"I understand," he whispered. "You have my cell if you need anything. I'll be back Saturday morning."

"We'll be fine."

"Thank you for doing this, Marin."

"I'm not doing it for you. I'm doing it for Julia and Wyatt."

CHAPTER TWENTY-FOUR

"So how did school go today?" Marin asked Julia as she came running across the school yard to where she and Wyatt were waiting.

"Good," she said. "Mrs. Larson gave me an A on my geography map."

"Let me see that!" she said excitedly.

Julia dug the map out of her backpack.

"Wow. This is amazing." Marin was truly surprised by the level of detail second graders these days were expected to know with regard to foreign countries. "You deserved an A."

"I got a star on my cursive letters," Wyatt said.

"You did?" Marin grinned. "I want to see that, too!"

He pulled the paper out of his backpack and Marin fawned over how well he'd made his letters. They walked home talking about this and that, recess and lunch.

Last night with the kids had gone off without a hitch. Getting the kids ready for school this morning had been a challenge, but fun. They said they didn't like the school lunches, so she made them turkey sandwiches, sliced their favorite kind of apples and walked them to school.

She would never have believed this could happen to her, but she actually enjoyed the domesticity of a life revolving around children. She was even entertaining the slim possibility of having her own kids someday. Unfortunately, there was only one man with whom she could ever imagine spending the rest of her life and that didn't seem very likely. Oh, but Adam had made such beautiful children with Beth. She couldn't help but imagine a little towheaded boy or girl pestering Julia and Wyatt.

"It's Friday," Marin said as they reached the house. "Did you kids want to have friends over?"

"No, we just want to be with you," Julia said with a smile. "Right, Wyatt?"

"Right."

They made homemade pizza, chocolate chip cookies and popcorn, built a fire in the fireplace, and piled onto the couch to watch a movie Marin had rented earlier in the day. After the movie, the kids were still not sleepy, but Marin had them change into pajamas all the same and read one book after another in front of the fire. The kids seemed starved for the stories and flipped pages the instant she'd finished.

When they came to the end of their stack of books, Marin said. "I have another story you might like."

"Which one?"

"It's a surprise. Wait here and I'll get it." Marin raced next door and back again.

She'd turned Missy's Lake Superior story into an actual book by typing up Missy's longhand, inserting pictures of all of Marin's paintings and printing it all up. Marin had even created a cover. It would be her parting gift to Missy, and it was time to try it out on Julia and Wyatt.

As she flipped through the book, the kids were mesmerized not only by the story itself, but also by her pictures.

"I like that one the best," Julia said.

"This is my favorite," Wyatt said.

"I can't believe you painted all of these."

"I think we all have surprises inside of us."

After they'd gone through Missy's book twice, both kids turned quiet. Soon, Wyatt fell asleep, his head tipping back and his mouth wide-open. Julia had inched herself right up against Marin's other side. Her hand rested on Marin's forearm and she brushed her fingers over Marin's skin in a slow absent pattern. "You feel nice," Julia whispered.

"What do I feel like?"

"Soft." Her head fell against Marin's shoulder. "Like a mommy."

Marin wrapped her arm around Julia and snuggled her close. She couldn't remember ever having felt this relaxed. This peaceful and content. As her eyes grew heavy and she began falling asleep, a wonderfully sad realization formed. She'd come to a new respect and understanding of her mother. Angelica Camden had never lost herself. She'd simply put her own needs aside for a while to do a very important job. Marin still wasn't crazy about most kids, not really, but somehow she'd fallen deeply and irrevocably in love with Julia and Wyatt. The same way she'd fallen in love with their father.

IT WAS A LONG AND GRUELING day of meetings and conferences with government officials. By the time all was said and done, Adam was exhausted, but they'd managed to appease the folks cutting the checks and had accomplished what he, Carl and Marty had set out to accomplish.

Marty said, "I think we should celebrate."

"Sounds good to me," Carl agreed. "How 'bout you, Adam?"

All day long, during any quiet moment, Adam's thoughts had filled with Marin. She was home with his kids and more than anything else he wanted to be with all three of them. If he didn't do something, Marin would be leaving for Manhattan without a backward glance, and suddenly he knew he couldn't let that happen. It was awfully late to be heading back to Mirabelle, but he had to cut this trip short.

"I'm going back tonight," he said. He'd have the long drive to figure out exactly what to do once he got there. "I need to get home. You guys have Marty's car, so you're fine, right?"

"Yeah, we're fine."

"Thanks for all your help today."

As if a fire was at his heels, Adam packed up and checked out of the hotel. He made good time on the highways, but he was no closer to an answer by the time he arrived in Bayfield.

Adam pulled the hood of his coat up over his head as the water taxi took him to Mirabelle. Chequamegon Bay hadn't frozen over just yet, but if these chilly December temperatures were any indication the bay would be impassable by boat very soon.

They arrived at the marina, and Adam grabbed his bag, laptop and briefcase and walked up the hill as fast as his legs would carry him. Although it was after eleven, it was Friday night. He hoped everyone would still be awake. As he approached his dark house, though, it was apparent his luck had run out.

He let himself in through the front door, set his things down and, as he was shrugging out of his coat, noticed a fire in the family room fireplace. Quietly, he walked into the room and found Marin and the kids sound asleep on the couch. The only sounds were their rhythmic breathing and the slight crackling of logs on the grate.

For a long while, he simply stood there and stared at the three of them. They looked so perfect, as if they belonged together. They looked like a family. They could be a family.

All this time, he'd thought he was protecting his kids, but they didn't need protection from Marin. She'd only leave Wyatt and Julia if Adam pushed her away. Maybe he didn't deserve a wife, maybe he wasn't entirely ready for this next step, but his children had done nothing wrong. Didn't they deserve a mother?

Marin stirred then. Her neck had been bent at an unnatural angle, so she cringed as she opened her eyes. "Adam." She stretched and yawned. "What are you doing home?"

"The meetings finished up and I wanted to be here." *With the kids. With you.*

As they'd done after the campfire that seemed so long ago, Adam picked up Julia, Marin took Wyatt and they carried the kids up to their bedroom. When they got back downstairs, it was obvious they were both remembering every kiss, every touch, every look that had passed between them. Trying to keep his distance from her all these months had been sheer hell.

"I've never seen you in a suit." Her gaze ran over him like a caress. "You look…impressive."

"Marin, we need to talk."

"I think we've talked quite enough." She spun around, grabbed her coat out of the closet and yanked it on. "I'll come back to get the rest of my things tomorrow." She reached for the doorknob.

"Not so fast." He grabbed her hand and pulled her toward him. "Stay with me," he whispered against her neck. "I came home to be with you."

For a moment, she resisted, and then she closed her eyes and her hands went to his waist and slipped under his suit coat. Over his back and up his sides and chest, she touched him almost reverently. "You feel so damned good."

"Marin—"

"No talking." She kissed him as she pushed him toward the family room. "You'll just screw it up."

He wasn't about to argue as she slid her hands up to his shoulders, gently slipped off his jacket and flung it over the nearest chair. Then she whipped off his tie and slowly, one by one, undid the buttons on his shirt. She moaned, a soft, sweet sound, as she buried her fingers in the hair on his chest.

He found he could barely breathe. Impatient now, he yanked the shirt the rest of the way off and tossed it over his coat. Then her fingers were working the buckle on his belt. Then the zipper. "Marin—"

Her hands ran down the length of his erection.

"Oh, Mar—" He stilled her hands, unable to take it any longer and held her arms out to her sides so she couldn't touch him. He kissed her, but her tongue dancing with his, licking at his lower lip, was driving him as crazy as her hands. "If I go upstairs to get a condom, do you promise to still be here when I come back?"

"Only if you make it quick," she said with a smile. "And only if you bring more than one condom."

As swiftly and quietly as he could, he went to his bedroom to get a few condoms from the box he'd made himself buy after that first time just to be safe. He closed the door to the kids' bedroom on his way down the hall, and when he returned downstairs, Marin was lying on the floor in front of the fire under a large blanket, every damned inch of her below her neck covered.

"Please tell me you're naked under there."

Lying on her back, she looked up at him and he'd never seen a more beautiful smile. "Why don't you come here and find out?"

"I want to see you first." As Adam drew the blanket away from her, he drew in a sharp breath. The only woman he'd ever seen naked had been Beth. She'd been beautiful, no doubt, but she and Marin were as different as women could be. Beth had been dark and lithe, while Marin was blonde and full. Everywhere. Full breasts. Full hips. As feminine as a woman got.

"Come here," she said softly.

He slipped out of his pants and boxers, dropped down next to her and, just in case, covered them with a blanket. "Seeing Daddy kiss Marin," he whispered as he covered her mouth with his, "probably wouldn't be as much of a shock to Julia or Wyatt as seeing my naked backside."

She laughed and then sobered as she cupped his cheek. "We're really going to do this? You really want to do this?"

"We are, and I do." He trailed kisses down her neck, across the gentle slope of one breast and licked her nipple as he nudged one knee between her legs.

He bit down gently on her pebbled nipple, and she

jerked and arched her back. Then she pulled away, slid under the blanket, down his body, down until her mouth connected with the head of his penis. She licked, sucked and tortured him for several long moments before she took him deep into her mouth. It was the most exquisite pain he'd ever felt, and he endured it for as long as he possibly could before he touched her cheek and gently drew her up to meet him. In true Marin form, she tortured him the whole way by leaving a trail of kisses up his abdomen and chest. Face-to-face again, she kissed him as she spread her legs over him, straddling him.

"I hope you're ready," he whispered. "Because you are driving me crazy."

"Adam, I was ready when you walked through that door in a suit." She smiled. "Hell, I've been ready ever since our first kiss that day I came out of the rain."

She was so slick and wet all she needed to do was press down on him and he was inside her. He was with Marin, as close as he could possibly be. The only place he wanted to be for the rest of his life. He felt wonderfully, blissfully, completely whole again.

Slowly, slowly, Marin moved over him. But the beautifully full feeling of him inside her...she had to stop. The whimper that escaped from her chest sounded like pain, but it was nothing short of absolute pleasure. She couldn't escape the feeling that she and Adam belonged together.

"You all right?" he whispered, his hip undulating beneath her, driving her wild.

"I just can't move," she breathed. "I feel like I'm breaking apart."

"Then let me." He rolled them over, smiled down at her and pulsed into her. "How's that?"

If her experience with Colin had left even one tiny shred of doubt inside her that she wasn't sexy or feminine enough, it dissipated with one look into Adam's eyes. This man wanted her more than his next breath. He'd been moved to make love to only two women in his life and she was one of them. She smiled and kissed him, felt her nails dig into his back.

He moved faster, thrusting into her. He brought her knee up higher, allowing him to penetrate deeper and Marin fell apart. "Adam!" she cried, then said softly, "I love you."

He muffled the sound with a kiss as he drove deeper and harder. Faster and stronger. Over and over. Then he groaned, and slowed, kissing her neck as he thrust into her one last time. He held still a moment, and then he moved again slowly, drawing out both their orgasms.

His breath buffeted her ear, his weight pressed down on her body, his lips kissed a sweet spot just under her jaw and his rough whiskers rubbed against her neck. Marin had never felt more loved in her life. She ran her hands over his back, down his spine, along his tight butt, his hips, his sides, wanting to memorize every inch of this man. The man she loved. The man she knew, without a doubt, was going to break her heart into a billion jagged pieces.

ADAM AWOKE ON HIS BACK, Marin tucked close against his side, her leg flung over him, her fingers buried in his chest hair, and all he knew was that he would've liked nothing more than to wake up like this every morning for the rest of his life.

She'd said she loved him.

Last night, he'd been so lost in the feel of being inside her, in the beauty of making love to her, that her words had simply felt an integral part of what was happening between them. So natural, as if he'd known exactly how she felt before she'd uttered one sound. Now the memory of that moment returned to him in a slow, quiet wave. She loved him. He was, at once, filled with a sense of rightness and yet an overwhelming feeling of uncertainty. Now what?

Julia's bed creaked above him. At any moment little footsteps would sound down the steps, and one of his children would see them lying here on the floor. Still, he couldn't make himself move other than to draw the blanket up over him and Marin, making sure they were covered. He didn't want this—whatever this was—to be over. But, then... maybe it didn't have to be over. Maybe—

"Daddy? You're home."

Julia.

"Morning, honey," he whispered as she came over into the family room. "I got in late last night."

"But…but?" She blinked. "Marin stayed here, too? You had a sleepover? On the floor?"

"It's a long story. Kind of complicated."

Marin stirred against him, purred as she stretched and rubbed her face against his neck.

Julia smiled. "You're getting married! I'm telling Wyatt." She skipped off to the steps.

"No," he whispered. "Julia, wait."

"Julia!" Waking with a start, Marin sat up, dragging the blanket with her and glancing around. "Is she up?"

"Yeah." He reached for his boxers and quickly pulled them on.

"Oh, no." Marin rubbed her face. "Did she come down here?"

She looked so pretty in the morning sunshine, her short hair sticking up all over. Her eyes sleepy and sweet. "Yeah," he said, smiling. "Julia was just down here."

"Oh, no." She stood, pulling the blanket with her and grabbing her pajamas. "You're on your own with this one." Then she ran out the back door and over to her own house, away from inquisitive minds.

MARIN FELT LIKE A CAGED animal. She'd showered and had breakfast. She'd tried painting, cleaning, cooking, even doing her nails, but she simply couldn't focus. What was Adam doing? What had he said to the kids? When was she going to see him again? This waiting was driving her crazy.

She changed into running gear and was about to head outside to try a good long jog when Adam appeared at the patio door. His features serious, he studied her through the glass panel, slid open the door and came inside.

"Hi," she said, her voice not much more than a squeak.

"Hi."

"Where are Julia and Wyatt?"

"I walked them to Maddie's house to play for a while." For a moment, he stood there, awkwardly, and then he came toward her, his eyes darkening, his gaze intent on her mouth.

She practically fell into his arms and they kissed as if they'd never been apart. He lifted her onto the counter, stepped between her legs and ran his hands up her side only to reverently cup her breasts, now squashed by the exercise bra.

She buried her hands into his hair, messing it up even more. Then she drew away. "What did you tell the kids?"

"That I got home late and we fell asleep talking." He looked into her eyes. "But Julia has something, you know."

Julia? What was he talking about?

"Marin, this is going to sound like it's coming from left field." He turned away from her, clearly unsettled. "And maybe it is, but it seems so right to me." He turned around, his expression so, so serious. "Marry me?"

"What?" Her heart leaped into her throat as she jumped down from the counter. "What did you say?"

"I don't have a ring yet, but we can shop for one today, if you want." He ran his warm hand down her cheek. "Will you marry me, Marin?"

Yes, she wanted to scream. *Yes, yes, yes!* He'd woken up. He'd come to his senses. He was finally, finally accepting the obvious. Or was he? The man wasn't smiling. This wasn't the joyous occasion it should be. *Wait a minute.* What was this really all about?

"Why?" she whispered, not entirely sure she wanted to hear his answer. "Why do you want to marry me?"

That's when he smiled, that quirky half smile he did when he was out of sorts. "I want to be with you. For the rest of our lives. We're good together. We want the same things in life. We fit. And the kids." He shook his head. "They love you, and you love them. You know that."

"I do. Love them. But I love you, too, Adam. The thought of never seeing the three of you again breaks my heart." As the undeniable truth hit her, she wrapped her arms around herself as if she might hold herself together.

His smile disappeared, his gaze turned wary. "But?"

"Tell me you love me," she whispered, going to

him and wrapping her arms around him, her heart racing. "Tell me you love me, and you will make me the happiest woman on earth. Then I will marry you tomorrow if you want. Tell me, Adam."

He looked as if she'd hit him, slapped him across the face with everything she had. He turned away, seemed to gather his thoughts. When he turned around, his resolve had returned.

Damn him. Damn him and his equilibrium straight to hell.

"I want to be with you, Marin. I want to come home at night to find you there. Night after night after night. I want to walk into your arms, feel your love and know at least one thing is right in this world. I want to watch you with my children. I want them to become your children. I want to laugh with you, cry with you, sleep with you, hold you. Forever. Isn't that enough?"

Don't do this, Marin. Oh, God, marry him. You'll make it work. He must love you. He just doesn't know it yet. Having a part of him is better than none of him. Any life with Adam is better than life without him.

Colin's accusations that she'd been content with mediocrity came back to haunt her. She could not do that again.

He reached for her. "Marin—"

"No." She stepped away. If he touched her, she would give in. "The truth is…you were right. I deserve better, Adam. I deserve to be with someone who loves me as much as I love him. Just as you deserve to be with someone you love." She took another step back. "So, no. What you're offering is not nearly enough."

"Marin, you don't mean that—"

"I do. I love you with everything in me. It's going to kill me to walk away from you—from Julia and Wyatt—but I would rather hurt now than die a slow and painful death loving someone who either doesn't love me back or can't—won't—admit to loving me. I won't accept anything less than everything from you, Adam. I could've married Colin for that."

He came toward her. "Marin, dammit—"

"Don't! Don't touch me." Finding no consolation in the fact that he was upset enough to swear, she held out her hands. "I mean it, Adam. I am not messing with you. You said it yourself—a wife needs to know she's loved. What makes you think I'm so different from Beth? If you can't love me the way you loved her, then I don't want you. For God's sake, you're still wearing your wedding ring. I will not live forever and ever jealous of a dead woman."

IN A SURREAL FOG OF EMOTION, Adam watched Marin run out the door and away from him. She moved, it seemed, almost in slow motion, her short hair catching on the breeze.

Go after her, you fool. She's the best thing that ever—ever—happened to you. The kids need her. You...need her.

But he couldn't. Everything she'd said had been right on the money. How could he go after her? He couldn't say what she needed to change her mind, any more than he could take this ring off his finger.

If you care about her at all, you'll let her go.

In a daze, he returned to his house, went into his office and closed the door. Let her go. That's what he had to do. She can—she will—move on. She would find someone else. She would find someone who wasn't broken, who could give her his whole heart and soul. It was no less than she deserved.

Still, the thought of her in another man's arms, of another man spending slow mornings in bed or quiet nights at home with her, of any other man simply loving her made everything inside him ache. Made everything inside him...simmer...boil...with anger.

"Dammit!" he yelled. "Damn you, Marin!"

She couldn't just leave well enough alone, could she? She couldn't just let him hide in his pain. No. She'd had to bring him back to life. She'd had to make him want again. She'd had to make him feel again. And for what?

Furiously, he swiped his hands across his desk, whipping everything, phone, paperweights, pens, pencils and laptop onto the floor. The crash barely penetrated his consciousness. Deliberately, he walked around the room, smashing lamps, over-turning furniture and pushing everything off the bookcase. Finally, he punched his fist through the drywall. By the time he was finished, the room

looked like Mirabelle had looked after the tornado
had ripped through the town.

Righting his chair, he noticed his hand was bleeding, but he didn't care. Nothing mattered right now.
Nothing. He sat at his empty desk, his head in his
hands. As the anger slowly subsided, a bone-deep
sadness settled. A storm had ripped through his soul,
pounded and pummeled his heart without mercy.

He could feel again. Too little, too late.

And this he couldn't fix.

CHAPTER TWENTY-FIVE

MARIN'S BAGS WERE PACKED and sitting on the front porch, and a carriage would be picking her up in a few minutes to take her to Mirabelle's tiny airport for her flight to Manhattan. She took one last look around the rental house and her throat tightened with emotion. There were more precious moments captured in her heart during the months she'd lived here on Mirabelle than in the past ten years of her life.

She could never regret what had happened here, but the sooner she was as far from Mirabelle as she could get the better. The only thing left to do was say goodbye.

Stepping out onto the front porch, she found Jonas there, of all people, waiting for her. "Hey," he said, avoiding eye contact with her, clearly uncomfortable with the situation.

"If Missy sent you over here—"

"Naw, she doesn't even know I'm here." Finally he held her gaze. "You sure you want to do this?"

"I'm not sure that I have any other options, Jonas."

"You could marry him."

She didn't say anything. There was nothing to say.

"He loves you."

"Did he say that? Have you been talking to Adam?"

"Hell, no, but any fool can see he's crazy about you."

"You calling me a fool?"

"Marin." He ran his hands through his shortly cropped hair. "Some men...some men just don't show their feelings very well. It took me a damned long time to show Missy how much I love her. It's not easy to show that kind of vulnerability. Goes against the grain for a lot of us."

"Are you saying I should settle? Settle for a man who loves me, but won't show it? Won't even say the words."

"No. I'm saying he'll figure it out. Give him time. He'll come after you. I know he will. Just don't give up, okay?"

She already had. She was a woman used to making things happen, but she'd accepted she couldn't make Adam love her.

Jonas hugged her and then carried her bags down to the end of the sidewalk. When they turned around, Missy was coming out of the house with the boys. As she approached Marin, it was clear that Missy was openly crying, but Marin refused to follow suit. "Oh, for crying out loud, Missy. We'll probably talk every day."

"I know, but it was so nice having you here. Right

next door. More than made up for all the years we lost."

"Yeah. That it did." She hugged her sister, gave Nate a kiss on his chubby cheek and then turned to Jonas and hugged him.

"You know you're welcome any time," he murmured in her ear.

"I know. Thanks." She kissed Michael.

"Buh, buh." Nate waved his chubby arm.

"Bye," Michael said.

"Oh, one more thing." Marin pulled out Missy's book complete with illustrations. "It's pretty cool, if I do say so myself."

Missy chuckled through her tears. "I knew you'd do it."

"Yeah, well, the publisher may hate the illustrations, but they were fun." She turned then toward Adam's house. The kids were coming out the front door.

"I told him what time you were leaving," Missy said softly.

"Good. That's good." She didn't want to say goodbye to Julia and Wyatt, but she had to, almost as much for herself as for them.

"Adam might come, too," Missy whispered. "He might come after you."

"He won't." Marin shook her head, too numb to cry. "It's over." Both kids were already crying by the time they reached her, so she forced a smile for their sake.

"I don't want you to go," Julia sobbed.

"Me neither," Wyatt added.

"I know." Marin knelt, grabbed them both, one in each arm and hugged them as tightly as she could. The three of them held each other for what seemed an eternity. "It's going to be all right, though," Marin finally said. "You'll see." She had to believe that was true. One way or another, they'd get over her.

"Carla's coming back," Julia said through her tears.

"See? That's what I'm talking about." Missy had filled her in on what had been happening at the Harding house for the past couple of days. "You two won't even miss me."

"Yes, we will," Wyatt said as he drew in a shaky breath.

"Will you come and visit us?" Julia asked.

She didn't want to lie, but the truth seemed too much even for her at the moment. "I'll try, but I'll probably be pretty busy at first looking for a new job. In the meantime," she said, "you can both write to me." She gave them each a box of cards with envelopes addressed to her Manhattan apartment. "You don't have to write much," she said, glancing at Wyatt. "Practice your ABCs. Draw me a picture. Whatever you feel like. I don't care."

That was enough. She didn't want to draw this out any longer. "As soon as you have a new address," she said, "send me a note, and I promise I'll write."

Then with one last look into their sweet faces, she turned and climbed up onto the carriage.

Adam never came outside, never even came to the window, but she could feel him there. Hurting. She wasn't foolish enough to think he didn't care about her. He just didn't care enough.

She finally, finally knew what she wanted in life, and she didn't care whether that life played out in Manhattan, Mirabelle, St. Louis or Mississippi. She just wanted Adam, Julia and Wyatt. What was a person to do when she couldn't have the only thing she wanted in life?

As the carriage drove away, her control wavered and crashed. The first of many, many tears slipped unchecked down her cheeks. The emotions she felt after quitting her job, Colin's betrayal and her parent's separation were nothing compared to this. This—this—was what it felt like for a life to truly fall apart.

ANGELICA STEPPED INTO HER Manhattan apartment and set her keys down on the hall table. As she kicked off her pumps, she breathed a contented sigh. It was Friday, the end of a long, but very fulfilling week. She'd discovered two very talented unpublished authors and was finally feeling comfortable in an office setting.

And someone was in her kitchen. A lemony, savory scent filled the air along with the sounds of pots or bowls and cutlery. A burglar having gotten into her apartment was a virtual impossibility. This building was as secure as it got in the city.

She tiptoed down the hall and peeked around the corner. "Arthur! What are you doing here?"

He spun around, two large salad forks in his hands. "Oh, you're home. I didn't hear you come in."

"I thought you had some state function you couldn't miss."

"Wilson can handle it." He shrugged. "Besides, I wanted to be with you."

Two salmon fillets lay on a baking tray, herbs and seasonings sprinkled over the dark pink flesh. A bottle of white wine sat opened and on ice beside two glasses. Apparently, he'd been tossing a fresh salad of romaine and cucumber.

"I hope you're hungry."

Actually, she was.

He poured two glasses of wine and handed one to her. "You look…so…happy. You must be liking your job."

"It's wonderful. The people are busy, but surprisingly welcoming. My senior editor is brilliant." She went on describing her week and within a few minutes they'd ended up, by unspoken agreement, on the couch in the living room. Arthur asked a few questions, but mostly he listened. They talked for so long that Arthur refilled both of their wineglasses.

"What about you?" she asked, surprised they'd focused so much of their conversation on her.

"Well, I have some news." He held her gaze and

took a long, deep breath. "I've decided to not seek reelection."

"What?"

"I'm done, Angie. I'm ready, like you, for a new stage in my life."

Sitting forward, she set her glass down. "You can't be serious."

"Oh, I'm very serious." He took a sip of wine. "It took a long while for it to sink in, but once it did, I can't believe how quickly my head has turned around."

"Why?"

"Quite simply. I want to be with you."

"Why? Why this sudden change?"

"I was in my office earlier this week. It was a day like so many others the last twenty years. Meetings, conference calls, one crisis after another. Wilson came in and tossed the society section of the *Post* onto my desk. Separate pictures of you and me. Then several of various women. Speculation I'd had affairs."

"I'm sorry."

"No. No. It's not your fault. Not for a moment. Wilson offered to call you to find out whether or not you'd seen the photos, and I told him not to bother. That you'd stopped watching the news or reading papers long, long ago. And that's when it hit me... what you've had to deal with all these years because of my public life.

"I'm stubborn, I know, and it takes me a while to

understand." He smiled slightly. "But I realized you were right. For thirty years you gave me, our children, our family your life." He reached out and ran his hand along her cheek. "So now is your time. It's my time to stand on the sidelines supporting you."

She almost couldn't believe it, but then she remembered this was Arthur. The man she'd fallen in love with. The generous, passionate man she still loved. It really wasn't surprising at all that once he'd made his mind up he'd wholeheartedly embraced his decision.

She kissed the palm of his hand.

He reached out to clink their wineglasses. "To exploring new horizons, Angie. Together."

CHAPTER TWENTY-SIX

"You did it, Adam!"

"You're Mirabelle's hero!"

To an uproarious rendition of the song "For He's a Jolly Good Fellow," Adam raised a glass of champagne and toasted with Mirabelle's residents. Standing in the new and improved Duffy's Pub, he wasn't feeling much the hero at the moment.

Yes, they'd met the town's deadline. Barely. The doors of every store, bar and restaurant were open for business, Duffy's being the last, and Christmas was still a couple of days away. Every building, inside and out, had been restored to at least its original condition, if not better. Every tree had been replanted. Every lamppost replaced. New sod laid. Sidewalks and signs repaired. The new library and stables rebuilt. Mirabelle was back to normal.

The town had done a good job of publicizing its renewal and Mother Nature had cooperated by giving the area more than adequate snowfall for winter activities. Mirabelle's winter business of snowmobilers, cross-country skiers and snowshoers had returned in record numbers and occupancy rates for all the hotels, inns and bed-and-breakfasts were climbing daily. At the rate the calls and online inquiries were coming in, their reservation listings would be busting at the seams before Memorial Day. The residents were happy.

The bottom line for Adam was that his company had been paid and paid well to do this job. For the sake of the islanders and their need to celebrate, though, he did his duty and joined in the revelry. He smiled when he was supposed to smile, took the pats on the back and toasted the rebuilding of Mirabelle with its residents.

For much longer than he'd wanted, Adam moved about the room doing his job, despite the fact that his heart wasn't close to celebrating. Brick by brick, he and his crews had renewed Mirabelle. Here on the island, he'd felt a few more bricks in his own life sliding into place, but he still wasn't whole. Not by a long shot.

Toward the end of the evening, there was one last thing he needed to do before leaving. He found Jesse by the bar with his friends. They patted Adam on the back. Erica Taylor was grinning widely behind the bar. "How do you like your new place?" he asked her.

"I love it, Adam!" A glimmer of tears shone in Erica's eyes. "It still feels like Duffy's. Only better."

His crew had managed to restore the original antique bar, but Erica and Garrett had made improvements to the layout of the place by ensuring both the pub and restaurant had equally beautiful views of Lake Superior. From the bar, and not just the restaurant, patrons could see the lake. Right now, snow was falling, but in the summer, this place would be hopping.

"Sarah and Missy's shops look great, too," Garrett added. "We can't thank you enough."

"You have. All of you have." He glanced from one face to the next, and then he settled on Jesse. "Can I talk to you a minute?"

Jesse raised his eyebrows. "Sure."

They stepped a short distance away. "I was impressed with the job you did here," Adam said. "I'm expanding my operations and I'd like to offer you a full-time position as one of my site managers. I'd need you in St. Louis for some training for a few weeks, but from there you'd be going from one job site to the next, managing your own operation."

"Like you did here, in other words?"

"Exactly."

As Jesse let go a long, slow whistle, he glanced at Sarah, his very pregnant wife.

"I need managers I can count on, Jesse," Adam explained. "I'll make it worth your while."

"I'm sure you would." He held Adam's gaze. "Sorry, Adam, but I'm not interested."

"When I say I'll make it worth your while, Jesse, I mean it. This is a lucrative business, and there's never shortage of work."

"Thanks, but no thanks."

"Maybe you should take some time to think about it. Talk it over with your wife."

"I appreciate the consideration, but I don't need to think about it." Jesse shook his head. "I know you'd be a good man to work for and you're offering me the best job opportunity that's crossed my path in well…hell. Ever."

"But…"

"I know what Sarah would say. She owns some property up the hill and has this dream house in her mind. We put it on hold while I was working for you, but I plan on building the home for her this spring."

"There's nothing I can say, no amount I can offer, to change your mind?"

"Nope." Jesse shook his head. "Tell me this, where you heading to after you leave Mirabelle?"

"A few weeks home in St. Louis over the holidays."

"And then?"

"Mississippi. A small town on the coast." They'd accepted his bid for their business just last week.

"See, me and Sarah, we have a son entering his teenage years, and there's nothing that could get me to uproot him like that. Besides, Mirabelle is where we want to raise our baby. In my mind, there are some things you can't put a price tag on, and one of them is finding the right home for your children. No offense, Adam, but I could never do what you do."

"None taken." But Jesse's words did sink in

deeply, almost painfully. He handed Jesse his business card. "You change your mind, give me a call."

Jesse nodded, but Adam had a feeling the small piece of paper would be going in the trash the moment he returned to the bar. As Adam drew on his coat, Missy caught his gaze from where she was standing with Jesse's group. Without a word, she came toward him. "When are you leaving Mirabelle?"

"Tomorrow morning. First thing. We'll spend the holidays with family in St. Louis and then it's on to Mississippi for another project."

"You know you're always, always welcome at Mirabelle. At my home, in particular."

"Thanks, Missy. You never know. Me and the kids might come back someday. See what this island's like in the summer."

She shook his hand. Just as he would've pulled away, she turned his hand over, opening his palm. Then she smiled, hugged him and handed him an envelope. "Do something with that sooner rather than later, okay? You can only tempt fate for so long."

He stuffed the envelope into his pocket. He knew what he'd find inside. He just didn't know, at the moment, what he'd do with Marin's address and phone number.

He left Duffy's and walked up Mirabelle's residential hill one last time. After reaching the top, he turned and looked down on the snow-covered village. With big, fluffy snowflakes falling gently from the dark sky, holiday lights strung down Main all the way to the pier, the town looked like something out of a dream.

There was something magical about Mirabelle, and he'd never, ever forget this place, but this island didn't mean to Adam what it clearly meant to Jesse or Garrett or any number of other residents he'd worked closely with over the past several months. Mirabelle wasn't his home. Home was something he wasn't sure he'd ever feel again.

MARIN THREW HER KEYS onto the hall table and walked into her apartment. She'd been back in Manhattan now for several weeks and still the place felt like a hotel. That is, except for one—or should she say two—things. "Ralph?" she called. "Raoul?"

She walked into her living room and found the Maine coon cats she'd adopted from the shelter, three-year-old brothers who'd been abandoned by their owner, curled up next to each other on the couch. Ralph, the darker of the two, yawned as he lazily stretched out a paw. Raoul, on the other hand, the smaller sibling, didn't budge even when she scratched his neck.

"Don't get up on my account." Smiling, she walked to the floor-to-ceiling windows and looked out over Manhattan. Once upon a time, this view had sealed the deal when she'd been considering buying this place, but now she could not have cared less. This city no longer felt like home. Oddly enough, though, Mirabelle wouldn't have felt like home, either.

Her cell phone rang and she snapped it open. "Hi, Mom."

"Hey, there. How are you?"

"All right. Still liking your job?"

"Like? Try love. Love, love, love it. That's what I'm calling about. I finally got word on Missy's books. We're going to publish them and they want you to do illustrations for every one in the series."

"That's great."

"I'm so excited. They just want you to tweak a few of the Lake Superior pictures and add a couple more. That kind of thing. And Missy has all kinds of other ideas."

"Sounds like the makings of a brand-new relationship." If nothing else it would give her something to do. "How are things between you and Dad?"

"Never been better. We get together every weekend, but the time away from each other is the best thing that ever happened to us. He made me dinner last Friday night."

"Good for him."

"It was actually good!" She laughed. "He's decided to not run for reelection."

"What? No way!"

"He's not retiring, but he said he's ready for something different, too. I almost can't believe it." She paused. "How are you, Marin?"

"Fine. Good."

"Liar."

Marin barely held the tears at bay. She missed Wyatt and Julia almost as much as she missed Adam. Before she could stop herself, she looked toward the bronze statue that Adam and the kids had given her and the photos they'd framed for her, all sitting front and center in her living room. The kids had both sent her notes. Wyatt's was short, but sweet and he'd included a drawing he'd done of their Christmas tree. Julia's was much longer than Marin had expected. She'd explained all about how nice Mirabelle looked now that the construction was done and how happy she was to see her grandparents in St. Louis. How strange for Marin's time on Mirabelle to be so bittersweet. She'd revived her relationship with Missy and was now closer than ever to her mom. She'd come to terms with the concept of motherhood, only to have the opportunity to be a mother swept out from under her.

"It's going to take a while for this broken heart to heal," she whispered.

"Yours broke three times over, sweetheart. It just might take three times as long."

CHAPTER TWENTY-SEVEN

SLOWLY, ADAM WALKED THROUGH the spacious, but empty rooms of the stately old house as the late afternoon sun shone brightly through the large windows. It was a pretty home, sturdy, with a versatile floor plan. The kind of house in which a young couple could and should raise a family. It was a shame, really, that it'd been left vacant all these years.

"Mr. Harding?" the Realtor called from the foyer. "The new owners are all set to take possession, if you're ready."

"Give me another minute alone, would you?"

She nodded, went outside and closed the front door.

The sound of the latch brought back the memory of the first time he and Beth had walked through this place. All he'd been able to think about had been all the work that needed to be done, but Beth had been enamored with this place from the moment she'd stepped through the front door and saw the decorative banister leading up to the second floor.

She'd then proceeded to dash through the house,

calling out something unique to love in every room. He smiled as he remembered. *Oh, Adam, you have to see the built-in burled oak china cabinet in the dining room. This pantry is every cook's dream. A claw-footed tub! Baby, that thing just might be big enough for two.*

As he glanced upstairs, his smile faded. He didn't want to go up there. He didn't want to face it, but it was why he'd come today. Resolutely, he went up the stairs, turned to the left and went into the bedroom he'd shared with Beth. It wasn't as hard as he thought it might be, looking at the window seat and imagining her there curled up and reading. The bathroom, on the other hand, would never be easy. He forced himself to turn and cross the threshold. There was the antique enameled tub she'd so loved. The tub in which she'd died.

"Dammit, Beth, you shouldn't have done it," he whispered, needing to speak the words out loud. "You should've told me what you were feeling. You should've talked to me. Given me a chance to help." His voice cracked and he wasn't sure he could get it all out.

"I was mad at you for a long time," he started again. "And I didn't even know it. Angry as hell at you for leaving…Julia and Wyatt. For leaving me. How could you do that? How?"

There were no miraculous answers awaiting him, but it was out of him. All these years, he'd held that inside. Maybe now he could let go of all the rest.

"I think I finally forgive you, though," he said softly as he looked around the room and did what he'd never been able to do. Imagine her final moments. "You were in pain. I know that now. More pain than I could ever comprehend. I forgive myself for not understanding…then and for not understanding now." There was nothing—nothing—he could've done differently.

"Mr. Harding?" the Realtor called again from downstairs. "You ready?"

He took a deep breath. There was nothing for him in this house anymore. It was time to let it go. "Yes, ma'am."

Pulling off his wedding ring, he set it on the vanity and walked down the hall, thinking it should be hard to let go. But it wasn't. It was time to close this chapter in his life and let another family make their memories—hopefully much happier memories than his—in this house.

Running his hand along the banister for one last time, he went down the stairs. "Tell the new family that I wish them the best. It was a good house."

He dropped the key into the Realtor's hand and went outside into the bright midafternoon sunshine. As he climbed into his SUV, pulled out of the driveway and left the house behind, a sense of intense relief passed through him. He felt unburdened, as if the weight of that place had been hanging over him all these years. Another brick in his life slid into place.

But he still didn't feel complete.

Resigned that maybe he'd never feel whole again, he stopped at his office to drop off a few things and then took the long drive across town to his parents' house on Lake St. Louis. By the time he arrived, it was dark. He went inside and hung up his jacket. His parents' house was decked out with all the traditional Christmas trimmings, lights, garland, a tree. You name it. His mother had pulled out all the stops for Adam's kids.

Quiet voices sounded from upstairs. Bedtime. Since his parents were out for the evening with friends, his kids were with Carla. She'd returned to them, a small consolation for the kids after Marin's departure. Carla's mother had lost her battle with cancer long before the holidays, and having settled her family's affairs Carla had asked to come back to care for Julia and Wyatt.

Adam climbed the stairs and paused at the bedroom door. The kids were snuggled in bed and Carla was reading.

"Daddy!" Julia said, looking up from the book. "You're home."

Smiling, he went into the room. "I'll take it from here, Carla. Thank you."

"Are you sure, Mr. Harding?" she said. "You look tired. I'm more than happy—"

"I've got it." Gently, but resolutely, he took the book out of Carla's hands. Not long ago, he would've either let Carla finish getting the kids off to sleep or, more likely, gone directly into his office to work, but those days were gone. Forever. Carla was just now understanding there'd been some changes these past few months.

"Sleep well, *niños*." She kissed each of the kids on the forehead and then smiled her approval at Adam. "Good night, Mr. Harding."

"Night, Carla, and thank you."

Pushing aside the chair, Adam climbed in bed between his two kids and snuggled them close. He put an arm around each of them and they took turns flipping the pages as he read. Toward the end of the third book, he could feel them getting heavier against his sides.

"Daddy?" Julia whispered sleepily. "How long do we get to stay here with Grandpa and Grandma Harding?"

"Yeah," Wyatt said. "How long?"

"About two weeks."

"And then where are we going?"

"Mississippi."

"We've never been there, have we?"

"No." But they had lived in at least six other states in three short years. Suddenly, Jesse's words that last night on Mirabelle came back to him.

There are some things you can't put a price tag on, and one of them is finding the right home for your children.

Adam imagined packing up and moving again, and he knew right then and there that he wasn't going to be able to do that to Julia and Wyatt. Not this time. Not ever again.

"What would you think if we stayed in St. Louis?"

"You mean like forever?"

"Yeah. Like forever."

Julia sat up and smiled brightly. "Can we live at the lake with Grandpa and Grandma Harding?"

"Well, no. We'll find our own house. A neighborhood with kids and good schools. Someplace you both like."

"Would we ever move again?"

"No."

"Good," Wyatt said, yawning.

That was it. They were staying in St. Louis. From now on, he'd be running his company from his home base and hiring on-site operations managers to run every new job.

He'd sold one home today, but there was another one out there for Julia and Wyatt and him. Someplace for the three of them to let their roots grow and new memories to be made. It was here in Missouri somewhere and he'd find it. The decision felt good, felt more right than any decision he'd made in the past three years. Finally, they were home.

Still, there was something missing.

"Daddy?" Julia whispered. "Are we ever going to see Marin again?"

"We miss her," Wyatt added softly.

"I don't know," Adam answered as truthfully as he could. "I just don't know."

"Do you think she misses us?"

"I'm sure she does." He squeezed them both tightly as a knot formed in his throat. "I know she does."

"Then why doesn't she come visit us?"

"Did we do something wrong?"

"Oh, no." He shook his head and kissed their foreheads. "Neither one of you did anything wrong. I swear."

"Maybe if we have a house, she'll come?"

"Maybe."

"You like her," Julia said. "I know you do. I saw you kissing. And she stayed over that one night. That means she likes you, too."

"Yeah, she likes me," he murmured, his heart breaking all over again.

"Then why don't you marry her?" Wyatt asked.

There was a time he would've lied to them and told them everything would be okay, but they'd been through enough in their short lives to know that wasn't true. Sometimes life just didn't work out the way we wanted it to.

"I did ask her to marry me," he said. "But I screwed it up. I asked her to marry me in the wrong way, and she—quite rightly—said no."

"Then ask her again," Julia said.

"The right way this time," Wyatt added.

"It isn't that easy."

"Why not?"

"It just...isn't."

"I'll ask her," Wyatt said. "I will."

Was it that easy? Is that all he had to do was ask her again, the right way this time?

That's when it hit him like a sledgehammer to the chest. All the pain, emptiness and uncertainty he'd been feeling these past several weeks hadn't been because of Beth. It didn't have anything to do with selling their old house. It didn't have to do with heading off to Mississippi. All of that was resolved, and he was still left with a yawning emptiness. Because he was missing Marin.

He'd turned away from the best thing that had ever happened to him other than Julia and Wyatt. He'd let Marin walk out of his life without lifting a finger to stop her. Apparently, he was the man, not any of his crew, in need of a swift kick in the ass.

"You guys up for a trip tomorrow?" he asked.

"Where?" Wyatt asked.

"New York City."

"But it's Christmas Eve, Daddy," Julia said.

"I know. With any luck, there'll be the most important present ever waiting there for us."

CHAPTER TWENTY-EIGHT

"How long do we have to wait here?" Wyatt groaned from the backseat of their parked car.

"Just a little while longer." His adrenaline running on high, Adam scanned the people walking up and down the sidewalks looking for one particular face. "Angelica said she should be home soon." Apparently, the Camden family had had Christmas Eve dinner at Angelica and Arthur's apartment and Marin would be on her way home.

"When she gets here, can we go with you?" Julia asked.

"Honey, I know you and Wyatt are as anxious as I am, but I need you two to wait in the car for a few minutes. I need to talk to Marin first. I need to make things right. If I can."

"What if you can't?"

As he fingered the engagement ring in his pocket, he refused to think about that possibility. If she'd truly loved him before, she had to still love him now. "One way or another, I will find a way. I promise."

Big, fluffy snowflakes fell from the darkening sky. Marin's apartment building looked imposing, cold, and for the first time in all of this he worried that maybe this hadn't been such a good idea. What if her feelings had changed? What if she'd met someone else?

As he drew his gaze back down he saw that beautiful head of short blond hair. Dressed in a red wool coat, Marin was crossing the street and heading toward her building, not twenty feet from him. But she was with another man. They were talking and laughing together as if they'd known each other their entire lives. They reached her building and she hugged him.

Son of a bitch! Adam had waited too long. It'd taken him too long to figure things out. He couldn't breathe. He couldn't—

"Daddy, there she is!" Julia said, pointing.

"Go, Daddy. Go."

Both kids pushed on his shoulder and Adam climbed out of the car. He took several steps and was almost there when she looked up. "Adam?" Her eyes grew wide and she stopped in her tracks. "What are you doing here?"

"I—" A violence Adam had never felt before raged through him. He wanted to punch the other man's face in, then rip his throat out, and then—

Stop it. It's your own damned fault if she's fallen in love with someone else.

Marin reached out and touched his arm, as if she could read his thoughts. "Adam, this is my brother Max."

Brother? Adam sucked in a deep, deep breath, and took a moment to clear his head. "Hello." He put out his hand. "Adam Harding."

"That, I gathered." Tentatively, her brother shook his hand, and then he turned to Marin. "You okay?"

"Yeah, I'm all right."

Max glared at Adam as if he had a thing or two to say, but thought better of it. "I guess I'll be going then."

"Good to see you, Max."

"Merry Christmas, Mar. See you later." He kissed her cheek, hailed a cab and disappeared down the street.

"I thought he was, that he might be—"

"A boyfriend? No. There's no one else."

He didn't know what to say, or how to start.

"You look like shit," she whispered.

"Thanks." He swallowed. "You look...you are... the best thing I've ever seen."

She crossed her arms. "Why did you come?"

"Can we go somewhere private? Someplace we can talk?"

"No." She shook her head. "This is good for me."

Traffic zoomed by on the street beside them. Horns honked. People walked past, bumping his arm.

"Mirabelle's finished," he said, trying to lighten things up, trying to find a way in. "Back as good as new."

"That's what Missy tells me. You should be very

proud. You did a wonderful job and rebuilt a lot of lives."

Now it was time for him to rebuild his own, and to do that he needed one thing. One person. Without her, he wasn't sure he would ever be truly whole again. "These past weeks have been...difficult, but I've had a lot of time to think about what you said. You were right about everything, you know."

"I don't want to be right, Adam."

"The thing is..." He looked away. "A man is lucky to find love in life once, let alone twice, and when I met and fell in love with Beth, I thought I was the luckiest man alive. When she died, I didn't know how I could ever live again. I didn't think I deserved to live, but I had to for Julia's and Wyatt's sakes. I had to keep moving on for them."

He turned to look at Marin, wanted to touch her, wanted to hold her, but he'd lost that right weeks ago. It was all he could do not to reach for her. All he wanted was to hold her for the rest of his life. "Then you came into my life, making me feel again. Making me want again. Making me imagine what could be." He stuffed his hands into his pockets. "You scared the hell out of me, Marin."

Say something, woman. Anything.

But then she didn't need to say a thing. He did. "I...love you...Marin."

The moment he said the words, another brick, a cornerstone, slid into place. Emotions welled up and rolled over him like a tidal wave, but he held them back for fear he'd bowl her over with the strength of them. There'd be time for letting go when they were alone—if he could get her alone—when they had privacy and, most important, a bed. He wanted, more than anything, to *show* her how much he loved her.

"God, how I love you," he said.

Marin stared at him. It was so good to see him again. To see his beautiful, soulful brown eyes. That mouth. That perfectly messy hair. These past weeks without him had felt like a lifetime, this day, Christmas Eve, had felt joyless. But now? Had he really said those precious words? "Say it again," she whispered.

"I love you."

"Do you mean that? Do you really, really mean that?"

"More than I've ever meant anything before in my life. I love you. I love you. I love you. I'll say those three words and mean them every hour of every day for the rest of my life if that's what it'll take to get you and keep you in my life."

A car door slammed. She turned to find Julia and Wyatt running toward her down the sidewalk. "Marin!"

She bent down, they ran into her open arms and the tears she'd been holding back fell unchecked. It finally felt like Christmas. "I missed you two so much."

"We missed you," Julia said.

"A lot," Wyatt added.

Julia drew away. "Are you going to marry Daddy?"

"I don't know. He didn't ask." Marin glanced up at Adam. "At least not properly."

"Daddy." Julia rolled her eyes at him.

"I didn't want to take a chance she'd say no again," he said, smiling softly. "Maybe you guys should ask her."

Wyatt looked innocently at Marin. "Will you marry us?"

"Not us, Wyatt. Daddy."

"Oh, yeah."

"The ring," Julia whispered.

Adam dug it out of his pocket.

"We helped pick it out." Julia smiled proudly as she held it out to Marin. "Do you like it?"

"It's beautiful." She hugged both kids and then stood, all the while holding Adam's suddenly very serious gaze.

"Will you marry me, Marin?"

"Say it one more time." She waited to hear those precious words.

"I love you. I don't want to live without you. Not one single day. Ever again."

"Yes. I'll marry you." She leaped into his arms and kissed him. "Yes, yes, yes."

EPILOGUE

"Tell Adam that Memorial Day weekend is a big hit!" Missy's voice sounded so loudly over Marin's cell phone that even Adam could make out her words. "The sun is shining, Mirabelle looks spectacular and Main Street is exactly the way it should be! Crawling with shoulder to shoulder tourists!"

Adam smiled at Marin, sitting there in the passenger seat of his SUV. "Tell her I said good."

"I heard him," Missy said. "So when are you guys coming to visit?"

Marin glanced at him.

"Whenever you want," he said, having the feeling that Mirabelle was going to become a second home.

"July Fourth," Marin said. "We're coming for the whole week."

"Yay!" Julia and Wyatt said in unison from the backseat.

As Missy and Marin chatted for a moment, Adam pulled into the suburban St. Louis neighborhood, found the address he was looking for and parked the car in front of the newly constructed brick home.

The kids hopped out of the car and ran across the thick green lawn.

"I gotta go," Marin said. "We're here."

Adam reached across the console and took her hand. "You sure St. Louis is okay with you?"

"It's better than okay. It already feels like home."

Adam followed Marin and the kids into the house. While Julia and Wyatt raced from one empty room to another, Adam slowly followed Marin into the spacious kitchen, which had the latest in new countertops, gleaming appliances, right off a huge family room with a fireplace.

She looked out toward the large wooded lot and smiled. The property bordered a park and there was a Little League game going on at the baseball diamond. A couple dogs barked. Most of the backyards in the neighborhood had play equipment, and there were young children swinging on swings.

Without a word, he and Marin went down the hall to the spacious first floor master bedroom and she spun around. "This is it. Our house."

"You don't want to see the rest?"

"You're not looking."

"If you're happy I'm happy. All I care about is a good school district, having a home office on the first floor—"

"Not that you're going to be spending much time in it," she said, grinning.

"No, but if I have to, I'll be near the family room

and kitchen, so I'll be as much a part of things as possible."

"That's all you want in a house?"

"And it's new. That means I don't have to do any work on the place. That means I get to spend more time with you and the kids."

Adam looked at her, standing in what would be their bedroom. The wedding ring on her finger. On his. Was this real? He reached out to touch her, ran his fingers through her silky, short hair. Yeah, this was real, very real. Life was good again.

She came into his arms and he kissed her. "I love you," he whispered against her lips.

"I'll never get sick of hearing that, you know."

"I get this room!" Julia called out from the second floor.

"This one's mine!" Wyatt responded.

He and Marin both chuckled and, hand in hand, walked upstairs to find the kids looking into closets and staring out windows.

"Are we going to live here, Daddy?" Julia asked.

"I don't know yet. Maybe."

"I love this house!"

"Can we go outside?" Wyatt asked.

"Sure. Stay close, though."

As the kids raced down the stairs and out the front door, he watched Marin move from one bedroom to the next. He loved watching her. His wife. His friend. His lover. He could look at her all day long and never tire of her face, her hands, her smile.

"So that one is Julia's. Wyatt wants that one. This one with the good light would make a nice art studio for my painting," she said, pointing at the big windows. "And this one...this room would make a beautiful...nursery." She glanced at him and whispered, "I'm pregnant, Adam."

For a second her words moved through his brain like molasses as he tried to comprehend. Pregnant. It felt as if his heart had flown into his throat, lodging there like a stone. They'd talked about having children together, and the way they'd been making love without any precautions, he shouldn't have been surprised. Talking was one thing. This was real, too.

"Adam, don't be sad."

"What if..." He turned away, his entire body breaking out into a cold sweat. *What if... Oh, God.* He couldn't even voice the terrible fears inside his own head.

"I know what you're thinking." Her arms came around him from behind, her hands ran up his chest and her cheek rested against his back. "Don't."

He focused on Julia and Wyatt running in the backyard, trying to push all the bad thoughts away. Soon, they were playing with the kids next door, climbing all over the play equipment, and laughing.

"We're going to have a baby, Adam," Marin said, a smile in her voice. "A baby. Can you believe it? It's actually a little overwhelming."

And wonderful. Absolutely wonderful. He shouldn't be sad, not for another moment. He should be filled with joy. Marin was going to have their baby. He put his hands over his wife's, took a deep breath and let the fear go, the same way he'd let that old house go. Marin wasn't Beth. Not by a long shot. Soft and strong, sensitive but tough, she was Beth and then some. The last brick, the last cornerstone, slid into place.

He turned within her arms and placed his hands on her warm belly. "You're going to be a wonderful mother."

"You think?"

"I know, Marin. I know." He cupped her face in his palms and kissed her. Then he whispered something he'd never get tired of saying. "I love you." Maybe he wasn't such a master at fixing things. Marin, after all, had fixed him. "Let's go tell Julia and Wyatt they're going to have a baby."

* * * * *